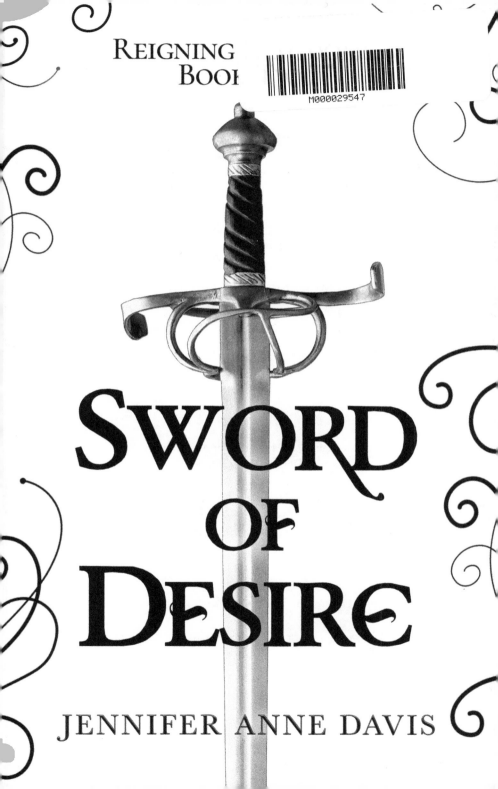

REIGNING
BOOK

SWORD
OF
DESIRE

JENNIFER ANNE DAVIS

Cover Design by KimG-Design
Editing by Jennifer Murgia
Proofreading by Appalachian Proofing

ISBN (Paperback): 978-1-7344947-9-2
eISBN: 978-1-7344947-8-5

Library of Congress Control Number: 1-10934128081

ALSO BY JENNIFER ANNE DAVIS

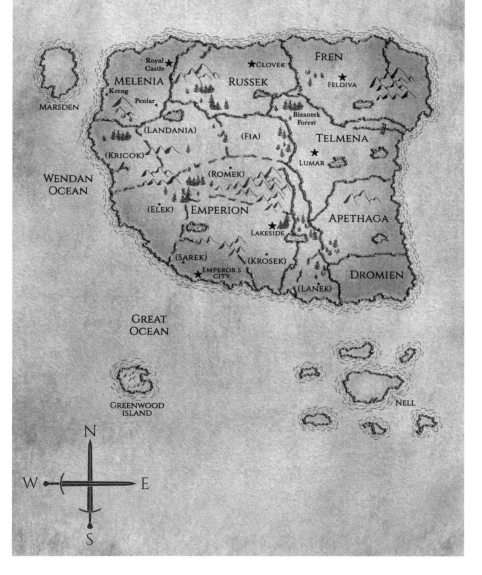

CHAPTER ONE

*H*arley stood on the open gorge tower. Everything had started here. The wind whipped around her body as the memories flooded in. Her brother's beheading, her cousins' brutal murders, and her aunt and uncle slaughtered before an army of cheering Russeks. She pinched her eyes shut, remembering how the blood poured down the side of the stone wall that fateful day Lyle, her own husband, had seized control of the royal castle.

Opening her eyes, she scanned the tents below. If she'd estimated correctly, there were a hundred tents which equated to about two hundred soldiers. She stepped closer to the half-wall, sliding her hands over the thick, rough stones.

So much bloodshed and heartache had happened here. She blinked the tears away, unable to believe she was at the royal castle again. This time, she was not here as a guest of the king and queen. Rather, she was the wife of the false king. Lyle had informed her she would be crowned in an elaborate ceremony

1

shortly after he returned. He'd been gone for almost two weeks now, and Harley expected him at any moment.

Shortly after Lyle killed Ledger, he'd gathered twenty soldiers and left, furious that both units he'd sent out had failed to assassinate their intended targets. He wanted to investigate what had gone wrong. Harley prayed Owen and Idina had made it safely to Kreng where they could seek refuge, guarded by the army there. She also hoped Ackley and Gytha were safely hiding in Kricok, protected by the Emperion empire.

Harley's hands started shaking. Did Ackley love her? Or had he only used her? Those two questions had been lingering in her mind, demanding an answer she couldn't give. Regardless, she had a job to do, and she would do it.

Ackley had given her Sword of Rage. During their time together, he'd been carefully feeding her information—like where to strike a man to kill him swiftly. The only conclusion she could fathom was that Ackley had known, or at least suspected, Lyle had taken the throne. Ackley had purposely embedded her with the enemy to kill Lyle. He had even said the more dangerous assassin was the one sleeping with the king, not the one sneaking into the castle.

Which meant the weight of the kingdom fell to her.

She needed to pretend to be loyal and passive toward her husband, so he didn't view her as a threat to his stolen throne. Lyle couldn't discover she was acting as a Knight, inserted in the royal castle for a mission. A new woman stood on the tower, one strong and capable of determining her own future. The naive person who'd married Lyle and allowed herself to be locked in closets, too afraid to go against her husband, was dead. She was so much more now. All because Ackley had given her another path to take.

Sucking in a deep breath, she made sure to keep her newfound strength and resilience hidden within. No one could know or suspect what simmered beneath the surface.

In the distance, a plume of dust rose. It had to be from a group of horses, which could only mean one thing. Lyle had returned.

During his absence, Harley had tried to come up with a plan to discover where he had hidden the Melenia soldiers' family members, figure out how to get information to Owen, and keep Ackley hidden from Lyle. If her husband ever found out that she had not only fallen for and slept with Ackley, but that Ackley had killed Lyle's father, there would be no stopping the wrath he would unleash. She had to tread carefully to keep her loved ones safe.

Ackley had said his profession required sacrifice. If she wanted to be a Knight, Harley needed to learn how to make those tough choices to succeed with the mission.

Slowly, she inched backward, being careful, so no one below would notice her. When she bumped into the wall, she reached behind and opened the door, slipping inside the castle. She made her way along the corridor, taking soft steps, and holding her dress up so it wouldn't swish. Thankfully the curtains hadn't been removed on this level, so she went behind one that concealed an entrance to the secret passageways. She opened the hidden door and stepped into darkness. Not having time to light a torch, she kept her right hand on the wall as she traversed through the corridor until she reached the third level where the royal residence was located.

Exiting the passageways, she paused, listening for anyone who might be nearby. A deafening silence greeted her. She crept to the right. While Lyle had never allowed servants in his home in Penlar, the same was not true for the royal castle.

Granted, there weren't nearly the amount the late king had kept, but a decent presence, nonetheless.

Since she'd spent so much time in the royal castle as a child, she knew her way around here like a second home. She passed the doors leading to her late cousins' rooms. When she reached the door to the king and queen's chambers, she pushed it open and went inside. Her arms trembled as she stood in the square anteroom. Even though she'd been here for two weeks, every time she stepped into this space, it felt as if she were doing something wrong. These private rooms still seemed forbidden to her.

She eyed the door on the left. On her first day here, shortly after Lyle had left for his mission, she'd considered going into that room. Since she knew Lyle well enough, she assumed he'd have some sort of trap in place. Not wanting him to know she'd been snooping already, she decided not to go in there. At least, not yet.

Taking a calming breath, she pushed open the door and stepped inside her aunt's bedchamber. Every time, the familiar smell hit her like a punch to the stomach, the distinct aroma of rosemary and honey that she always associated with her aunt. Tears filled her eyes. Eventually, the smell would fade. The memories of her aunt would dull. But not until after Harley had sought her revenge.

Rushing into her aunt's dressing closet, she stepped inside the small room containing dresses, nightclothes, and jewelry. Her fingers trailed over necklaces and other trinkets, and she wondered why the Russeks hadn't stolen these items or ransacked the room. She'd have to think on the matter later. Right now, she needed a shawl.

She grabbed a blue one, then exited the closet and glanced at the vanity mirror, verifying what she suspected—her hair was a raging mess. She hastily brushed it, knowing Lyle would expect her to look the part. As she stared at herself in the mirror, she considered the role she must play.

Lyle had to believe she was the same woman he married. Someone who listened and obeyed him. He couldn't suspect she was snooping for information or intended to kill him. But she also couldn't act too naive. Lyle knew she wasn't an idiot and probably suspected she wasn't quite as compliant as she let on. After all, he'd locked her in the closet numerous times and belittled her on multiple occasions for a reason.

The difference now—she knew what he was capable of. He'd been in love with another woman before he married Harley. He only broke off that engagement to marry Harley to have a legitimate claim to the throne once he killed off the royal family. His desire for power outweighed all else. She couldn't forget that fact.

She needed to tread carefully since Lyle had no love for her. She was simply a means to an end for him. Once Owen was dead, he'd probably kill her as well. But she had no intention of letting Lyle kill Owen. And she had every intention of putting Owen on the throne and killing Lyle. It would be justice for all her vile husband had done.

The weapon Ackley had given her was safely hidden in one of the guest suites. Harley decided to leave it there for now. She'd stashed it there along with the letters Lyle's father had sent him. The letters implicated not only that she was the king's illegitimate child, but that Beck had been blackmailing the king. Harley had no idea what to do with the letters, but she didn't want Lyle to have them. She'd put the sword and letters behind a drawer in the armoire—another piece of advice Ackley had deliberately told her.

She moved away from the vanity, then exited the room.

Since the day she was brought here, she'd been wanting to get to the stables. However, the sentries on duty prevented her from leaving the third floor. While she'd traversed through the passageways over the past two weeks, she hadn't left the castle, not wanting to be seen and questioned. With Lyle's return, this may be her only chance.

Holding her head high, she glided along the hallway. After making two turns, she neared the staircase leading to the lower levels. Two soldiers stood guard. She considered addressing them but decided against it. She would play the part and treat them as servants.

Without saying a word to either man, she strolled past them and descended the stairs.

"May we assist you with something, Lady Harley?" the soldier on the left asked.

"My husband has returned," she answered. "I am eager to see him." The lie felt like cow dung in her mouth.

"I will escort you," the other soldier said. He pounded down the stairs after her.

Not bothering to answer, she kept her pace quick as she headed to the first level of the castle.

None of the usual sounds of her cousins joking or her aunt's laugh came from within. Instead, an eerie silence filled the halls. She headed down the corridor to her left, toward the kitchen. She occasionally came across another sentry on duty, but she couldn't discern any reason for where the guards were placed or why. Maybe she could make a map of the castle, marking where the sentries were stationed. That could either offer valuable insight or come in handy at some later point in time.

Opening the side door, she exited the castle. The trampled ground had turned muddy from a recent rain. Taking the gravel pathway, she headed toward the stables. Dozens of tents and soldiers filled the entire space to her left. She tried not to look that way for fear she'd recognize someone, and her resolve would crack.

At the entrance to the stables, a flurry of activity took place. Harley was there for one purpose—and it had nothing to do with Lyle. She scanned the horses, finding most saddlebags still attached as the animals were led inside. Slowing her pace, she searched for Lyle. He stood off to the side speaking to a group of soldiers.

Harley didn't have long until he spotted her. Wanting to remain unnoticed, she dodged into the fray, staying closer to those around her than customary. She just needed to make it into the stables without being seen. Since the soldier from inside still followed her, she kept moving, never giving him an opportunity to question her.

She neared the doors where the horses were being led inside. Lyle remained with his men, speaking to them. Sidling up next to one of the horses, Harley glided through the doorway. She blinked, her eyes adjusting to the dimmer light. Scouring the stalls, she looked for Ledger's horse. None of the animals on the left appeared to be his. Searching the other side, toward the back she spotted Ledger's horse in a stall next to the one she'd been riding. Her heart pounded, and her hands started to shake.

Stable boys led the horses into empty stalls, rubbing them down, and filling up water buckets.

"Lady Harley," the soldier following her said. "I believe King Lyle is outside. I can escort you there."

She glared at him over her shoulder. "I know perfectly well where my husband is." And how dare this common foot soldier refer to Lyle as the king. The false title made her want to vomit. It was a boldfaced lie.

"I'm not sure it's appropriate for a lady to be in the stables," he stuttered, a tinge of red covering his cheeks.

Her eyes narrowed. "When I was brought to this castle two weeks ago, someone neglected to bring my belongings inside. Since I'm here, I'd like to see if my bag is still with my horse." She folded her arms, tilting her head to the side just as she'd seen her mother do a hundred times. "Does that meet with your approval?" Her voice dripped with sarcasm.

"I'm, uh, sorry, Lady Harley. Forgive me for questioning you." He motioned for her to proceed.

She raised her eyebrows, staring at him a moment longer than necessary before turning and heading to the other end. He gave her more space this time. Her shoulders relaxed as she neared Ledger's horse. When the animal noticed her, it nodded its head. Pretending the horse was her own, she opened the door and stepped into the stall. As she cooed to the animal, it nuzzled her hand, allowing her to quickly survey the area. A saddle hung on the back wall. In the corner, a bag had been thrown, its tethers flung open indicating someone had gone through it.

"There's my bag," she exclaimed. Rushing over, she knelt, tying the tethers before sliding the strap over her shoulder.

"I can get that for you," the soldier said, coming into the stall. The horse snorted, and the soldier took a step back.

"I would appreciate that," Harley replied as she stood. She didn't want to be seen carrying the bag and raise any unwanted suspicions. "Please see that this goes directly to the queen's chambers."

"Yes, Lady Harley." He reached for the bag, so she handed it to him. "Is there anything else?" he inquired, holding the stall door open for her.

"I'd like a moment alone with my horse." She quickly grabbed the brush off the wall, patting the animal's neck.

The soldier hesitated.

"You may go now." She gave no room for him to linger or question her.

He nodded and left.

Harley tossed the brush in the corner, then rushed to the adjacent stall where her horse was. Since a young stable boy was mucking the area, she didn't want to step inside and disturb him. She glanced around for her bag, not finding it. When she backed up, she bumped into someone. "I'm sorry," she said quickly, turning to see who she'd run into.

"No worries," a soldier mumbled before hurrying into the next stall with a bucket full of water.

Since she'd gotten what she'd came there for, it was time for her to go. Walking toward the exit, she suddenly felt off kilter. Something poked her arm, so she reached inside her sleeve, finding a piece of paper that hadn't been there moments ago. She glanced around, wondering when it had been put there and by whom. Her breathing sped up, but she tried to remain calm in case someone was watching her.

Several boisterous voices came from the entrance. Harley spotted Lyle striding past the threshold, the setting sun at his back.

She shoved the paper back up her sleeve, hoping no one noticed. She headed toward Lyle with a fake smile plastered on her face.

"One of my men mentioned he saw you in here," Lyle said by way of greeting. "What are you doing?" Clasping his hands behind his back, he scanned her from head to toe.

"I heard you'd returned. I was eager to greet you. Welcome home." She bowed her head and curtseyed in submission. When she righted herself, she met her husband's assessing gaze. As usual, his blond hair had been combed back, the sides shorter than the top. His brown eyes remained flat, no depth to them as he stared at her. His squared jaw had a few days' worth of stubble on it, making him appear more rugged. "Is it time for supper?" she asked through hooded eyes, hoping to deflect his astute attention.

"It is." He gestured for her to exit before him.

She tried not to flinch as she made her way past him. They walked side by side along the gravel pathway toward the castle, Lyle towering over Harley by at least a foot. He wore a black leather shirt under a mustard-colored tunic. When she glanced down, she noticed a dagger tucked inside his knee-high boots. The sword strapped to his waist swayed lightly as he moved. His shoulders appeared even wider than the last time she saw him. She shivered.

Lyle peered down at her.

Needing to say something, she asked, "Do you have a cook or does that duty fall to me?" For the past two weeks, a soldier had been bringing food to her room three times a day. However, now that Lyle had returned, she didn't know if he would insist on her taking care of their meals. At their house in Penlar, Lyle had expected Harley to assume all duties that servants normally handled, regardless of her status as a lady. Which meant Harley cooked all meals and cleaned the house. Lyle had been too paranoid to allow servants inside. Now she understood why since he'd been planning to overthrow the royal family. If only she'd been more astute and could have prevented him from doing so. Maybe her brother would be alive today. Pain gripped her heart, and she shoved it away, forcing a pleasant smile on her face.

"The kitchen here is fully staffed," Lyle replied. "There are also sentries guarding each level. My captains have access to the first-floor offices."

Shock rolled through Harley that he allowed his officers inside. And through her shock, some of the unease and building tension seemed to melt away. She wouldn't be utterly alone inside with this murderous man. If someone could hear her scream, maybe Lyle wouldn't mistreat her so badly. However, with Lyle, she could never be sure.

"Since you will soon be Melenia's queen, it isn't prudent for others to see you doing such mundane tasks," he explained. "You are royalty and must behave as such. Your purpose is to be seen when needed and to look the part. Understand?"

"I'm not the queen yet," she whispered, not intending for Lyle to hear. He held no right to the throne until she was officially crowned. However, since Owen was still alive and older than her, that meant Owen was the true heir. If Harley was crowned knowing that information, she would be guilty of treason, and her fate would be sealed along with Lyle's. She shivered. It was her job to assassinate Lyle and save the kingdom.

"That situation will be rectified shortly," he murmured, his deep voice rumbling through her. They reached the door and Lyle came to an abrupt halt, grabbing her arm and squeezing it harder than necessary. "You will support me and do as I say." He leaned in closer, his hot breath brushing her right ear. "Otherwise, I will take my knife and slice you open." He released her and smacked her stomach. "Here." He hit her inner thigh. "And here. I won't kill you. I'll take my time and make it as painful as possible." He took a step back, his eyes hardening as he watched for a reaction.

She nodded, believing he meant every word he said.

The mysterious paper she'd acquired in the stables started sliding from her sleeve, and panic shot through her. If Lyle discovered her true intentions, she would be better off dead than in his hands.

He opened the door to the castle, gesturing for her to enter.

Harley steeled her resolve. Even though Lyle had been here for some time now, he didn't know this place as well as she did. Every nook and hiding spot, every twist and turn, every room and closet, she'd explored as a child. Even the hidden passageways she could navigate with her eyes closed. Lyle didn't know the castle's secrets like she did. This had been Harley's second home—it would never be Lyle's.

She stepped inside, squinting in the dim light of the corridor. Lyle went around her, taking the lead, expecting her to follow. His boots thumped over the stones, echoing in the corridor. Now that his back faced her, Harley slid the paper from her sleeve, her fingers curling around it. She pretended to cough, the sound loud. As she did so, she shoved the paper down her neckline to her bosom, where it rested safely against her skin.

Let the games begin.

CHAPTER TWO

ACKLEY

*a*ckley sat on his bedroll, a single candle lighting the small tent. The same question he'd asked himself a thousand times popped in his head again. *What did I do?* He sucked in a deep breath, releasing it slowly, trying to remain calm. He'd done something that no one else in his situation would've done. He'd gambled with the life of someone he loved.

He pulled Sword of Desire from its scabbard, examining the blood-red leather grip. His fingers slid around it, clutching tightly, his knuckles turning white. When he'd first found the letters written between Commander Beck and his son, Lyle, he realized Harley was the late king's illegitimate child, putting her in line for the throne. The letters also revealed that Beck and Lyle had struck a deal with Russek to overthrow the royal family to put Harley on the throne, making Lyle the legitimate king.

Which led Ackley to suspect that Lyle was alive.

When Ackley and Gytha were attacked by those soldiers

and the man he'd questioned said another group had gone after Owen, Ackley knew for certain Lyle was the one claiming to be Melenia's king.

And now Harley was with her husband—and it was Ackley's doing.

Grabbing his whetstone with his free hand, he slid the blade along it, satisfied with the crisp sound of steel slicing through the air.

What did I do? His hands shook slightly. He set the whetstone aside since the blade remained sharp. He pinched his eyes shut. *What did I do?* He'd knowingly sent Harley back to her husband in the hopes she could kill him and avoid a bloody war. He opened his eyes. Before parting, he'd given her his sword's match—Sword of Rage. As if a sword could protect her from the monster that was her husband. The issue wasn't Lyle killing Harley since the man needed her alive to cling to the throne. The problem was what he'd do to her mind and body.

Ackley set his sword down and rubbed his face. He didn't know if Harley was strong enough to survive Lyle. He wasn't even certain she could kill him. But if she was strong enough and if she did kill him, she would single handedly save the kingdom. Ackley was either a fool or a genius, and a fool was the more likely of the two.

He refused to consider Harley sharing Lyle's bed. His stomach twisted, and he forced himself to think of something else.

Owen and Idina should be safely in Kreng by now. Although Owen was probably still furious with Ackley for letting Ledger take Harley to the royal castle. Ackley rubbed his cheek. The bruise had faded, but he still remembered Owen swinging and punching him for what he'd done. That was about the time Idina started questioning the reasoning behind it and figured out Lyle was on the throne and Owen and Harley were half siblings instead of cousins. Owen still hadn't acknowledged any of it.

"Are you awake?" Gytha whispered loudly from the other side of the tent flap.

If he'd been asleep, that would have woken him. "Yeah."

"Edison told me you'd arrived," the warrior woman said as she ducked inside. "Why are you in here?"

Since it was after midnight, he hadn't wanted to take the time to pitch his own tent, so he'd asked to borrow the tent of the soldier on duty—figuring he wouldn't be using it any time soon. Instead of passing out as he'd expected, he tossed and turned until he finally sat up and lit the candle.

He raised a single eyebrow. "I think the better question is why aren't you in your own tent sleeping?" After all, one of them needed a good night's rest.

"I told them to notify me the moment you arrived." She sat across from him. "Since you're here and not out murdering people, I assume your sister is safe?"

He nodded, thankful he'd managed to warn Idina and Owen before they were ambushed.

"What about Harley and Ledger?" Gytha leaned forward, visually inspecting Ackley's sword.

His right hand made a gesture, giving his permission for her to pick the weapon up.

She shook her head and leaned back.

Ackley plucked the sword and sheathed it before tucking it under the bedroll. "No one went after them, if that's what you're asking."

"I guess Harley isn't important enough to kill." She snorted.

"The opposite, actually." He rubbed a hand over his face,

not wanting to have this conversation right now. However, it was better to just get it over with rather than prolonging it. "Her husband, Lyle, is the false king. Ledger took her to him."

Gytha's eyes widened.

"The answer to your next question is no," Ackley continued. "She had no knowledge of him being alive or on the throne." He stretched out on his bedroll, extending his legs. It felt good to be off the horse.

Brows drawing together, Gytha slowly nodded. "Of course, she didn't."

Surprise washed through Ackley. He expected Gytha would accuse Harley of being involved since the warrior woman didn't care for Harley.

"I may not like her," Gytha explained, "but I know she'd never be involved in the assassination of her family."

He nodded, thankful Gytha wasn't asking more intimate questions. Ones he had no intention of thinking about, let alone answering. "I'm going to get some sleep." It had been days since he'd had a decent night's rest.

Gytha stood. "When did you figure out Lyle is the one on the throne?"

"I've suspected for some time."

"And you *let* Ledger take Harley to the royal castle?" she asked carefully.

"I did." He closed his eyes, knowing her questions were leading somewhere he didn't want to go.

Her feet shuffled over the dirt. "Sometimes I can't figure you out."

He kept his eyes shut, not wanting to meet her assessing gaze. Not when he hadn't come to terms with what he'd done yet.

"I couldn't figure out why you liked someone who couldn't

wield a sword. You tried telling me she was strong in other ways. I just didn't see it." Another shuffling noise. "What do you think she's going to do for you? Spy on her husband?"

"Among other things," he mumbled, not wanting to think about what Harley could be doing right now. The image of her sharing a bed with her husband was more than he could stomach. He rubbed his throbbing temples.

"Do you truly care for her? Or are you only using her to do your bidding?"

At that Ackley opened his eyes and glared at Gytha.

She raised her hands in surrender. "Sorry I asked." She ducked out of the tent.

His heart pounded. He hoped Harley wasn't wondering the same thing. Reaching over, he snuffed out the candle, sending the tent into darkness.

When he'd first considered training Harley to be a Knight, he'd done so because she was intelligent and genuinely seemed interested in becoming one, though he hadn't pointedly asked her. Now that he'd sent her to the royal castle, he had a sick feeling in his stomach that he'd made a mistake. He should have trained her more, taught her how to kill, practiced with her. At the very least, told her what he was doing instead of training her without her knowledge.

His fingers curled inward, and he made two fists. He needed to stop second-guessing himself and trust Harley could handle the situation. She was smart, intuitive, and stealthy. And she may be the best bet they had at preventing a bloody war where hundreds of lives would be lost. Maybe if he hadn't fallen for her, or spent the night with her, he wouldn't have this queasy feeling in his stomach. Regardless, he needed to pull himself together. By tomorrow morning, every Marsden soldier would know he was there. Which meant he'd have to address and lead his men. Be the prince they expected and needed, not a love-sick man pining over a married woman.

Traveling with seven hundred men on foot wasn't nearly as slow and tedious as Ackley feared. Gytha had organized the men into smaller groups of fifty, each one setting out in fifteen-minute intervals, which resulted in less wasted time. The food was cooked, and the tents were set up and taken down while a portion of the army was traveling. Being structured this way allowed them to cover almost twice as much ground as they had when under Owen's command.

As the sun set, Ackley and his group neared the Landania border. In the distance he could see a row of heads on spikes indicating where Melenia ended. Based on the topography, it appeared they were on track to avoid all major towns. He headed down the hill, toward the spikes, leading his horse. There was no point in being the only mounted soldier in his group.

"Your Highness," a familiar voice said, coming up behind Ackley.

He allowed Finnegan, one of his most trusted men, to catch up with him.

"Captain Gytha is asking if we should set up camp in Melenia before nightfall?"

As the first group, they determined how far the army traveled each day. "We're crossing the border." They were too close to Landania not to seek refuge there.

"Yes, Your Highness," Finnegan said.

Not wanting Landania—and Emperion by extension—to think Ackley was invading with his army, he'd written a letter to the empress of Emperion stating his case and asking for asylum. "Lieutenant, I need you to do something for me." He withdrew the letter from under his tunic. "Take my horse, this letter, and this map." Ackley pulled out another paper, handing everything to Finnegan. "See that this letter is delivered to the empress. Bring her reply to me immediately."

"Yes, Your Highness."

Finnegan tucked the letter and map into his belt before mounting the horse and taking off.

Gytha joined Ackley. "What's going on?" she demanded. "Are we making camp for the night?"

"Eventually."

"Are those...heads on spikes?" Gytha asked, her voice rising higher pitched than usual.

"Unfortunately." He was surprised she hadn't seen them before when she and Ledger had met him and Harley near the border.

"Are you certain you don't want to set up camp here?"

Ackley snorted, as if here was safer. "We need to enter Landania before we stop." That way if Lyle attacked them, they'd be on Emperion soil, and it would be seen as an assault on the empress.

Gytha shivered. "You never did tell me what you were doing in Russek." They continued down the hill, toward the spikes. She didn't say anything else. If she suspected why he'd gone, she gave no indication she knew.

"I met with Kerdan," he revealed.

"The Russek prince in exile?"

"Yes."

"And?"

He didn't feel like discussing it now—especially with so many soldiers around. "Russek isn't the enemy."

19

"Even though they did all this?" Gytha waved a hand at the spikes.

"The late King Drenton is responsible for this." He nodded at the severed heads. "He's dead. One day soon, Kerdan will sit on the throne. He is not evil like his father was." However, the Russek soldiers were ruthless and would require someone strong and capable like Kerdan to keep them in line.

The smell hit Ackley like a boulder so he pulled his tunic up over his mouth and nose. Flies buzzed. Most of the heads were severely decayed with missing eyeballs and rotting flesh. A few vultures flew overhead.

The stench caused several soldiers to vomit. Ackley forced one foot in front of the other, focusing on the ground in front of him.

"I assume there aren't any towns nearby?" Gytha asked.

"No." While there could be a small village or two, there weren't any cities around for miles. It was one of the reasons he chose this location. The other was the low rolling hills. Once they went over the one up ahead, they would set up camp and no one looking from Melenia would see them. They'd be close, but not too close. Plus, he didn't want to encroach too far into Landania and upset the empress. He had no idea what sort of woman she was. He'd never heard of a woman lording over a kingdom, let alone one the size of Emperion. She had to be smart, mighty, and not one to trifle with. Ackley would have to tread carefully.

He'd already told Gytha where they were going and why. He suspected she'd asked the question to take her mind off the row of death. They stepped foot into Landania, and Ackley's shoulders relaxed.

"Where did Finnegan go?" Gytha asked, nodding up ahead where the soldier disappeared over a low hill.

"He's taking a letter to the empress." Ackley didn't know how long it would take for his man to reach Rema and return with an answer.

After traveling about two miles, he gave the command to stop. His men immediately got to work setting up the tents and cooking food. The second group arrived and got to work. Three and a half hours later, all seven hundred of his men were accounted for. Darkness had descended as he stood outside his tent, looking over the camp they'd erected. He made a list of tasks that needed to be completed.

He tilted his head to the side, cracking his neck. Then he whistled, garnering the attention of Morton.

"Your Highness," he said sardonically.

His men knew he hated to be addressed so formally. "Gather my captains. Inform them that I want them running drills with their units daily, so they remain busy."

"Anything else?"

"Once you've dispersed that message, gather my Knights. It's time to work."

A wicked smile spread across Morton's face. "It's about time." He gave a curt nod.

"Why is she here?" Warner asked, pointing his sword at Gytha's approaching form.

"I invited her to join us," Ackley said, wiping his brow with his free arm.

"You've never invited someone from the army to join us before."

Ackley shrugged. "Doesn't matter what I've done in the past." He lifted his sword and swung. Warner barely parried the hit. "Only thing that matters is what I'm going to do in the future." Ackley stepped in closer, lifted his sword as if to strike him, and then swung his leg, knocking Warner onto his back. Ackley aimed his sword at his fellow Knight's chest.

Warner growled. "I concede."

Gytha now stood alongside his other Knights. "You asked me if I wanted to spar," she said. "Well, I'm here. Let's get to it."

Ackley sheathed his sword. "Sparring is over." He motioned for his six men and Gytha to come closer.

"If sparring is over, why am I here?" Gytha asked.

"Assignments?" Neville guessed.

Ackley nodded. They'd wasted enough time traveling. Now that his soldiers were safe, it was time for him to focus on what needed to be done. "Morton and Galvin, you'll be numbers one and two, and will head north to the royal castle. Rikter is already there. Your job is to support him and make sure information gets to me in a timely manner."

They both nodded in agreement.

"Warner and Neville, you'll be numbers three and four, and you two will stay nearby. You will be my eyes and ears in Landania. Keep watch for troop movement in the area."

"What's the radius?" Neville asked.

"Ten miles," Ackley answered. "And Fletcher and Dalton, numbers five and six, I want the two of you in Kreng. If Owen or Idina need to get word to me, it will be through you."

"And me?" Gytha asked. "I assume you have a job for me as well. Otherwise, I wouldn't be here."

"Gytha and I will be going on a mission. Ruthar will remain here in my place."

Each of the six men raised his right hand, made a fist, and placed it over his chest. Ackley nodded in acknowledgment.

Ackley watched his men walk back toward the camp. When he and Gytha were alone, he let out a long breath, considering all he needed to do today.

"You're in your element among your Knights," Gytha commented.

"How so?"

She shrugged. "You seem more commanding and sure of yourself."

He looked at her sidelong. "You mean my roguish charm is gone?"

Gytha punched his shoulder. "Charming is not a word I'd use to describe you."

His brows pulled together. "What word would you use?"

She pursed her lips. "Distanced, detached, pig-headed, loner."

"I said one word, not a list." He rolled his eyes; he was none of those things.

They started walking back toward the camp.

"You're also smart, conniving, and an excellent planner. You're just not a strong leader."

He never should have asked Gytha in the first place. Growing up, third in line to the throne, he never thought he'd have to rule, so he never bothered learning how to. When the line shifted to his cousin, Dexter, he was thrilled. But now, here in Melenia, he realized his lack of training on the subject proved to be a weakness. While he understood his responsibility to ensure his men were taken care of and made it home alive, he couldn't be the figurehead they needed and wanted.

"What are you thinking?" Gytha asked. "Because I don't like the look on your face right now."

He raised a single brow. "And what look would that be?"

She shook her head. "That you have a plan you know I won't like."

He smiled wryly. "Do I ever do anything you like?"

She glared at him. "What is it?"

The odd thing happened to be that Gytha would actually like this plan. "We're going to meet with the Emperion empress."

"Didn't you just send a man to arrange that?"

"I did."

"So, when he returns, I'll go with you to speak to her?"

"Not quite." He wanted to have an idea of what they were getting themselves into before he met with Rema. To discover that information, they needed to see where the empress lived and learn what her people thought of her. In other words, they had some reconnaissance to do.

"Then I'm afraid I don't understand you." She stopped walking.

"We're leaving in an hour. Be prepared." Not having time to discuss it further with Gytha, he hurried away. A lot needed to be done before they left.

If everything went as Ackley hoped, Kerdan would be crowned the king of Russek in the coming weeks. Once that happened, Kerdan wouldn't support Lyle, thus lending credence to Owen's quest for the throne. If Ackley could get Emperion to support Owen as well, they could force Lyle to step down. However, Ackley was only supposed to ask permission for his troops to remain in Landania. Owen hadn't said anything about negotiating a deal on his behalf. Since Ackley wasn't from the mainland, he had no business getting involved. Too bad he considered himself working on his sister's behalf and would do whatever necessary to secure her throne. He wouldn't leave here until he believed her safe. If that meant going behind Owen's back, so be it. It was a sacrifice Ackley was willing to make.

When he reached the tents, he sought out Ruthar. Though Ruthar wasn't a Knight, Ackley had used him a handful of times.

"Your Highness," Ruthar greeted him.

Ackley scanned him from head to toe. They had the same long lanky legs, brown shaggy hair, and shoulders. Even though Ruthar was an inch shorter, he'd do.

"Walk with me." Ackley led the way between two tents to an unoccupied area where no one could overhear them. "I need you to do something for me."

"Of course, Your Highness." Ruthar nodded. "Anything you need."

"I'm going on a mission. However, I don't want anyone to know I'm gone."

"Okay," Ruthar said, his voice drawling the word out longer than necessary. "What do you need from me?"

"I need you to be me." Ackley folded his arms, assessing Ruthar's poor posture.

"I'm not sure I can do that..."

"You don't have a choice. My personal guard will assist you. Make a point of leaving the tent once or twice a day, with my cape on, so my soldiers see me. Other than that, remain inside."

"Where will you be?"

Ackley didn't respond. Ruthar didn't need to know anything. "Make sure the cape's hood is up, you stand tall and straight, and speak as little as possible."

"Okay."

"You'll also need to walk like me."

Ruthar nodded again. If there was one thing he excelled at,

it was imitating those around him. It was one of the main reasons Ackley had used him on missions in the past.

"Meet me over that ridge in twenty." He pointed south.

"Yes, Your Highness."

Ackley headed to his tent to gather what he needed for his journey. Once he packed his provisions, he brought his six guards inside so he could explain the plan to them. He made it clear no one was to know he was gone. They were to address Ruthar as the prince, follow him around as if he were Ackley, and make sure no one discovered where Ackley had gone. He then proceeded to tell his men where he was going in case something happened, and they needed to get a hold of him.

Satisfied, the seven of them exited the tent, heading to the other side of the ridge Ackley had pointed out earlier. When they arrived, they found Ruthar there waiting for them.

"Here." Ackley tossed a sack at Ruthar.

Ruthar opened it, pulling out Ackley's pants and tunic.

"Put those on." He unlatched his cape, handing it to Ruthar.

Once Ruthar was dressed, Ackley made him walk back and forth a few times until he moved like Ackley.

"The ones who'll seek you out are either us or the six you sent on missions," Harper said. "We shouldn't have any problems."

It was time to be on his way. "Head back to camp. Find Captain Gytha and send her this way. Harper, you're in charge. If any decisions need to be made, if the camp needs to move, anything at all—the decision is yours."

"Yes, Your Highness."

"Your priority is protecting my men."

"Of course, Your Highness."

Ackley watched the seven of them head back toward camp. Thirty minutes later, Gytha approached, leading two horses.

"You don't think anyone is going to notice two of our six horses are gone?"

A smile spread across her face. "It's taken care of." She mounted her horse.

He had no idea what she'd done, but he trusted her.

Ackley also mounted, and the two of them set out.

"I'm glad you're taking me along instead of trying to do this on your own," Gytha said. "Maybe you're not as pig-headed as I thought."

If she could take a jab at him, he could take one at her as well. "It's safer to travel with a female. Less threatening."

Her shoulders stiffened.

Ackley chuckled. "Thankfully, appearances can be deceiving."

They rode in companionable silence for several minutes. "I'm surprised you didn't want to wait a day or two to make sure the camp was running efficiently before we left."

He'd considered it. "I wanted to get out of there before anyone realized I was gone. There was still so much commotion setting up camp, it was the perfect time to slip away unnoticed."

"I'm shocked you trust anyone enough to leave them in charge."

He still grappled with it. "If there's a deal to be made with the empress, it has to be with me." And waiting for his man to reach the empress and then for the empress to send word back to him would take too long. This was far more efficient. And he hated sitting around doing nothing. To ensure his sister remained hidden and safe, and for Harley to not be under

Lyle's command for too long, Ackley needed to speed things along.

While he hoped Harley killed Lyle and saved them a lot of trouble, he couldn't depend on it. He had to have a backup plan—and this was it.

"Don't get me wrong," Gytha said as they continued along, "I'm glad I'm not going to have to sit around camp for a couple of weeks. Traveling—even with you—is preferable to that."

Ackley chuckled. He always enjoyed spending time with Gytha. She amused him with her lack of filter and blunt way of speaking.

"I hate traveling over open land," Gytha mumbled. "I feel so exposed."

"Don't worry, there's a forest up ahead." Which was why he chose this route.

As they crested the last hill before the forest, a lone rider sat atop a horse, a sword in hand. Gytha withdrew her sword and cursed. Ackley squinted, trying to see the person better. There was nothing remarkable about him—his shoulders were slightly hunched forward, his hair hung loose around his face, and his horse was on the smaller side. To Ackley, the man appeared to be a commoner. If it weren't for the sword in hand, he wouldn't be concerned. But one thing Ackley had learned through the years, anyone trying to look normal had to be anything but.

He slid his dagger from his sleeve. "Let me do the talking."

"There's going to be talking? I'd rather not waste our time with pleasantries."

Ackley chuckled. That was when he noticed another man out of the corner of his eye. Suddenly, he realized they were surrounded.

CHAPTER THREE

HARLEY

*H*arley sat across from Lyle at the dining table. The last time she'd sat there, her uncle had been in that seat. No, not her uncle, her father. She still couldn't get used to the idea that the father she'd grown up with wasn't hers biologically. Rubbing her temples, she shoved the thought aside. She'd deal with that later. One of the benefits of being here in the castle was that she could investigate to see if it was true. Clearly, Lyle believed it. Deep in her heart, she knew it as well. But her brain still screamed that it was impossible. Perhaps it was wishful thinking on her part.

A servant entered, set plates in front of Lyle and Harley, and then left.

Harley glanced at her chicken and potatoes, her stomach growling. She didn't think Lyle would poison the food since he needed her alive, so she took a bite.

Lyle sat there, staring at her, not touching his plate.

She set her fork down, the food feeling like bark in her

throat as she swallowed it. "Is something the matter, dear?" she asked, trying to sound pleasant.

His eyes narrowed. "Nothing is the matter." His right pointer finger tapped on the table as he stared at her. "I'm just trying to figure you out."

"How so?" The words slipped from her mouth before she could think better of it. She prayed he didn't suspect her of treachery.

A slow smile spread across his face. "I'm going to ask you a series of questions. You will answer them."

She nodded, suddenly unable to speak. She feared he'd ask her if she was working for Ackley. If so, he'd kill her right there. Sliding her hands back on the table, she clutched her fork and knife, forcing herself to eat. At least the utensils would serve as weapons if Lyle came at her. Her hands started shaking. She was ill-prepared to deal with a man like him.

"Who did you travel with these past few weeks before joining me here?" He picked up his utensils and started eating, as if this were normal conversation.

"Owen and his soldiers." She felt him staring at her. Peering up at him, his eyes had narrowed into slits. "But his soldiers left him and came to you." It sounded more like a question than an answer. She didn't want to say anything about Ackley, Idina, or the Marsden soldiers unless she had to.

Lyle took a bite of his chicken, his jaw moving as he chewed, staring at her. He swallowed. "Did you overhear anything about my father?"

She dropped her fork. Quickly picking it back up, she stabbed a potato, shoving it in her mouth. She kept her gaze on her plate. Lyle couldn't know that Ackley killed his father. "I... uh...did hear something." Ackley had once told her when lying, the best lie stemmed from truth.

"What, exactly, did you hear?" He set his fork down, reaching for his goblet.

"Owen mentioned Commander Beck died in Marsden." She chose her words carefully, not divulging that Beck tried killing Owen, and Ackley had killed him as a result, branding the commander a traitor to Melenia. She was curious to hear what, if anything, Lyle knew about the situation. Ledger had asked about Beck's death, demanding to know who murdered him. Just before Lyle killed Ledger, Ledger had been about to reveal that Ackley ran him through with a sword.

He set his goblet down. "Not everything went according to plan." He looked across the long table at her. "My father wasn't supposed to die. Neither was your brother."

It felt as if he'd punched her. Her hands moved to her lap, her fingers curling inward, making two fists. Her eyes filled with tears. "So only my uncle, aunt, and cousins were supposed to die?" she ground out. As if sparing Hollis would have made everything better.

"Coden wasn't your uncle, he was your father."

She closed her eyes. Hearing it from Lyle caused an unsettling feeling to wash over her. She still didn't understand the circumstances surrounding her conception. Not when the king was married to her mother's sister. Harley's last encounter with her mother came to mind. Her mother had said there were things she didn't know. She'd been trying to tell Harley something. She rubbed her forehead, a headache forming.

Lyle stood, pulling his sleeves down. "I have duties to attend to."

She nodded and resumed eating, ignoring him.

"How long?" he asked as he headed toward the exit.

"Until what?"

"You bleed."

It felt as if a bucket of cold water had been poured over her head. She struggled for what to say. If there was a way to postpone having to share a bed with him, she would. She was about to lie and say she was bleeding. It would buy her a week.

"I need to know that you're not with Ledger's child before we can resume relations. I don't want to question whether my heir is really mine."

She blinked, understanding the gift she'd been given. Since Lyle had been gone for two weeks, she couldn't stretch it out too long. "Next week I should bleed," she lied.

"Good. I want proof." He exited the room.

She slouched in the chair, relieved. She'd just bought herself two weeks until she had to share a bed with her husband.

Harley paced inside the queen's bedchamber. With Lyle's return, so much had already changed. She eyed the door leading to what she presumed to be his room. Of course, it could be another closet, but she didn't think so. After hesitating a moment, she finally summoned her courage and went over to the door. Her hand shook as she pushed it open, peering inside. Instead of the king's personal bedchamber as she'd expected, she found a smaller room containing a gigantic bed with dark blue curtains. No other furniture adorned the area. The only purpose of this place was to perform one's marital duties.

A small part of her considered that she might have been conceived there. She shook her head. Only royalty used this bed. If the king took a mistress, he'd entertain her in a suite established solely for that purpose. The mere thought made her stomach sour, especially the idea that her own mother had been intimate with the king. She couldn't help but contemplate if it had been a mutual relationship where they enjoyed one another's company. Or, if the king had simply wanted Lady Mayle and she'd had no choice but to give her body to him. Harley backed up a step, wanting to get away from this room.

She closed the door, wondering if the king had taken many lovers through the years. When Harley stayed at the royal castle, he often threw parties filled with nobility. She'd never paid attention to whether he spent any time with other women or not. Her aunt had never hinted at being unhappy with the king. However, Harley had never really asked or talked with her aunt about such things. Her mother had taught her conversations like that weren't polite. So, as it stood, Harley felt as if she didn't truly know those closest to her.

Harley took the chair from the queen's writing desk and placed it under the door handle to the adjoining suite. Then she went over and locked the door leading from the antechamber to her room. Satisfied no one could come in, she grabbed Ledger's bag which had been placed on the chest in her room.

Sitting on the floor, she untied the straps and opened it. Inside, she found a pair of pants and a tunic. At the bottom, there were two pouches. She carefully pulled both out, setting them on the floor next to her. After wiping her sweaty hands on her dress, she opened the first pouch, careful not to touch its contents.

A tangy smell greeted her. Peering inside, she saw a handful of bright green leaves. She set the pouch aside. Opening the second one, she found what looked like several light brown roots, though she couldn't be certain. Perhaps Ledger had used these items to make the poison he put on the horse's reins to paralyze her hands. Or it could be what he put in her mouth to knock her out. Regardless, she needed to discover what these items were. Maybe she could take the leaves and roots to the library and do some investigating. There had to be at least one book on poisons. Closing the pouches, she picked them up and scanned the room, searching for a place to hide them. Somewhere no one would accidentally find them. She thought about all the places Ackley had shown her.

On a hunch, she reached down and pulled back the corner of the area rug. One of the wood planks appeared more worn than the others. Smiling, she knelt and tried prying it up. When it wouldn't move, she pushed on the end, and it flipped upward. Inside, she found a handful of trinkets, a few sketches of flowers, and some money. Tears welled in her eyes, and she had to stifle a gasp. It felt as if her heart were being squeezed. These precious items belonged to her dear aunt. They weren't meant for her to see, so she left them there undisturbed.

Harley put the pouches inside. She was about to close the wood plank when she remembered the piece of paper she'd received in the stables. She pulled the paper out from the neckline of her dress.

Harley—

If you need immediate extraction, light the candle on the queen's dresser and place it in the north window. If you need to communicate, light the candle on the queen's vanity table and place it in the south window. We have a common friend, and he asked me to watch out for you. Best of luck.

It wasn't signed. Harley hoped the mutual friend this person referred to was Ackley. If so, then this changed things. No longer was she isolated and alone in her endeavor to kill the false king. Not that she needed help, but knowing she had some sort of support emboldened her. She placed the letter in with the pouches and closed the wood plank. Standing, she settled the rug back in place.

Glancing over at the dresser, she eyed the six-inch tall candle sitting in a glass holder. It had three wicks and was the width of a hand. On the vanity, she spotted a long skinny candle about a foot high with a single wick. It, too, was encased in a glass jar. On either side of the queen's bed, two narrow windows were situated. The windows on the right had to be the north windows, the other ones, the south.

Things started falling into place.

Somehow, some way, she was no longer alone.

After changing into nightclothes, she climbed into bed. Sleep didn't come. The stillness around her brought up thoughts she wasn't ready to face.

Thoughts of Ackley.

Had Ackley planned on sending her to the royal castle this entire time? Since he had one of his men here to help her, she had to consider the possibility. As far as she knew, the last time he had contact with his men had been before the two of them traveled to Penlar together. That was before they could tolerate one another.

Harley didn't think Owen knew Ackley's suspicions. Surely her cousin wouldn't approve of Ackley's endeavors either. If Ackley had surmised way back then that Lyle was on the throne, why hadn't he said something to her?

His actions left her wondering if he even cared for her, let alone loved her.

But she knew Ackley. He would not have incorporated her into his plans if he didn't think her capable. Which meant regardless of what he felt for her, she had a job to do. Ever since her brother was murdered, she'd wanted retribution. This could be her one shot to get it. She needed a plan, and she needed to set it into motion tomorrow morning.

A cool breeze floated against Harley's hair. When she rolled onto her back, the wind wafted against her face.

"Harley," a soft voice crooned. "Wake up."

Her eyes flew open. She found herself in darkness, the outline of a man hovering above her. Her heart pounded, and fear coursed through her. That smell—horse and steel—meant it was Lyle.

"Why is there a chair wedged against the door adjoining our rooms?" he asked, his voice low.

Harley blinked, wondering how he'd gotten in there. She swallowed, trying to keep her head on straight and not let fear override common sense. "I don't know how many men you have on the castle grounds. Any one of them could sneak in here for a multitude of reasons. This is the queen's room. There are valuable items in here someone might want to steal, or I could be kidnapped for ransom. I don't know." She prayed he bought the lie. It seemed plausible to her. "A queen usually has some form of a royal guard." She swallowed again. Her body turned hot, sweat beading on her forehead. She could barely breathe.

Silence extended between them, making her skin crawl with dread.

"Your doors are to remain unguarded—by lock or chair. I

have men stationed at the top of the staircases. No one is permitted on this level except for the two of us."

No one would be able to hear her cry for help.

"Understood?" he asked.

"Yes," she whispered. She wanted to ask him how he'd gotten in, but she kept her mouth shut. If he'd broken one of the doors, she would have heard it. He could have picked the lock to the one door. However, there was another possibility she had to consider. There could be another entrance she was unaware of. She thought she'd learned everything about this castle. However, this was the queen's room, and she'd only been in here a handful of times. There had been no need for her to know the secrets of this room. As to how Lyle had discovered it, she didn't know. But she would be sure to find out.

He stood, making no move to leave.

"Is there something else?" she asked. As soon as the question was out, she wished she hadn't asked it.

"We need to talk."

Exhaustion consumed Harley since she hadn't slept much. By the time Lyle left her room, dawn was on the horizon. When he'd first started questioning her about Owen, she hadn't understood why he did so in the middle of the night. Then she realized that the more tired her body became, concealing certain truths turned increasingly difficult.

He'd grilled her on what Owen told her, if she knew anything about Commander Beck's death, what she'd been doing in Penlar, and if she'd seen the letters Ledger claimed she had. She didn't think she slipped up at all. She tried to stay as close to the truth as possible. But it had been so late, and she'd been so tired.

After dressing, she went to get something to eat. She wanted to make friends with the servants who worked in the kitchen. The more people she knew, the better. Having eyes and ears on her side could only help.

Nearing the kitchen, she stopped, remembering the last time she was in there and had spoken to Kerdan. He'd given her the only key to the dungeon and told her to free her family and to get as far away from the castle as possible.

While she'd never been in the dungeon, she didn't think it large enough to accommodate a significant number of people. If Lyle still had the soldiers' loved ones hidden, it couldn't be there. Her gut told her he had them holed up somewhere. Given the number of soldiers on the castle grounds, she doubted those men were there out of pure loyalty. They had to be there because Lyle still had their family members. Which meant she had a job to do. She needed to figure out where the soldiers' loyalties lie.

As their soon-to-be queen, they had to listen to her. She snorted, the sound loud in the empty hallway. Perhaps she could be the one to command the army, not Lyle. She smiled and stepped into the kitchen, envisioning a woman leading an army of men.

CHAPTER FOUR

ACKLEY

"We're surrounded," Ackley mumbled. Given the barren terrain, the area didn't seem conducive for attacking someone. So far, the men hadn't advanced or drawn their weapons. At least not yet. No one waved or shouted out in greeting, leading him to believe they weren't friendly either.

"Who do you think they are?" Gytha asked. "Melenia soldiers?"

"No." Lyle wouldn't dare send soldiers to Landania and risk starting a war with Emperion until he secured his throne. And even then, that would be a stupid move. Ackley didn't think these men were from Russek since they didn't have the right build. "Let's keep moving."

The pair continued southeast.

Ackley's dagger remained in hand, at the ready. "Keep your fingers away from your sword," he whispered. "And don't make any sudden movements. Try to act nonthreatening." Maybe this was some sort of Landania unit who watched the border.

As they neared the man directly ahead of them, the others came in closer, forming a circle around Ackley and Gytha, effectively blocking an exit. Each man wore nondescript clothing—plain pants and tunics with no distinguishing marks. Nothing stood out about any of the seven men, which made Ackley even more uneasy. This was no regular guard, and they weren't soldiers dressed as civilians. He stretched his neck, loosening it up, in case he needed to defend himself.

"Do you plan on just riding right up to the leader?" Gytha nodded her chin toward the man in front of them, now about thirty feet away.

"It's easier to have a conversation if we're close, don't you think?" The man in front of them looked six feet, one hundred and eighty pounds. Based upon the way he held his horse's reins, he was right-handed.

"I doubt we're going to have a civil conversation." She glanced behind her. "They're getting closer."

"Who said anything about civil?" While Ackley knew the men were gaining ground on them, they still hadn't made a move to attack. Trying to keep his posture casual, he slid a second dagger from his sleeve into the palm of his hand. Things were about to get interesting.

They stopped fifteen feet from the man directly in front of them.

"I understand you speak for the hundreds of soldiers now camped on Emperion land," the man said, his accent thick.

"Where'd you hear that?" Ackley asked. At least the man hadn't insinuated the army was invading or attacking. Camping sounded neutral, making him speculate further about this group of men. He kept his shoulders down, listening for any sounds of attack coming from behind him.

The guy leaned forward on his horse, eyeing Ackley. "I read your letter."

Ackley inwardly cursed.

"Your man is fine, if that's what you're wondering."

Finnegan was not only well-trained but had specific instructions to not be taken alive. If Finnegan was unharmed and had handed over the letter willingly, then these men had to work for the empress. Most likely, they monitored the border for threats. Since this group hadn't attacked Ackley and Gytha, they must be trying to determine their intentions. It was probably why the man hadn't yet withdrawn the daggers tucked under his sleeves, or gone for the knives in his boots, or even the short sword strapped to his back hidden by the hood of his cloak. Funny that Ackley had similar weapons in the same places.

"Well?" the man asked. "Do you speak for the soldiers or not?"

"Yes," he answered, choosing his words carefully. "I speak for the men temporarily camped just inside Emperion's border."

The corners of the man's lips pulled downward. "You're Prince Ackley?" Although he asked it as a question, the man said it with purpose, demanding an answer.

Trying not to roll his eyes, Ackley took a deep breath, pulling the necessary facade over his face as he prepared to play the part he needed to. "Yes," he drawled, using his refined voice. "I am Prince Ackley of Marsden. I'm here assisting King Owen of Melenia as he fights for his crown, trying to rid the kingdom of the traitor sitting on the throne. King Owen remains in Melenia while I am here with my men seeking temporary asylum. I want an audience with Empress Rema."

The man's eyes shifted over to Gytha. "And you?"

"I'm Captain Gytha." She said each word slowly so the men could understand her. Though they used the same language, the men spoke with a higher tone and clipped syllables.

Ackley raised a single eyebrow, awaiting the man's response. Just looking at Gytha with her dark hair slicked back into a single braid, her squared shoulders, tanned skin, brown eyes, and muscled arms gave no question—this woman was a warrior through and through, strong enough to take on anyone here.

The man's attention returned to Ackley, and their eyes locked. Ackley got the impression that this man was trying to decide what to do with him.

To diffuse the building tension, Ackley decided to speak first. After all, he needed to meet with Rema. Idina, Owen, and Harley all depended on him. "I assume you're some sort of guard working for the empress?"

The man didn't respond.

Ackley smiled. "I suggest you either take me to meet with Empress Rema, or you deliver my letter to her." He leaned forward on his horse, casually placing his arms on his horse's neck. "As a prince from another kingdom, I have the right to demand an audience with your ruler."

Gytha added, "I'm sure your empress would want to know why there are soldiers on her land."

"That's why I'm here," the man finally replied, scratching the side of his neck.

Ackley tensed, knowing the man had just communicated something to his men who still surrounded them.

"We'll take you to a nearby inn," the man said. "You will

42

remain there while one of my men takes your letter to our empress."

"Very well," Ackley said as he eyed the men around them. They hadn't questioned where Marsden was located, why he was helping Owen, or why they needed asylum.

The leader tilted his head to the right and nudged his horse that way, turning his back to Ackley.

Ackley steered his horse alongside the man. "What's your name?"

The man smiled. "You can call me Brodek."

"Tell me, Brodek, do you have a title to go along with that name?" If that was even the man's name.

"A title as in captain or lieutenant?"

"Or knight or assassin." Ackley knew this was no ordinary soldier.

"I suppose it takes one to know one."

Ackley chuckled. "I suppose."

Gytha rode behind him not making conversation with anyone. With her protecting his back, he felt more comfortable to speak freely with Brodek.

"And your men," Ackley said. "What are their names?"

"Ridek, Olek, Tarnek, Herek, Erek, and Rettek."

Ackley mulled over the names. For some reason, he felt as if he were missing something. Instead of voicing his suspicions, he said, "And what town are you taking us to?"

"We're going to an inn."

"And is this inn not in a town?" He'd studied the map of the area enough to know the names of the nearby towns and villages.

"No."

Maybe it was some sort of hunting lodge. Unease took root. He didn't like the idea of not being near civilization.

"Relax," Brodek said. "Unless you don't trust me." He shrugged.

Ackley neither trusted him nor would he relax when he didn't know where they were going.

They rode all day. When the sun set and the sky darkened, Ackley began to worry since they'd gone farther east than he'd intended.

Just when Ackley was about to question how much longer they'd be traveling, Brodek whistled, and Ridek joined them. "Sweep the road ahead," Brodek ordered. Ridek nodded and nudged his horse, taking off. A few seconds later, he disappeared over the next hill.

Gytha shifted on her saddle but kept her mouth shut.

After another twenty minutes, complete darkness engulfed them. Ackley could no longer see the road ahead and feared his horse would stumble and injure itself. He was just about to insist they stop for the night when they rounded a bend and light shone up ahead. The group headed straight for the light.

As they got closer, the shape of a large stone castle came into view. It appeared to be a simple square building with a turret at each corner. The only light came from the handful of torches at the front entrance.

"Where I'm from," Ackley said, "our inns are usually wooden structures on the brink of collapse." All his senses remained on high alert. He scanned the land, searching for threats.

"This isn't a usual inn," Brodek replied.

"Tell me," Ackley said, hoping they weren't walking into some sort of dungeon, "are you from Emperion or Landania?" He could feel Gytha tense behind him.

"Landania is part of Emperion."

"Isn't that a new status?" The last thing he wanted was to be some sort of political hostage.

"Does it matter?" Brodek asked.

"I've told you I'm a prince," Ackley said as they neared the castle.

"And?"

"You don't treat me as one." Perhaps Brodek didn't believe Ackley or held him and Marsden in so little regard that he didn't care about Ackley's status.

"I've been around enough royalty to know some don't like to be treated differently." He raised his eyebrows, as if daring Ackley to disagree with what he said.

Perhaps once Ackley learned more about Emperion and its politics, he could understand Brodek and where he came from better. As it stood, Ackley wasn't certain if this man was on his side or not.

At the front doors, they dismounted. Herek and Erek took the horses while Brodek led Ackley and Gytha inside, followed by the remaining three men—Ridek, Olek, and Tarnek. Now that it was four against two, Ackley felt more comfortable with those odds. Should the need arise, he was confident he and Gytha could not only handle these four but do so without sustaining any major injuries.

A single torch lit the vestibule. Brodek grabbed the torch and led the way along a narrow corridor. The smell of mold and thick dust permeated the air.

"Is anyone else staying here?" Ackley asked, noticing the filth kicked up by their feet as they walked. For that much to accumulate, this place had to be abandoned. They left a trail of footprints in their wake.

"That is none of your concern."

Being in an abandoned castle with a group of men was his

concern. Especially since he was certain about one thing: these weren't ordinary soldiers. They had to be a special unit like his Knights back home. That being the case, he and Gytha needed to remain alert. Even if these men didn't intend to harm them, it didn't mean they could be trusted.

They went up a flight of stairs. Up was certainly better than down. After traversing through another corridor, Brodek stopped.

"The two of you will sleep in here." He opened a door, ushering them inside.

Ackley stepped around Brodek, unable to see much. "Do we get a light?"

"Not tonight." Without another word, Brodek closed the door.

"Maybe there's a window," Gytha mumbled.

Ackley stood still, not wanting to stub a toe. Gytha moved around the room cursing as she stumbled into furniture. Finally, she yanked a curtain aside, and moonlight shone through a filthy window, illuminating part of the room. There was a single bed, a desk, an empty fireplace, and a few trunks scattered about. Cobwebs hung between two of the bed posts.

"I'm tired and need to sleep." Ackley shrugged. At least they'd have a roof over their heads for the night. "You take the first watch. Wake me up in four hours."

"I need to get my weapons situated," she mumbled, pulling her knives from her boots.

"Something tells me these men don't need weapons to kill." Each one could probably snap a neck or incapacitate someone in less than a minute using just their bare hands. Ackley plopped on the bed, dust wafting in the air. He sneezed from the smell.

"Do you think they intend to kill us?" Gytha whispered, looking at the door.

"I haven't decided. But don't give them a reason to. Be your wonderful, pleasant self."

Gytha cursed. "How can you be so calm?"

"I'm too tired to worry right now. Once I've slept, then I'm sure I'll feel differently."

"Sometimes I want to strangle you," she ground out.

"I know." Smiling, he closed his eyes and fell fast asleep.

Ackley leaned against the wall, keeping watch. The door to the room remained unlocked, tempting him to walk out into the hallway and search through the castle. However, he refrained from doing so because he felt as if he were being tested. Exiting the room implied he was nosy. His training as a Knight begged him to investigate to see what he could learn. However, since his objective was to meet with the empress, he thought it best to remain in the room, to show he could be trusted. Trying to act like a normal prince would act. Staying in there proved far more difficult than he'd thought it would be.

Gytha still slept in the bed, her right arm thrown over her face.

He glanced through the dirty window. Outside, a thick fog coated the land making it impossible to see the surrounding area. He'd been on watch for five hours. During that time, he hadn't heard a single sound other than Gytha's incessant snoring. When he'd first gone on watch, she'd told him it sounded like three men had left. Assuming the only people here were the seven men, that meant four remained. Perhaps the three had gone to deliver his letter to the empress.

He really wanted to know if these men hailed from Landania or Emperion. While Brodek had claimed they were the same kingdom now, Ackley knew Emperion had only recently acquired Landania. After Russek invaded Melenia, the small kingdom of Landania felt threatened and joined Emperion to be protected. There had to be some people unhappy with the alliance.

Tapping his pointer finger on the window ledge, Ackley considered the machinations of the mainland further. Originally, he'd believed Russek had only invaded Melenia for soldiers and to acquire more land in order to overthrow Emperion. However, Lyle and his father had made a deal with Russek. They allowed Russek to take Melenia soldiers and civilians in exchange for the throne. Ackley continued tapping his finger, trying to speculate if he was missing anything.

"Do you have to be so annoying?" Gytha moaned. "I'm trying to sleep." She yanked the pillow over her head.

"You should be awake by now; it's well past sunrise."

She flew upright, rubbing her eyes. "It is?"

"Yes." The thought of sitting around this abandoned castle for days made him itch for action. He started pacing at the end of the bed, considering his options. He and Gytha could sneak away and locate the empress on their own. That might speed things along.

Gytha slid out from under the covers and stretched. "Are you worried about Harley?"

"Why do you ask?" He stopped pacing and faced her.

She shrugged. "You look upset. I thought maybe it was about her being with Lyle. You know since they're married and all." She ducked her head and reached down, pulling on her boots.

Every time Ackley thought about Harley being at the royal

castle with Lyle, uncertainty and dread filled him. Even though he had a man in place to aid her, there was nothing his man could do to stop Lyle from verbally abusing Harley. At least he didn't have to worry about Lyle physically harming her. Lyle couldn't kill her until he secured his throne. That wouldn't happen until the surrounding monarchs acknowledged him as the king of Melenia. Since Kerdan was battling with his stepmother, Jana, for the throne, Ackley had some time. Once Ackley met with Rema, he would know how she felt about Melenia and if she planned to acknowledge Lyle or support Owen. If Rema believed Lyle the successor, Ackley would have to immediately get Harley out of there because her life would be forfeit.

As for Harley being with her husband, he purposefully ignored all thoughts relating to that. He couldn't even consider Harley sharing a bed with another man. The mere thought made him want to slit someone's throat, bash his fist into Lyle's face, or scream and tear things apart.

Someone knocked on the door, garnering Ackley's attention. At least the person hadn't barged in. The day seemed to be getting off to a good start.

"Enter," Ackley called out. He stopped pacing and folded his arms, waiting to see who walked through the door.

CHAPTER FIVE

HARLEY

*H*arley entered the kitchen, curious what she'd find since Lyle hated having servants around. A handful of people rushed about, some chopping vegetables, others tending to pots over the fire in the hearth. Not nearly as many as her uncle had employed, but a lot for Lyle.

An elderly woman slid a loaf of bread onto a table before glancing at Harley. "You must be our new queen," she said with a warm smile revealing a missing front tooth. "What can I get for you?"

Harley took note that while the woman had acknowledged her status as the future queen, she hadn't addressed her as a lady. She was immediately on edge. "I came for something to eat."

The woman sliced off two pieces of bread and placed them on a plate. "Here you go. There are some apples in the basket behind you."

No one else in the kitchen acknowledged Harley's presence.

"Thank you." She took the plate and grabbed an apple. "Are you cooking for supper already?" It seemed like too much food for just her and Lyle.

The woman shook her head. "We're cooking for the soldiers outside."

"Then I don't want to get in your way." Harley hurried from the kitchen. Lyle wouldn't let anyone he didn't trust inside the castle. The people working in the kitchen had to be servants employed by the late Commander Beck. The sentries in the castle had probably served under Lyle.

Harley made her way to the library. Curling up on one of the four sofas, she kicked off her shoes then ate her food, contemplating the organization of the room. As a child, she'd been limited to the south wall, which consisted of simplistic picture books, detailed encyclopedias about animals, and books on the kingdom's history along with information on the noble families. As she got older, she'd been granted permission to read anything on the east wall. Those books contained wonderful stories told from writers around the mainland. Romance, adventure, dragons, pirates. She'd been so wrapped up in these fantastical stories that she'd never bothered to discover what the last two walls contained. The library was for members of the family and special guests; still, the late king rarely granted anyone permission to use the room.

Setting her plate aside, she stood and perused the shelves on the west wall, looking for anything related to poisons. Toward the right, she found a dozen or so whose titles seemed promising. *Plants, Leaves, and Trees: Various Uses* sounded interesting, so she pulled the book from the shelf and continued investigating. Along the north wall, she found several books on weather, crops, and metals. She'd just reached the end of the bookshelf and was about to head back to the section where she'd found the plant book when she felt Lyle behind her. Instead of acknowledging him, she pretended she didn't know he was there. Scanning the books on the east wall, she pulled a book off the shelf entitled *Love on the Sea* while furtively sliding the plant book into its spot since she didn't want Lyle to see her with it.

"I don't understand your fascination with reading," Lyle said, his low voice loud in the empty room.

Harley jumped, clutching the book to her chest while pretending to be startled. She turned and faced him, curtseying. "I fear there are a great number of things you don't understand about me since we haven't been married very long." She forced a smile on her lips. "I find reading a wonderful way to pass the time."

Lyle strode farther into the room, his hands clasped behind his back. "And I find a woman who spends her time reading useless."

The smile vanished from her face. "Did you need something?" Surely he wasn't there to enjoy her company since they could barely stand one another.

He silently read some of the titles before saying, "I have a question for you." His focus remained on the books.

"What is it?" she asked, not sure how he could possibly have another question after last night. Unless he'd caught her in a lie. Her spine tingled with fear.

He passed the section on poisons. Hopefully, he hadn't noticed the missing book. He turned to face her. "While traveling with your cousin, did you meet a man by the name of Ackley?" His eyes remained focused on her face, carefully watching her.

Her heartbeat sped up, and perspiration coated her

forehead. "Yes." She couldn't lie about that since several of the soldiers saw them together on multiple occasions.

"What can you tell me about him?"

She shrugged. "Not much. He is from a kingdom called Marsden." It took all her strength to remain calm and unruffled. "Why do you ask?" Under no circumstances could Lyle discover Ackley had killed his father. She had to protect Ackley, no matter the cost.

"Is he a prince?" he asked, slowly moving toward her.

"I believe someone referred to him as a prince; however, I don't think he's in line to the throne. I'm not certain, though."

"I want to make sure I understand this correctly. A prince from another kingdom is here with his soldiers."

She didn't recall saying anything about Marsden soldiers being there. Ledger must have told him. "Yes," she replied, seeing no need to contradict him since he already knew this information. "Ackley is here offering aid to Owen. They reached a treaty of some sort, though they never discussed the details with me."

Lyle stopped two feet in front of her. "He's quite skilled, isn't he?"

Clutching the book to her chest, her brows drew together, pretending not to understand him. "Skilled?"

Lyle's eyes darkened. "I've been told he is more soldier than prince." He took a step closer to her, now only a foot away.

"I wouldn't know," she whispered, the room suddenly cold.

"You wouldn't?"

Harley needed to tread carefully since she didn't know what Lyle had heard. "Ackley is like Owen. They are both princes and swordsmen. That is all I know."

"Ackley is my enemy."

She hated Lyle and considered him her enemy. "I understand."

"I want him dead."

She would never let it happen. Lyle would be dead before he touched Ackley. She would make sure of it or die trying.

"Do you know where Ackley is?" He leaned toward her.

She had to force herself to remain in place, not backing away from him. She shook her head, unable to speak. Lyle had sent a group of soldiers after Ackley and Gytha, but they'd failed to kill the Marsdens and instead, Ackley and Gytha had managed to kill the Melenians. It was what had sent Lyle away from the castle for two weeks, investigating what happened. She had no idea if Ackley and Gytha had met up with their soldiers and made it to Kricok.

"So, you don't know where he is headed?"

She shook her head. "Owen never discussed his plans with me. I don't know where he sent Ackley."

"We can't be sure Ackley is even following Owen's orders. Ackley could have gone rogue, seeking land or title here."

Ackley wasn't interested in any of that, but she refrained from saying so. Lyle wanted information, and she had to be careful not to give it. "I don't know what his intentions are." Tears threatened with the truth of what she said. "After all, I'm married to you, and I had no idea you intended to overthrow my family and take the throne." It was a bold, reckless thing to say.

"There are times when I wonder if you're that stupid." The corners of his lips rose ever so slightly. "Or if you're that smart."

Harley wondered the same thing. They were on dangerous ground.

Lyle turned and headed toward the exit.

"Where are you going?" she blurted out.

He glanced back at her, a wicked smile on his face. "Hunting."

After he left, two sentries entered the library. Afraid to garner suspicion, Harley took her romance book and headed back to her room. Later, when no one hovered over her shoulder, she'd return for the book on poisonous plants.

Pretending to read near one of the larger windows in her bedchamber, Harley furtively watched the soldiers outside, taking note of shift changes, eating times, and patrol runs. Occasionally, she'd catch a glimpse of Lyle walking among the soldiers, barking out orders.

While Harley despised the man, she didn't think she could plunge a sword into his throat or heart as Ackley had instructed. To end him, she would have to be more discreet. The most logical plan she'd come up with so far had to do with using the poison in the sacks, assuming the leaves and roots could kill a man. She just needed to find a way to convert the materials she had into something useful. Then all she'd have to do would be to slip the poison into his food or drink.

One of the soldiers brought a horse out of the stables, handing the reins to Lyle. He mounted the animal and took off, heading away from the castle.

Harley rose from her chair. She couldn't waste this precious gift of time she'd just been given. Setting her book aside, she contemplated her options. A paranoid man like Lyle who didn't trust many people, including Harley, would have his room rigged so he'd know if anyone entered.

Of the two entry points, if she used the one from the

adjoining room, he'd know without a doubt she entered. Which meant the main door off the antechamber would be the safer option. It would still be rigged, but at least Lyle wouldn't know who'd entered that way.

Wiping her sweaty palms on her dress, she exited her room and entered the antechamber, standing before Lyle's door. Her entire body shook. To pull this off, she needed to believe she could do it.

Not knowing how much time she had, she reached for the door and opened it. Nothing exploded or fell on her head. Remaining at the threshold, she surveyed his room, taking it all in. She was about to step inside when she noticed a white substance on the floor covering a three-foot area. It appeared to be sugar or salt. If she stepped on it, she'd leave a footprint. She knelt, considering how Lyle entered and exited his room. If the substance remained there, he'd track it everywhere. Which meant he had to clean it up every time he entered.

Harley went back to her room, grabbed a cup, and then returned to the threshold. Kneeling, she used her hands to gather the salt into a pile before scooping it into the cup. After setting the cup aside, she stood and entered Lyle's room.

Her skin tingled. If Lyle found her there, he'd kill her. She stepped farther into the king's room. Like hers, a large bed took up the far wall. There was also an armoire and a dressing closet. She remained standing in the middle of the room, taking it all in, as Ackley had shown her. She looked for anything odd, out of place, or inexplicably worn. Nothing jumped out at her. A drop of sweat trickled down the side of her face. Taking a deep breath, she tried to calm her nerves so she could focus on the task at hand.

Nothing appeared out of place. Not a single item of clothing littered the floor, the bedsheets were pulled taut, and not a single piece of paper rested on the writing desk. Harley turned in a slow circle, searching for something, anything. In Lyle's house, he'd hid some important items under a floorboard in his bedchamber. She glanced around the room, not seeing any boards with a worn edge.

She scanned the area again. Ackley had told her the most typical hiding places were behind pictures, in drawers, and in furniture. Three tapestries hung in the room. She rushed over to one, glancing behind it. Nothing. She quickly checked the other two, not finding anything behind them. Kneeling, she peered under the bed, not seeing anything under it. Rushing over to the armoire, she quickly threw open the doors and checked inside the drawers which were all filled with Lyle's clothes. Shoving her hand into each corner, her fingers searched for something out of place.

Frustrated, she took a step back to close the doors. Two pine needles rested on the floor. Her heart pounded even harder. When she'd searched the floor, those hadn't been there. Which meant when she'd opened the doors to the armoire, she'd knocked the needles onto the floor. It had to be one of Lyle's ways of knowing if someone had been in his room snooping around. With shaking hands, she reached down and picked them up. She carefully placed each needle under a door, praying she'd put them in the correct locations and Lyle wouldn't notice.

Another bead of sweat slid down her cheek. She was a fool to think she could do this without any formal training. Lyle was cunning, and she was in over her head. Taking a step back, she realized how stupid it had been to come in there, especially since she hadn't even found anything. She took another step back and bumped into the chair at the writing desk. She went to straighten it when something caught her eye. A loose string hung from the one corner of the seat. On a hunch, she reached down, prying the cushion up. Beneath it, she discovered a handful of papers.

If she took the papers, Lyle would eventually discover they were missing. Then he'd know whatever information they contained could be in the hands of his enemy. The only option she had was to read through them and try to retain the information.

Her heart pounding, Harley scanned the first page. It listed each province and one city. The next paper had the names of captains along with the number of soldiers under each one's command. The third paper had the kingdoms Marsden, Greenwood Island, and Nell written on it. Then, next to each kingdom was a list of three to five ships. The last piece of paper had a map of Russek along with three spots marked near a mountain range.

Harley glanced up, noticing the lighting in the room had turned to an eerie shade of orange. The sun had to be setting. She'd been in there far too long. Carefully setting the papers back, she replaced the cushion on top of them. She went to push the chair back in but couldn't remember exactly where it had been. All the way in? Partially in? Her stomach twisted, and she felt as if she was going to vomit.

Somehow, some way, Lyle would know she'd been in there and make her pay. Scurrying over to the door, she grabbed the cup and exited the room. She stood at the threshold and sprinkled the salt on the floor, trying to keep it in the same three-foot area as before.

Loud voices came from out in the hallway. She was about to slam the door shut when she thought better of it. Not wanting to disrupt the salt, she slowly closed the door, then ran toward her room. The voices sounded as if they came from right out in the hallway. She flung her door open and threw the cup inside, immediately pulling her door shut to cover the sound.

The door to the antechamber opened. "Harley," Lyle said, as he entered the room. "I was just coming to get you. Come with me."

"I'm on my way to get something to eat from the kitchen," she said, trying to keep her voice steady, though she felt as if ice filled her body.

"That can wait," he replied, holding the door open and motioning for her to exit the antechamber.

She did as he requested and moved into the corridor. Two soldiers led them toward the staircase while two additional soldiers followed close behind. If he'd discovered she'd been snooping in his room, he'd punish her. Back at his house in Penlar, whenever she did something that upset him, he locked her in the closet or withheld food and water from her.

"Is everything all right?" she asked.

"It is now," Lyle said. "We finally have Ackley, the prince from Marsden."

She gasped. It felt as if a sword had been plunged into her heart. She would find a way to save Ackley. As she descended the staircase, she prayed Lyle didn't intend to kill him right then and there. If Lyle threw Ackley in the dungeon, she could break him out.

"We technically don't have him in our possession, but we know where he is. I'm sending a group of men in to extract him."

Relief filled her. "Are your men competent enough to get him this time?" she asked, unable to avoid making the jab.

"I've assembled a group of my fiercest soldiers."

They entered the great hall where a dozen armed soldiers waited. Harley scanned their faces—the faces of the men who intended to kidnap the man she loved. All had wide shoulders and muscled arms. However, compared to the Russek soldiers, these men looked like whelps. All had swords prominently displayed. While they may be Lyle's most proficient men, they would be no match for Ackley.

Three men strode through the side door. Harley peered around Lyle to get a better look at them. Each man wore solid black, no weapons visible.

"Excellent," Lyle said. "I'm so glad the three of you are here."

The newcomers joined the others.

Harley slunk back a step. There was something about these three men...their eyes revealed no emotion, their faces had hard edges, and each had to be at least a foot taller and wider than the others. They reminded her more of the Russek soldiers—deadly and lethal.

"My wife has met Ackley," Lyle said to those assembled. "She will describe him to you so you can be sure you have the right person. I have a half dozen men ready to hand him over when you arrive."

"What's with the assassin squad?" the soldier to Lyle's right asked, pointing at the three men in black.

"They will accompany you to ensure things do not deviate from the plan. If things go badly, they will step in." Lyle turned to Harley and waved his right hand, indicating for her to speak.

Everyone focused on her.

She needed to tell them something. "Ackley is, well, he's taller than me." She couldn't be too specific. "He's skinny, has dark hair that goes to his shoulders, and he has dark eyes." Other than the dark hair, that described half the soldiers stationed on the castle grounds. Unfortunately, Ackley's distinct hair would give him away.

"What else?" Lyle demanded.

She had to say something. "Ackley speaks with an accent. His words sort of run together."

"Anything else?"

She shook her head.

The men's attention returned to Lyle. "You know where to go and what to do. When you return with Ackley, my wife will verify it's him, and you'll each be generously rewarded. Don't mess this up. If you do, I'll kill you myself. Dismissed."

The soldiers exited the room.

"Would you kill them?" Harley asked.

"The last time I sent men after Ackley, he killed every single one of them. If they don't succeed, I'm sure Ackley will do the job for me." He turned and strode away.

Harley shivered, unable to believe Lyle had managed to find Ackley. However, since Ackley was with hundreds of soldiers, locating him would be a lot easier than if he traveled alone.

Not knowing how long it would take the soldiers to reach Ackley, Harley had to do what she could to warn him. Rushing back to her room, she snatched the tall, skinny candle from the vanity table. After lighting it, she placed it in the south window. The sun had only just set, so she didn't know if anyone would even notice the candle until it got darker.

Ten, twenty, thirty minutes passed, and nothing happened. She didn't know how long she should leave the candle lit. When it came time for supper, she snuffed it out and headed to the first floor. As she casually strolled down the steps, she took note that in addition to two guards posted at each landing, the second-floor hallways had every other torch lit, not casting enough light for the sentries to notice if someone lurked about. To retrieve her sword and the letters from the guest suite, she should be able to use the secret passageways.

She entered the dining hall and found Lyle already seated and waiting for her, a goblet in hand. "Sorry I'm late." Even though she was early. "I didn't realize you were in here already."

"It has been a long day." He swirled the wine in his goblet, not looking her way. "My father should be here to help me navigate through this."

Something must have happened since the last time she saw him. "Your father may not be here to help, but I am," she said kindly, batting her eyes and trying to come across as sincere and demure. Inside, she wanted to gouge his eyes out.

He peered over the rim of his goblet at her.

A servant entered carrying two plates of food. She set one before Lyle and the other in front of Harley, her hand trembling as she put the plate down.

"Thank you," Harley said, trying to help calm the woman's nerves.

The servant didn't respond. Facing Lyle, she asked, "Is there anything else, Your Majesty?"

"That will be all."

The servant bowed, then left the room.

Harley picked up her fork and took a bite of her potatoes. A piece of paper hid under her food, the butter and gravy soaking into it. Taking another bite, she read the words: *Midnight. Oriana's room.*

CHAPTER SIX

ACKLEY

Brodek stood in the doorway. "Sleep well?" he asked, glancing between Ackley and Gytha.

Ackley chuckled, the sound low and sultry. "When Gytha is with me, I always sleep well." He winked. In all honesty, he spoke the truth. There were very few people he trusted to keep watch over him.

"Really Ackley?" Gytha mumbled. "Don't you think it's early to be annoying the hell out of me already?" She shoved past him. "I'm starving. Where can I get some food?"

"Is she always this lovely in the morning?" Brodek asked wryly before rushing after her.

"She's like this morning, noon, and night," Ackley said as he followed them down the hallway.

When Gytha came to an intersection, she turned right.

"We're actually going to head this way," Brodek said, going to the left.

"Even though we came from this direction last night?" she asked, her eyes narrowing in suspicion.

Brodek smiled. "You're welcome to go that way; however, this way is faster."

Gytha hesitated.

Ackley decided to follow him. So far, Brodek and his men hadn't given any indication they intended to harm him. That wasn't to say things couldn't change. As they traversed through hallway after hallway, Ackley took note of the width from wall to wall, intersections, doors, and anything useful in case he did find himself in the middle of a fight.

A hint of smoke wafted in the corridor. Brodek stopped before an open archway, waving the two of them forward. Ackley entered the kitchen where he saw two skinned rabbits skewered on sticks resting over a fire in the hearth off to the left. In the center of the large room, a long wooden table took up most of the space. He sat on the bench, resting his elbows against the table. "I take it this place is abandoned?"

"It is," Brodek said, sitting across from him.

Gytha plopped next to Ackley. "I thought we were going to an inn."

"This used to be an inn."

Ridek entered, rubbing his hands together and blowing into them. "All clear. Olek just went on duty."

Brodek nodded. "And Tarnek?"

"He's not here?" Ridek looked at the hearth. "I see two rabbits cooking."

Shaking his head, Brodek said, "He went back out for more. That was twenty minutes ago."

"Right at shift change," Ridek mused.

"With the thick fog, it'll be hard to see someone coming," Ackley pointed out. It was one of the many reasons he both loved and hated fog.

"Is that a threat?" Brodek asked, his voice low and lethal.

Ackley blinked, finding it interesting that Brodek felt as uncertain about this situation as he did. "It's an observation." The tension increased, and he wanted to diffuse it. "I need to speak with your empress to ensure my soldiers' safety. I'm not going to do anything to jeopardize that, and I suggest you don't either."

"And that, my dear Brodek," Gytha drawled, "is a threat."

Brodek watched the two of them for an uncomfortable minute before glancing at Ridek. "Was everything quiet during your watch?"

"Eerily quiet."

"Put the fire out," Brodek commanded.

Ridek grabbed a bucket of water and tossed it on the flames in the hearth. They sizzled out, filling the room with smoke.

"Who could be out there?" Gytha asked.

"Besides your men coming to rescue you, I have no idea." Brodek stood and unsheathed his sword.

"I don't need to be rescued," Ackley said. He had the inclination to lean back and put his boots on the table. However, he was on a bench seat so that wasn't feasible. "How many men did you send to the empress with my request?"

"Three."

"And you plan to remain here until you hear back from them?" Perhaps someone knew the plan and had come to intervene.

"If there's someone out there, I have no idea what they'd want." Brodek exited the room, Ridek right behind him.

Gytha jumped up and followed, a sword already in hand.

Reluctantly, Ackley stood and headed after them. He hadn't even eaten, and the possibility of a fight already presented itself. Pinching the bridge of his nose, he cursed, wishing things could either go according to plan or be simple for once.

They headed along a dark hallway.

"I don't think we should fight," Ackley said as he brought up the rear. They were probably outnumbered, and he had no desire to get into a scuffle this early in the morning when he had more important things to attend to.

"Who said anything about fighting?" Ridek muttered.

When everyone had a sword in hand, fighting was implied. Instead of saying that, Ackley simply followed, observing everything. He would decide what to do once he had a better read on the situation. He tapped Gytha and motioned for her to sheath her sword. Her eyes widened, but she conceded.

A low whistle echoed in the hallway. The four of them froze. The whistle came again.

Brodek's shoulders relaxed. "Olek," he whispered to them. Then he whistled back.

They stood there for about two minutes until Olek joined them.

"Tarnek can't make it back to the castle," Olek said. "He's hiding outside about half a mile away."

"Hiding from what?" Ridek asked.

"There's a group of Landania soldiers patrolling the area."

"Is that a problem?" Ackley asked. "After all, Landania falls under Emperion jurisdiction." Which meant they were on the same side. If these men feared the Landania soldiers, perhaps they weren't who they said they were.

Brodek's shoulders stiffened, as if he weren't used to people questioning him. "We're trying to do this as quietly as possible. The less people who know we're here, the better."

"Why?" Ackley demanded, leaning forward into Brodek's personal space.

He didn't flinch. "Because I don't know how trustworthy the Landania soldiers are."

Ackley could understand that. However, he still thought there was more to it than that. "I suggest you start talking. Now." In that moment, he was only an assassin, not a prince. And he wanted answers.

"Don't threaten me," Brodek snapped, his knuckles turning white as he gripped the hilt of his sword.

"Who are you?" Ackley demanded. If Brodek didn't answer, Ackley planned to jam his fist into the guy's throat, followed by a stomach punch. Gytha could handle Ridek and Olek.

"I've already told you my name." Brodek shifted his feet.

Ackley stepped to the side to avoid the strike. It barely missed him. "Don't forget I'm a prince," Ackley snarled, unable to believe this guy had tried punching him.

"And you're a foreigner on my land."

"Your land?" Ackley leaned in, forcing Brodek to take a step back. "You're not a common foot soldier, are you?" He suspected Brodek belonged to either a group of mercenaries or an elite unit in the Emperion military.

"I will defend this land until the day I die," Brodek snarled. "I took an oath."

Interesting. "Do you intend to broker a meeting between me and Empress Rema?" Or perhaps this entire thing had been a set up to get rid of Ackley and Gytha.

"If Her Majesty wishes to meet with you, my men and I will make it happen."

That was all Ackley needed to know. He patted the man's shoulder. "Then let's find a way to sneak out of here so that meeting can happen sooner rather than later."

"And you said the border assignment was going to be boring," Ridek mumbled.

"We could stay here and hide," Olek suggested. "There's plenty of places in the castle."

"No." Ackley refused to remain there since they hadn't been careful not to leave a trace. If people came in, they would immediately see the dust had been recently disturbed and half-cooked rabbits rested over hot logs. The castle would immediately be searched.

"I agree," Brodek said. "We'll leave out of the entrance closest to the forest, heading straight for the cover of the trees.

"What about the horses?" Gytha asked.

"They're in the stables at the other end of the castle," Brodek replied. "We can't possibly reach them without being seen."

Ackley wanted to get out of there as quickly as possible. If word reached Melenia that Ackley was in Landania, Lyle might figure out what Ackley intended to do and try to stop him. That, or Ackley's army would be in danger of an attack. Either option was not acceptable. So, if he had to avoid the Landania soldiers, he would. "Brodek, get us out of here. Now."

Brodek nodded and went down the hallway to the right. When he came to a door, he paused, listening. Satisfied, he cracked it an inch. After a moment, he pushed it open and stepped outside.

Ackley followed him into the crisp morning air. The thick fog still hung above the ground concealing everything in sight. There could be someone standing three feet away, and he wouldn't know. Sticking close together, the five of them silently headed south. After about a quarter of a mile, they reached some trees, and the fog thinned. Brodek continued, leading them deeper into the forest.

"Do we need to wait for Tarnek?" Ackley whispered.

"He'll catch up," Ridek replied. "Eventually."

Gytha's stomach growled, and Ackley glanced over his shoulder at her, smiling. She smacked him. "I'm too cold and

68

hungry to deal with you right now," she mumbled. "I should have stayed with everyone else back at camp. This is not turning out how I thought it would."

"And miss the chance to meet the empress?" Ackley asked. Gytha rarely complained, which meant she must be hungry.

"That's the only reason I'm still here. Otherwise, I would have left your sorry arse by now."

"You're a soldier in the army?" Ridek asked Gytha.

"I am. Do you have women fighters?"

"No, we do not."

"Why?" she demanded.

He shrugged. "The thought never crossed my mind."

Ackley chuckled as Gytha's fingers curled into fists. She managed to restrain herself from hitting Ridek...this time.

They spent all day traveling by foot along the edge of the forest. At night, they slept under a tree with low hanging branches. Not having the luxury of time, Brodek suggested they "borrow" horses from a field they passed on the second day. It meant riding bareback, but Ackley didn't complain. At least they weren't walking.

The group continued to follow the edge of the forest, hunting for food and avoiding cities and villages. The farther south they went, the lusher the landscape became. On the fourth day, Tarnek caught up with them carrying a bag with additional provisions.

After about a week, Ackley's patience began wearing thin. Now he understood why Knights couldn't marry—he'd been spending far too much time and energy worrying about Harley rather than preparing for his meeting with the empress.

On the eighth day, Ackley's four male companions began joking and laughing with one another.

"Are we almost there?" Ackley inquired.

"Why do you ask?" Brodek said.

"Things feel...different."

"We're in Romek, which was the northern part of Emperion before Landania, Fia, and Kricok joined in."

Which meant they were in the heart of Emperion now. These four men had to be at ease since Landania soldiers wouldn't be patrolling this land. "Are we going to the empress's castle?" From what his spies had gathered, there were two royal residences, one in the south toward the ocean, and another in Lakeside in the middle of Emperion. Given the direction they'd been traveling, he guessed they were closer to the one in Lakeside.

"No. We're going to stop some place safe and wait for further instructions."

They traveled away from the forest and over low rolling hills. The thick grass became a deep shade of green. Dark clouds covered the sky hinting at rain. At a dirt road, Brodek led the way toward a simple manor with smoke billowing from the chimney.

"Another inn?" Ackley asked wryly.

"Not quite." Brodek pulled his horse to a stop in front of the house and dismounted, his men following suit.

Ackley scanned the area, not seeing anything of concern.

"Where are we?" Gytha asked as she climbed off her horse. A low fence surrounded the right side of the manor, a few sheep roaming in it.

"Some place safe." Brodek knocked on the door. "The three of you," he pointed to his men, "take the horses around back to the stables. Get them out of sight."

The three men did as they were told.

The door swung open and a tall, skinny man with red hair stood there.

"His hair is the same color as your sister's," Gytha said, jabbing Ackley in the side with her elbow.

"This man's hair is much darker. It's not nearly as lethal as Idina's." Regardless, it was a rare hair color to see.

"Brodek," the man said, waving them inside. "I hope everything is okay."

"It is," Brodek replied once he was inside the manor. "I'd like to introduce to you Prince Ackley of Marsden and Gytha, a fierce soldier in his army."

Ackley and Gytha entered the house, closing the door behind them.

The man smiled. "Welcome to our humble abode." He bowed with a flourish. "My name's Audek. My wife, Vesha, is around here somewhere."

The low ceiling was only a foot above Ackley's head, making him feel like a giant in the small room. A fire crackled in the hearth, warming the place. The paintings on the walls were simple, mostly involving plants or landscape. The few knickknacks around seemed to have been etched from wood. By all accounts, the manor was simple.

"Please have a seat," Audek said, motioning toward the sofas.

Ackley and Gytha sat together while Audek and Brodek sat across from them.

"It's not often we have royalty here," Audek said. "I mean royalty other than Rema and Darmik. But I don't think of them as being royal although they are." Audek scratched the side of his head. "Do you want something to eat or drink?"

"That would be nice," Ackley said, speaking slowly to ensure Audek could understand his accent.

Audek nodded and left the room.

"Your men?" Ackley asked.

"I don't expect there to be any trouble out here," Brodek said. "However, I asked for them to remain on watch just in case."

Audek returned and took his seat. "My wife will bring something out shortly." He rubbed his hands together and looked at Brodek expectantly.

"I sent a letter to the empress," Brodek explained. "We're awaiting her response."

"I assume this has something to do with..." Audek nodded toward Ackley and Gytha.

"Yes," Ackley answered. He then quickly explained his situation and why he needed an audience with Empress Rema.

As soon as he finished, a woman in her late forties entered carrying a tray of tea and pastries. She introduced herself as Vesha, then set the tray on the low table and sat on the other side of Audek.

Vesha looked between Ackley and Gytha. "My husband tells me you're both from a kingdom called Marsden?"

Gytha nodded.

"And you're a soldier?" Vesha asked her.

"I am," Gytha said with pride, sitting up a little straighter.

Vesha smiled. "Back in my younger days, I was also a soldier of sorts, though not as formidable as you."

Ackley glanced up at the ceiling. This was all he needed—Gytha's ego stroked.

Audek placed his hand on Vesha's thigh, squeezing it. "Oh, I don't know. You've always been intimidating to me." He smiled sheepishly.

"It's nice to meet a fellow warrior," Gytha replied.

"Did I hear correctly that the two of you sent a letter to Empress Rema?" Vesha asked as she poured five cups of tea.

"Yes," Ackley replied. "I have soldiers camped just inside Landania's border. Their lives are in danger, and I need the empress's permission for them to remain there until further notice."

Vesha handed Ackley a cup of tea.

He took it, automatically smelling for poisons. Not finding any, he took a sip. "How long until we hear back from the empress?" he inquired.

"We should hear back shortly," Brodek answered.

Ackley raised a single eyebrow. *Shortly* was not an adequate measurement of time.

"Tomorrow or the day after," Brodek clarified.

Instead of waiting to be offered a cup of tea, Gytha grabbed one, slurping it down.

Ackley glared at her.

"Sorry, I'm starving," she muttered. "I've been traveling with the lot of you and haven't had something warm to drink in days."

Now he questioned bringing the warrior woman along to meet the empress. Choosing to ignore her lack of manners, he asked, "How do you two know the empress?"

"We knew Rema before she became the empress," Vesha answered. She handed Audek and Brodek each a cup of tea before taking one for herself.

"We met back on Greenwood Island," Audek added.

"Greenwood Island?" Ackley asked. He'd never heard of it before.

"It's an island southwest of the mainland," Vesha said.

"We all became fast friends. We helped Rema overthrow the

illegitimate king, putting her on the throne." Audek leaned back on the sofa, lost in thought.

Ackley wondered about the empress's husband and what sort of man he was to be married to someone so powerful.

"Anyway," Audek mused, tapping his free hand on his knee. "It feels like only yesterday. Yet so much has happened and changed since then."

Brodek finished his tea, setting his cup back on the tray. "I'm going to check on my men. I'll remain outside with them for the night." He stood and left the house.

"We have two extra rooms," Vesha said. "I'll go and get them ready for you."

"Is there a place I can wash up?" Gytha asked. "Since I've been traveling with men, I haven't had the chance to bathe in over a week."

Vesha smiled. "Yes, of course. Right this way." The two women exited the sitting room.

Now that Ackley was alone with Audek, he was certain he could get the information he wanted out of the man. "Are you a member of this prestigious group of men?" He wouldn't classify Audek as a fighter, but he asked the question nonetheless to get the conversation going. He stretched his arms across the back of the sofa, relaxing for the first time in days.

"Me?" Audek said. "No. My wife hates fighting. We've seen enough to last a lifetime and avoid getting involved. It's one of the reasons we live all the way out here."

Audek hadn't denied these men belonged to a prestigious group. Ackley needed to push a little harder. "Back where I'm from, even though I'm a prince, I'm also a Knight."

"And what do Knights do?"

"Protect the kingdom, go on secret missions, that sort of thing."

"The Brotherhood is the same."

And he had a name for the group. Brotherhood. He rather liked that. The men he'd been traveling with...Brodek, Ridek, Olek, Tarnek, Herek, Erek, and Rettek...the first letter of their names spelled brother. *Clever.* "Is the Brotherhood independent of the army?"

"Yup."

Ackley contemplated this newfound knowledge. Brotherhood. A secret band of warriors who protected the crown, like Knights. And the group had to be all men as the title implied, which would irk Gytha to no end. His smile widened. The Brotherhood could aid him without anyone knowing. A slew of possibilities opened.

CHAPTER SEVEN

HARLEY

*H*arley cut her meat, allowing the gravy to spread out, fully covering the note that had been hidden under her food. She tried to keep her hands steady though they shook ever so slightly. With any luck, Lyle hadn't noticed the piece of paper. She needed to act normal so he wouldn't suspect anything.

The note instructed her to go to Oriana's bedchamber tonight at midnight. She'd have to sneak out of her room, go through the antechamber, and out into the hallway without waking Lyle. Since sentries only stood guard at the top of the staircase, she should be able to reach Oriana's room only a few doors down. She assumed Ackley's man planned on meeting her there. Or perhaps he'd leave another letter.

"Harley?" Lyle said, startling her.

"Sorry, I was lost in thought," she mumbled.

"Obviously." He took a bite of his food, watching her across the table. "What are you thinking about?"

A loaded question she needed to answer carefully. "Do you

want me to be honest?" She stabbed another piece of meat, swirling it around her plate to help conceal the note.

"Always. I am your king and husband—I deserve your honesty."

He deserved nothing. She ate the piece of meat while thinking. Scooping up a potato along with a piece of the soggy paper, she shoved both in her mouth. After she swallowed, she finally looked at him. "I've been thinking about how much I miss my brother." Tears filled her eyes, exemplifying the fact.

His eyes widened infinitesimally, and a sense of satisfaction filled her. The first jab had been made. She awaited his response.

"He wasn't supposed to die," Lyle said, a hint of remorse to his voice.

Harley knew he lied. Lyle didn't care about Hollis, and he wasn't capable of remorse.

"Owen is all I have left," she said, pretending to play with her food all the while ensuring the note dissolved. "I don't want to lose him, too." Both statements were true. She found it easier than lying to her husband who always seemed to know when she wasn't being honest with him.

"At least your parents are still alive." Anger flashed in Lyle's eyes. "I will make Owen pay for my father's death."

She almost burst out laughing at the absurdity of his statement. "Your father's death is a casualty of war—a war he instigated. That's what happens when you try to take over another kingdom. My brother, uncle, aunt, and cousins, they didn't start this. You did."

Lyle went very still.

She'd said too much, been too forceful with her words. Anger and hurt swelled within, making it difficult to regain control. She wanted to reach across the table and strangle Lyle. Since he was stronger than her, she couldn't physically hurt him. As Ackley had hinted at during their parting, she would have to kill Lyle at night while he slept. Sneaking into his room with him sleeping in it would be nearly impossible. She'd have to do it while sharing his bed. Even though she wanted to kill him, she didn't know if she could plunge a sword into his chest.

"You've spent too much time with Owen." Lyle practically spit out Owen's name. "You need to come with me and see your people firsthand so you're clear on where your loyalties should lie."

As if he knew a thing about loyalty. She hated him.

"You should understand what the kingdom was truly like under your *father*. You will see the poverty, disease, and filth. Then you will witness the changes I'm making. The jobs I'm creating, the way I'm helping our people live better lives. They finally have food and shelter—necessities."

She ignored the jab about her uncle being her father. "I'm sure after the Russek army decimated the land, it's easy to sweep in and look good to the people."

Harley wanted to run from the room, but a corner of the paper remained on her plate. She couldn't leave a trace behind. If a servant found it, it would be shown to Lyle, and he might end up killing her sooner than planned.

Stabbing another potato, she made sure to get the rest of the soggy note, shoving it in her mouth and chewing with far more force than necessary.

"You think I'm the bad guy," Lyle said, leaning back in his chair. "But I'm not. Your father was the evil one. He was the one destroying this kingdom, not me."

"Uncle," she snapped. And how dare Lyle claim he wasn't

the evil one. He'd locked her in closets and belittled her countless times.

"You need to acknowledge Coden was your father."

She had to do no such thing. "How do you know that?" Even though she saw the letter implying her true parentage, she wanted verification from her mother before publicly acknowledging it.

"Tomorrow you will go with me. Be prepared to leave at sunrise." He took a long drink from his goblet before shoving his chair back and striding from the room.

Harley sat up, listening. Not hearing any sounds of movement, she carefully pushed her blankets back and slid out of bed. Grabbing her dressing robe, she wrapped it around her body, tying it at her waist. She decided not to wear her slippers and opted for remaining in socks to make the least amount of noise possible.

She'd heard Lyle's door open and close about two hours ago. While she assumed he'd retired for the night, she couldn't be certain. She methodically turned her handle, cracking her door an inch. No light came from under Lyle's door, so she entered the antechamber, closing her door behind her. Ever so slowly, she tiptoed to the next door. Knowing Lyle, he probably had this door rigged so he'd know if someone opened it or not. Considering her options, she came up with a plan to enact after she went to Oriana's room.

Harley opened the door and slid into the hallway. With her back to the wall, she made her way to the left, maintaining a steady pace as she passed the first two doors. When she reached the third one, it wasn't closed all the way, so she had to be careful not to push on it, opening it farther.

With a pounding heart, she finally reached the fourth door. She slowly turned the handle. Once the door was cracked far enough, she stepped into Oriana's room, closing the door behind her. The open curtains allowed moonlight to filter in.

The smell hit her first. Roses—just like Oriana. She breathed in deeply, savoring the familiarity, as if her cousin were still alive. Unable to help herself, she went over to the nightstand, picking up the small wooden box with a rose carved on the top. Lifting the lid, she saw the necklace with a tiny yellow rose on it, the one her cousin wore every single day. However, at her birthday celebration, she had worn a fancy diamond necklace. But this one here, this was the essence of Oriana. Tears slid down Harley's cheeks. She set the box down and wiped her face with her sleeve. She hadn't considered what being in here would do to her. Sniffling, she dabbed her nose.

"Sorry," a gruff voice said from behind her. "I had to be sure."

She startled at the sound and whirled around to face a man stepping out from the dressing closet. When he came into the moonlight, she noticed the roots of his hair were dark like most Marsdens, but his ends were blond like most people from Melenia. "Who are you?" she whispered.

"The name's Rikter."

"Are you the one who gave me the notes?"

"I am."

"What did you mean when you said you had to be sure?"

"Ackley trusts you—and I trust Ackley—but I wanted to see if being in here would affect you. If it didn't, I was going to leave. I've been watching you, and I couldn't tell if you had Ackley or Lyle fooled. Maybe both." He shrugged.

"And now?"

"As always, Ackley is right." The corners of his lips rose.

She nodded. "Coming here, I considered the possibility that you might work for Lyle, not Ackley."

"And now?" he asked, repeating the same words she'd used.

"I see your hair is dyed." That was all the proof she needed to confirm this man wasn't loyal to Lyle.

The man nodded, seemingly satisfied. "We don't have a lot of time. I need to leave in ten minutes, during the change in shifts."

Harley moved toward the window, intending to look outside, when the man grabbed her arm, pulling her away.

"Sorry," he said, releasing her. "I just don't want anyone to see you or a shadow."

She nodded, feeling stupid for not thinking about that. "Can you get a message to Ackley?"

"I can get messages to Ackley and Owen. Whatever you need, I'll try and make it happen."

A sense of relief filled her. This man, Rikter, was her lifeline to the outside world. Knowing he was there to support her, emboldened her to do more to take Lyle down. "Lyle said he located Ackley. He sent a unit after him."

"I saw a group of heavily armed men leave earlier today." He folded his arms.

"That was probably them." Unease filled her. "Will you be able to get word to Ackley before those men reach him?"

"I'll do my best. Is there anything else?"

She shook her head.

"Thank you for this information." He squeezed her shoulder. "I'm glad you're on our side."

"What if we just killed Lyle now?" Before he had the chance to harm those she loved and cared about.

"His death would solve a lot of problems."

"Can you sneak into his room and slit his throat?" They were only a few rooms away. Maybe if the two of them worked together, they could overpower Lyle.

"If I could, I would. Why do you think Ackley allowed you to come here?"

She already knew the answer.

Seeing the understanding on her face, he continued, "When Lyle goes to sleep at night, he sets a series of traps. If I so much as turn the door handle, a knife will be embedded in me. If I climb up the side of the castle to go in through the window, a guard will see me. Even if I go through your room to the adjoining room, the second I turn the door handle for Lyle's room, I'll be impaled by a sword. The man is paranoid. And for good reason."

She shivered, thankful she'd never tried going into her husband's room when he was in there. "Truly, the only way to kill him is for me to do it?"

He nodded. "When you're lying next to him while he's sleeping," he said dryly. "Assuming he even allows that."

Back in Penlar, they'd shared a bed nightly. Here, since they had separate rooms, she didn't know what would happen once they reestablished marital relations. He very well could send her back to her room once he finished with her.

"Have you ever killed someone before?" Rikter asked.

"No." When that man had grabbed her in Penlar, threatening her with a knife, she'd tried stabbing him to get free. However, she'd been so consumed with fear that she hadn't thought properly about where to strike the man and how much force to use. She'd barely made a scratch. She didn't know if she could stab Lyle hard enough, deep enough, to kill him. She didn't know if she could murder someone—even someone she hated.

"Are you okay?" Rikter asked.

"How did you learn to tolerate killing another person?" Maybe if she detached herself from the situation, she could manage it. However, that almost made it worse. Somehow, the rage was what fueled her to do something so violent.

He pursed his lips. "Why do you think I'm able to tolerate it?"

"I just assumed." She hugged herself, considering what had to be done in order to save her cousin and her kingdom. "Why would Ackley send me here to kill Lyle?" She wasn't physically or mentally strong enough to do it.

"Because you're the only one."

"I don't know if I can." Tears filled her eyes.

He nodded, as if he understood the emotions twisting through her head like a windstorm. "Consider this. If you don't kill Lyle, then it'll have to be on a battlefield with hundreds of lives lost."

Her shoulders drooped, as if the weight of the kingdom rested on them.

"I must go." He turned and left the room.

Harley stood in the middle of Oriana's room feeling utterly useless and alone. Ackley should have prepared her better. He should have trained her how to kill, how to spy, how to take down a monarch. Throwing her in here like he did...did he even love her? Or did he love the idea of her? Maybe she was simply a means to an end, and he was only using her.

She wiped the tears already falling. Her night was not over. She needed to enact the second part of her plan. She exited Oriana's room and headed back to hers. Inside her own bedchamber again, she ruffled her hair to ensure it appeared she just woke up. Then she went over to her door, throwing it open. She didn't want to make too much noise—as if she were trying to, but she couldn't be too quiet either. Then she went through the antechamber and opened the door to the hallway. She rushed to the guards.

They both stood straighter, startled to see her.

"Is something the matter, Lady Harley?" the one closest to her asked.

"I just had a terrible nightmare and am in dire need of some warm milk." She hugged her body.

"I'll go and get you a cup. Wait here."

She nodded, hiding her smile. Now when Lyle questioned why the antechamber door had been opened in the middle of the night, she'd have a verifiable reason.

Harley tossed and turned, thoughts of killing consuming her. Unable to sleep, she finally gave up and got out of bed. She dressed and went downstairs just as first light approached. One of the sentries on duty led her to the stables where Lyle was saddling two horses.

"You'll use this one," Lyle said as he tightened the girth strap of the smaller animal.

Harley took the reins, and Lyle helped her mount. She settled on the saddle as Lyle climbed onto his horse. He took hold of her reins and led them out of the stables to where a group of three dozen mounted soldiers waited.

"Where are we headed?" Harley asked. The sky had cleared, not a cloud in sight as the sun crested the land.

"A village about an hour from here."

The soldiers formed a loose circle around the two of them as they headed north.

"I grew up in Penlar." One of the largest provinces. On the outskirts of the city, there were plenty of farmers. She knew how people lived and behaved. Taking her to a small farming village would do nothing to change her impression of her uncle.

"You were sheltered and have no idea what's out there."

Not wanting to argue, she remained quiet and instead, tried to enjoy being outside on this lovely morning. The crisp air felt refreshing on her face.

They traveled until they came to several fields planted with corn, potatoes, carrots, and a few other vegetables. Just past the fields, she could make out a dozen or so wooden huts. As they neared the village, Harley heard children laughing. The mere sound filled her with warmth. It had been too long since she'd heard such joy.

"Why isn't this village burned like the others?" she inquired.

"We're north of the royal castle."

Owen had sent out scouts to investigate the status of the kingdom. While a few towns had been spared, no one had ever said anything about the northern portion being safe from Russek's slaughter. Her understanding was that most places had been destroyed.

"The Russeks came from the north," Lyle explained. "They didn't start ravaging anything until after they infiltrated the castle. Then they headed south, taking every man, and burning everything in their path."

"What happened to the men they took?" When Ackley and she had met with Kerdan, he'd assumed those taken had been released and that they'd probably fled to the nearby kingdoms seeking refuge.

Lyle shrugged. "No idea. They're most likely dead."

Harley had a feeling he knew more but was keeping the truth from her. Immediately on edge, she asked, "Do you know why Russek suddenly withdrew from Melenia?" Kerdan had told her he'd called his men back after his father was assassinated, but she doubted Lyle knew this information.

"We can continue this discussion later at a more appropriate time."

They neared the huts that had been constructed in a circular fashion. They rode their horses into the middle of the circle, fanning out. Over two dozen people were scattered about, some sorting through a cart of vegetables, a group of children playing, and a few elderly residents sitting on chairs. Most had stopped what they were doing and simply stared at the intruders.

"Greetings," Lyle said to the villagers from atop his horse. "I want to introduce you to my wife, Lady Harley. She will soon be crowned your queen."

Her heart started pounding, and she felt a headache coming on. The villagers all stared at her with cold, uncaring eyes. She had the urge to back up, distancing herself from Lyle and his soldiers.

"Why are you here?" an elderly woman with brown weathered skin asked.

Harley pursed her lips, thankful these people didn't address Lyle as the king. If anything, they appeared wary and uncertain of him. She patted her horse's neck, wanting the animal to remain calm.

"I wanted to come by to see how everyone is doing. That is

all. We'll be on our way in a few minutes." Lyle maintained an even voice and a warm smile as he spoke.

"Do you plan on taking our food?" the elderly woman demanded, her hands clamped onto the arms of the chair.

"No," he assured her. "I am not like the last king. I do not intend to take what is rightfully yours."

The woman squinted, trying to find a lie in his words, as if she could see it if she looked hard enough.

A group of children ran by, laughing and squealing, oblivious to the tension between the villagers and soldiers.

"Besides stealing your food, what else did the late king do that you did not agree with?" Lyle inquired.

The villagers looked at one another. No one answered, though it appeared they had plenty to complain about.

On a whim, Harley asked the old woman, "Why isn't your village burned?" She didn't believe what Lyle had told her about it being unharmed simply because it was north of the castle.

"Burned?" she asked.

"I've traveled through the kingdom," Harley explained. "Hardly any villages were spared."

She blinked. "Because of the large man and his wolves. They kept the others away when he was sick in bed."

Harley wondered if she was referring to Kerdan and his men. They all wore fur wraps and had black markings on their faces. The night of the takeover, when Kerdan had realized he'd been poisoned, he'd said his supplies were stashed not far from the castle. He'd also said that he would be quite ill. Perhaps he'd fallen so ill that he'd had to rest here until he was well enough to travel. Harley had seen his men and knew they were more than capable of keeping this town secure. Also, the Russek soldiers would've had to listen to their prince.

"Don't talk nonsense," Lyle snapped. "Tell Lady Harley how things were before I took over."

"They were awful." The elderly woman spit on the ground. "The old king was a fool. He took all our food, never paid us for it, and squandered what he had."

"And now?" Lyle asked.

"Now?" The woman waved him off. "So far, it's better. You don't steal from us. We'll see how long that lasts."

"You have my word what food you grow remains your own." With that, he steered his horse away from the huts and toward the road.

Harley followed him. Back on the road, the soldiers once again formed a loose circle around them.

She'd learned two valuable things this morning. One, that Kerdan had saved this village and these people were alive because of him. And two, even though her father had seen to her education, he'd left out some important political information—like how her uncle collected taxes and food. She hadn't studied how other kingdoms handled these issues, so she couldn't compare her kingdom to others.

Somehow, Harley's lack of education in that respect didn't surprise her. If her uncle truly was her father, then there were a lot of things that had been kept from her.

An overwhelming sense of worthlessness inundated her. She had been ill-prepared to marry Lyle, be involved in politics, act as an assassin, be a spy, and help Ackley. All she excelled at was being pretty and looking the part of a noble woman. She hated herself and how naive she was. These things would have to be rectified. She would find a way to learn more, be more, and do more. She would figure out how to do these things, and she would do them well.

When they arrived back at the castle, two dozen men were in the process of dismounting near the front doors. One shouted something about the king. Lyle nudged his horse and rode ahead to see what the commotion was.

Harley dismounted at the stables, handing her horse over to a stable boy. Two of the soldiers who'd accompanied her on the journey escorted her toward the side entrance of the castle.

"What's going on?" She pointed to the front of the castle where all the activity was.

"I don't know," the man on her right answered.

"I want to see what's happening." She hurried over toward the group of people that had gathered.

When she got closer, she heard Lyle barking out orders for his men to stand back. They immediately complied, forming a tight circle around someone.

As she neared, she caught a glimpse of a man kneeling on the ground, a brown potato sack covering his head. Her arms tingled—there was something familiar about his shoulders and the way his back remained erect despite his situation. Though the man's wrists had been tied together, he'd managed to undo his bindings. His hands slowly moved to his sides, his fingers curling into fists.

"Don't even think about attacking," Lyle sneered. "You're vastly outnumbered."

The soldiers all had their swords drawn and pointed at the prisoner.

"We confiscated several weapons from him," one of the soldiers said to Lyle. "He's clearly a trained fighter. It took all of us to get him here."

Harley started shaking. Her first instinct was to rush

forward and defend Ackley. However, Lyle would kill her on the spot for embarrassing him. She had to be calm and smart. After all, Ackley's life depended on it.

She vaguely wondered if Ackley could attack this many men and survive. If he had his weapons, possibly. But not bare-handed. He could probably hold his own for some time. However, with over two dozen armed men, there was only so much he could do.

Lyle stepped into the circle. Harley hoped he got close enough so Ackley could kill him. She'd love to see Ackley's hands wrapped around Lyle's neck, squeezing the life from him. She wondered how loyal these soldiers were and if they'd help Lyle. Either these men were loyal to the crown, or Lyle had their loved one's held somewhere to ensure their loyalty.

"You killed dozens of my men," Lyle said, five feet away from Ackley. "You brought soldiers from another kingdom here to Melenia to overthrow me. You are a traitor and must be executed."

While Harley knew Lyle intended to kill Ackley, she didn't know if he planned to do it right there on the spot or if he'd throw him in the dungeon for a few days and drag it out. Her brain ran through several plans, none of them feasible. Terror took hold.

Lyle reached forward, grabbing the top of the potato sack. In one swift motion, he removed the cloth from Ackley's head.

CHAPTER EIGHT

*T*hree days passed. While Ackley enjoyed his time at Audek and Vesha's quaint home, the waiting began to drive him nuts. Gytha tried to keep him occupied. They sparred, shot bows and arrows—Audek really could use a new bow, and hunted on the nearby land. Through it all, Ackley kept imagining ways he could utilize Brodek and his men if needed.

On the fourth day, Ackley woke up just as the sun rose. He made his way to the kitchen where Vesha was already preparing a pot of cornmeal.

"Where is everyone?" he asked her as he took a seat at the table.

"Gytha is still asleep." She spooned some of the food into a bowl for him. "Audek and Brodek left about an hour ago to see if any messages came from Rema."

He noticed Vesha rarely used the empress's title and instead, always spoke of her with easy familiarity.

"Thank you." He ate a spoonful of cornmeal while

91

wondering where Brodek and Audek went to check for messages. He didn't think there was a city or village nearby.

The side door flew open, and a gust of wind came whipping into the kitchen. Brodek and Audek stomped inside. "Word just came from the empress," Brodek said, slamming the door closed. "Her Majesty wants to meet with you immediately."

Relief coursed through Ackley. The Emperion empress had agreed to see him. "Excellent," he said. "When and where?" He hadn't realized until then that he'd feared she would deny his request for a meeting.

"Some place Audek is familiar with." Brodek sat at the table, and Vesha handed him a steaming bowl of cornmeal.

Audek kissed Vesha's cheek before sitting alongside Brodek.

"Her instructions are very specific," Brodek said around a mouthful of food. "Audek and I will escort you. No one else is to come. We are to leave immediately."

"I suppose I should go and pack." Not that Ackley had much to gather, but he wanted to get his thoughts in order before they left. After he finished his cornmeal, he stood and headed to the hallway. "By the way," he said as he turned back toward the kitchen, addressing both men. "Gytha is coming with me." Under no circumstances would he leave her behind. Not only did he not want them to be separated, but he didn't want to waste time coming back here once he met with the empress. And he knew Gytha would enjoy meeting a powerful woman. Besides, he wouldn't go into a meeting with one of the most powerful rulers without having someone watching his back.

Audek opened his mouth, as if to say something, but snapped it shut.

Brodek's eyes narrowed, considering Ackley. "I understand

why you'd want to bring her, but I have to follow the empress's orders."

"Got it," Ackley said. "I'll just have Gytha follow us at a safe distance. You can pretend you don't know she's there."

Brodek rubbed his temples. "I suppose nothing I say will convince you to leave her here?"

"That is correct." Ackley smiled.

"Fine. She can come," Brodek conceded, "but when we get there, if Empress Rema is mad, that's on you."

Less than thirty minutes later, the four of them set out on horseback, traveling at a quick pace. Audek talked incessantly, driving Ackley mad. He'd never met a man before who enjoyed blabbing so much. Audek commented on every little thing. Even the color of the leaves, as if that mattered.

"Do you talk because you're nervous?" Ackley inquired, interrupting Audek's speech on the lines of a boulder in the distance.

"What would I be nervous about?" Audek asked, glancing around.

Gytha chuckled. "I assume it's because he's bored."

"How can I be bored when I'm traveling outside like this?"

Ackley shrugged. "You're with two people from another kingdom. How do you know we won't slit your throat while you sleep?"

Audek's face paled. "Well, now I'm nervous."

Brodek chuckled. "Audek may not look like a soldier, but he fought alongside Empress Rema to reclaim her throne."

"Yes, he told me." Now, not only did he need to ask the empress's permission for his soldiers to be on her land, but he wanted to know how she reclaimed her throne. Learning how she overthrew the person ruling Emperion could be vital in Owen's quest to retake his kingdom.

The four of them nudged their horses across a low creek, reaching the other side and heading southeast. Massive trees towered above them and the ground turned from moist dirt to a covering of thick, bright-green moss. A light rain started to fall, but the thick foliage above protected them from getting wet.

"Tell me about your empress," Ackley said, curious to know about the woman he'd be meeting soon.

"Rema?" Audek asked. "She's great. Never wanted to rule which makes her perfect for the job."

"It's her husband you need to watch out for," Brodek said. "Darmik is the commander of the Emperion army. A position that suits him exceedingly well."

Ackley found all this fascinating. A woman ruling a kingdom; her husband a lethal warrior. It didn't get any better than that. "How long has she been the empress?"

"About twenty years," Audek responded. "Since she's been in charge, we've never had to fight a war."

"Does she avoid fighting?" he asked. Maybe she wasn't as strong as he'd presumed.

"Not at all," Brodek answered. "She isn't afraid to fight, and she does what needs to be done, which makes her even more scary." He adjusted his reins before continuing. "When she says something, she means it."

"If she hasn't fought since taking the throne," Gytha said, "then how do you know she isn't afraid to fight?"

Good question, and one Ackley had been wondering the answer to.

"She's sent men to fight, she just hasn't sent her army into war," Brodek clarified. "Take right now, for example. She has her army lined up at Russek's border. They are just standing there ready and waiting to be unleashed."

"What's the empress waiting for?" Ackley asked, mulling over the possibilities. "Didn't Russek kidnap and kill her daughter, the princess?" If the empress was as commanding and lethal as they'd implied, it seemed reasonable to assume she would immediately send her army in to kill those responsible for taking her daughter. "Does Empress Rema not know who killed the princess?" Ackley doubted it was Kerdan, which left Jana. Perhaps the empress was waiting to see if Kerdan killed Jana for her, so she wouldn't have to start a war. If that were the case, it was efficient but lacked the revenge the empress probably desired.

"Rema never does anything in haste," Audek said. "Each decision is carefully thought out and calculated. It's what's best for the kingdom, not one person or just the royal family. She puts everyone before herself. That is why she's the greatest leader we'll ever have. She is selfless."

Empress Rema seemed too good to be true for Ackley's liking.

"But I've also known Rema for a long time," Audek continued. "If Russek killed Allyssa, Rema will wipe them out. Which makes me wonder if that's what really happened."

"You don't think the princess is dead?" Gytha asked.

Audek shrugged. "When they kidnapped Allyssa, Rema lined her soldiers up along the border threatening war if her daughter wasn't returned safely. Her daughter wasn't returned; yet, she hasn't attacked. Which makes me wonder what else is going on."

Ackley realized Audek was more astute than he'd first thought. "Since Kerdan and Jana are fighting for the throne, a lot could have happened that we don't know about." Ackley liked Kerdan and had a hard time believing the man would've allowed Allyssa to be killed. He seemed to want what was best for Russek, and killing Emperion's crown princess was the fastest way to ensure its destruction.

Days passed. They traveled hard and fast, going straight through several towns and villages simply because it was the most direct route to take. The land reminded Ackley of Axian— the southern region of Marsden. Everywhere he went, he saw well-tended fields, well-kept homes, vibrant markets, and people dressed appropriately. The people seemed happy— smiling and greeting them as they passed through.

Where he'd grown up, the towns consisted of rickety wood structures, most falling apart. The people rarely had new clothes and instead, wore ones tattered with holes. Most homes were in shambles, and food was scarce. His father had overtaxed their people without sympathy, leaving most destitute. Ackley hadn't even known there was another way, a better way, until he went south and met Dexter. Traveling through Emperion made one thing abundantly clear—their ruler cared for them.

A light rain had fallen for the better part of the day. They now traveled on a narrow dirt road, a dark, dense forest lining both sides of it. The four of them crested a low hill. At the top, Audek pulled his horse to a halt. He sat there scanning the area before them.

"What are you looking for?" Ackley asked, wondering why they'd stopped. The road descended on the other side of the hill, disappearing amongst the foliage. Treetops covered the landscape as far as he could see.

"I'm waiting for them to acknowledge we can enter."

Ackley didn't bother asking what it was they would be entering because as soon as Audek spoke, Ackley felt a presence nearby.

A single whistle rang out, and Audek nudged his horse forward, down the slope. Ackley followed him, more excited than nervous, and Gytha and Brodek rode close behind. About half-way down, Audek veered off the road and to the right, entering the forest. He continued to head downward at an angle.

Ackley noted small boulders every ten to fifteen feet and wondered if they were markers. At the bottom of the hill, they turned left, riding alongside a stream for about a mile until they came to a cliff. The water from the stream cascaded over the side, spilling into a lake about fifteen feet below. A stone castle stood in the middle of the water.

Audek dismounted. "We'll leave the horses here." He tied his to a tree, everyone else doing the same.

"Are we going to that castle?" Ackley asked. He didn't see a bridge and had no idea how they'd reach it. The castle appeared to be about a mile from shore, too far to swim.

"Yes. And to answer your next question, we'll get to it by boat."

Gytha chuckled but didn't say anything.

Ackley glared at her. A short boat ride on calm water wouldn't cause him any issues. Only the turbulent sea made him become violently ill.

Audek led the way down the side of the cliff. At the bottom, an old, dilapidated boat had been stored in a shallow cave. Each of them grabbed hold, dragging it out and sliding it into the water. Ackley steadied the end while everyone else climbed in, then he shoved the boat forward, off the bank. He sprang into the boat and sat on one of the benches. Brodek and Audek each grabbed an oar and rowed the boat toward the castle.

During the journey there, Ackley studied the five-story structure and four turrets, searching for signs of life. All the windows appeared dark; no movement came from within. He didn't spot anyone patrolling the roof. Two crows flew overhead, cawing. The wind whipped across the lake, dropping the temperature even further.

"A little to the right," Brodek murmured.

Audek nodded and adjusted their course, lining the boat up with the iron gate that extended from the bottom portion of the castle into the water.

When they were twenty feet away, the gate shook and then groaned as it opened upward. Nearing it, Audek and Brodek pulled their oars into the boat, letting the boat drift beneath the gate, water dripping down the iron spikes above them.

After floating fifteen feet, the gate closed behind them. Up ahead, torches lit the way, the only evidence of life in the castle.

The walls widened as they entered a thirty-foot-by-thirty-foot squared room. At the south end, a wooden dock extended into the water. Audek used his oar to steer the boat over to it. Brodek grabbed a rope hanging from the dock and tied it to the boat.

Ackley climbed onto the five-foot long dock that led to an iron door. "Should I knock?" he whispered, his voice loud in the enclosed space.

"No need," Brodek answered.

The four of them stood on the dock, waiting. The water

gently lapped against the stone walls providing the only sound. A minute later, the iron door screeched open.

Ackley stepped into a narrow hallway, the ceiling only inches above his head. A man stood at the other end, a torch in hand, waving him forward. As he moved toward him, he glanced over his shoulder to ensure his three companions followed.

"Prince Ackley of Marsden?" the man asked when Ackley reached him.

"Yes."

"Empress Rema is expecting you. This way." He led them up a stairwell and onto the first level of the castle.

They walked through an empty great hall to a staircase at the back of the room, then up to the second level and down a long corridor. No paintings or tapestries adorned the walls. Ackley didn't spot furniture in any of the rooms they passed. However, torches lined the walls providing light.

Dripping water echoed from somewhere inside the castle. A damp, moldy smell permeated the air as Ackley traversed through the place. He got the feeling that the castle had been there for hundreds of years, but it hadn't been used for quite some time. No one spoke as they moved deeper into the interior of the place.

Behind him, he heard Gytha's breathing speed up. Ackley knew she still had nightmares from when she'd been trapped beneath the castle in Axion. It had taken her a couple of days to escape from the underground labyrinth. Her heroic act had saved Ackley and his cousins from certain death. He wanted to reach back and squeeze her hand, reassuring her that she wasn't going to be trapped like that again. However, one thing he knew for certain, he couldn't make such assurances.

The man escorting them paused before an open doorway on

the left, mumbling to someone inside. He nodded, then gestured for Ackley and his companions to enter.

Ackley stepped into a room, thirty feet wide, lit only by two torches. A dozen men stood around the perimeter in the shadows, watching. Gytha entered behind him.

A young man stepped forward, toward the center of the room. He appeared to be only seventeen with shaggy light-brown hair and a muscular build. "You didn't bother taking their weapons?" he asked, addressing Audek.

"They're not prisoners," Audek said. "Blasted, I can't get over how much you look like your mother."

"And you are?" the young man asked.

"This is my dear friend, Audek," a woman said, emerging from the shadows and into the dim light. This had to be Rema— the empress of Emperion. Simply put, she was stunning, leaving Ackley momentarily speechless. Rema's clear blue eyes glistened under the low light, her long, wavy blonde hair rested against her back, and her refined posture gave her a regal appearance.

Audek rushed forward, hugging her. When he released her, he remained at her side. "This is Prince Ackley and Captain Gytha," he said, gesturing toward each of them.

Ackley didn't recall telling him Gytha's title.

Rema's attention went to Gytha. "You're a soldier?"

"I am," Gytha said, speaking slowly so Rema could understand her.

"That is something I'm interested in," Rema replied, "but a conversation for another day since we are short on time."

The young man who hadn't yet introduced himself took a step back, closer to the empress. They both had the same cheekbones and skin tone. Ackley figured the young man had to be her son.

Rema's attention shifted to Ackley. "Why are you here?"

He appreciated her bluntness and getting right to the point. "I'm here on behalf of my soldiers." Ackley quickly explained how Owen had come to Marsden and the events that transpired there. Then he told her that he'd traveled to Melenia with his soldiers to aid Owen in his quest to reclaim the throne. He ended with his abrupt retreat to Landania to keep his men safe while Owen regrouped.

When he finished, the empress nodded, as if thinking through all he'd said. "What are King Owen's intentions toward Russek? Does he plan to seek retribution once his throne is secure?"

The fact that Rema addressed Owen as the king was a promising sign. However, Ackley was slightly thrown off by her question. As the empress for the largest kingdom on the mainland, she had to be concerned about any upcoming wars or conflicts. Somehow, he felt his answer would determine Emperion's next move. After considering different options, he decided to go with the truth—at least a limited version of it. He cleared his throat. "I secretly met with Prince Kerdan a couple of weeks ago. I believe he will soon be King Kerdan."

"You met with him?" the young man asked, a hint of disbelief coloring his voice.

"Savenek," Rema said, touching the young man's forearm. She gestured for Ackley to continue.

"Yes, I met with him." Ackley folded his arms. "I'd been told Kerdan did not intend for Melenia's royal family to be executed. I wanted to ask him about the takeover and find out what really happened. My sister is now married to King Owen, and I want to make sure her throne is secure and there won't be another event like this again." He made sure to maintain eye contact so the empress would know he spoke the truth and intended to follow through with what he said.

"What did you discover?" Savenek asked.

"That Kerdan is a good man." Ackley feared the empress wouldn't agree with him since Russek had kidnapped the Emperion princess. However, he knew Kerdan had nothing to do with it.

The corners of Rema's lips pulled into a tight smile. "How can you be so sure?"

He couldn't tell if she was being patronizing, condescending, or knew something he didn't. "Kerdan is a formidable man to be sure. Yet, the way he treated me when I went to Russek, and what he said to me, revealed his integrity. I also witnessed how his men respect and follow him. To me, that speaks to his character."

An uncomfortable minute passed without anyone speaking. Finally, Rema said, "I happen to agree with you."

Savenek glared at the low ceiling, as if he couldn't believe his mother had said that. When he focused on Ackley again, he asked, "So neither you nor King Owen intend to seek retribution against Russek?"

"No," Ackley answered without hesitation. When he'd met with Kerdan, one of the things he insisted upon was that those responsible for the invasion be brought to justice. "Kerdan and I have an agreement."

"I know," Rema revealed. "Kerdan informed my husband that he'd met with and trusted you. I wanted to see for myself —which is the only reason I'm here today."

Shock rolled through Ackley along with a deep respect and understanding. Rema was the empress not only because of her bloodline but because she was an intelligent, shrewd woman. However, this meant she wasn't there to bargain with him; she was there to determine Ackley's character. It also meant she'd been in contact with Kerdan. "When he's successful in taking control of Russek, you don't intend to invade the kingdom either, do you?"

"I do not."

"Why?" He had to be missing something. "Russek tried waging a war against Emperion. And they killed your daughter. Don't you want revenge?"

"Kerdan is not Russek," she replied. "And we're in the process of striking a treaty of sorts with Kerdan."

"Do you seek a treaty with Melenia?" Ackley asked.

"I don't think you're in a position to negotiate on Melenia's behalf." Rema pulled her shawl around her arms and took a step closer to Ackley. "You want Owen established on the throne so your sister's reign is secure. You want peace so you don't have to worry about conflict. Am I missing anything?" She tilted her head to the side, carefully watching him.

"Yes. I want my men to stay in Landania until Owen needs them. Then they'll join with his forces to retake the throne."

Rema rolled her shoulders back, considering what he'd said. "In order for your men to remain here, *we* must strike a deal. You are in effect trying to force me to choose sides. If I allow your men to stay in my kingdom, then I am siding with Owen, not Lyle."

So, she knew who sat on the throne. Ackley suddenly felt ill-prepared for this meeting. Rema clearly had the upper hand, and he couldn't let it rattle him.

"Lyle claims to have a legitimate right to be king," she added.

"As you so kindly pointed out, I am not in a position to make deals on Owen's behalf, even if he is my brother-in-law." Ackley had to figure out what Rema wanted. "The claim Lyle holds to the throne is through his wife." Calling Harley Lyle's wife tasted like ash. "Lady Harley is the old king's illegitimate daughter, so she is in line for the throne after Owen. Lyle thought he killed Owen thus allowing Harley to ascend to the throne. However, Owen is alive and is next in line."

"So, when you kill Lyle and Harley, there will be no other heir to the throne except for Owen." She said it as a statement of fact and not a question.

The temperature in the room dropped. The thought of Harley being killed felt like a knife across his abdomen.

"What are you proposing?" she asked, her voice all business, revealing no emotion. "Surely you didn't come all this way simply to ask for me to graciously allow foreign soldiers in my kingdom. If word got out, I'd be seen as weak."

"Of course not," he said, taking a slow, measured step toward the empress of Emperion. Every single person in the room tensed, preparing to strike him down if necessary. He smiled, trying to appear disarming. "Let my men camp on Landania's soil. When Owen needs them in Melenia, they'll go. Once the false king is overthrown and Owen and Idina are crowned, I will return to Marsden with my soldiers. I will also ensure Owen has no intention of seeking retribution against Russek for the damage done to his kingdom and people—which, by the way, is quite extensive. Then, I will ensure Owen meets with you and establishes an open relationship." He considered if he should leave it at that. "The previous king was a bit of a...what's the right word?" He pretended to think for a minute. "He was a weak ruler. He didn't do what was best for his subjects. I suspect that this is how Russek was able to strike a deal with Lyle so easily."

"Your point?" Rema asked.

"Owen is not weak. He will do what is best for his

kingdom. I suspect you understand that better than anyone."
He hoped he'd hit on all the necessary points. It was hard to
tell since her face remained impassive, giving no hint as to
what she was thinking. He found it disconcerting not being
able to read her.

She folded her hands together, ready to deliver her decision.
"The problem is that I must give something with the *hope* of
getting something in return." She looked at Savenek. "What do
you think?"

Ackley knew she had already made up her mind. However,
she consulted her son for a reason, as if she was training him
in negotiations and diplomacy.

"Why did Melenia try to take over Marsden?" Savenek
asked. "To gain more land? Money? What was the end goal?"

"The commander of the Melenia army invaded us because
he sought power." Ackley didn't want to reveal Marsden had
mines filled with stones worth a fortune. It was best to keep
that a secret; they didn't need anyone else invading.

Savenek tapped the hilt of his sword while considering
what Ackley had said. "If Commander Beck sought power, and
his son is carrying out his father's plans, then I must conclude
that Lyle also seeks power. What's to prevent him from
invading another kingdom again?"

Rema nodded. "A good observation. What else can you
deduce?"

"Lyle hasn't attempted to communicate with Kerdan, has
he?" Savenek asked.

"No."

The two of them knew far more than Ackley had suspected.

"But he is in communication with Jana?" Savenek said.

"He is."

"And Darmik is still on track with that plan?"

Rema nodded. "He is working with Kerdan."

Ackley knew she'd thrown him that boon of information.

"If something happens and they are not successful, we need a backup plan," Savenek said.

"And you think our backup plan should be to forge a treaty with Owen?" Rema asked.

"Yes. We don't need another situation like we have with Russek looming over our heads. I'd rather be proactive."

"I agree," Rema said.

"Do we have a deal?" Ackley asked.

A man rushed into the room, breathing heavily. "Did anyone else come with the four of you?" he asked Audek.

"Uh, no. Just the four of us. And the horses."

"What's the problem?" Rema demanded.

"We have visitors. And they don't appear to be friendly."

CHAPTER NINE

*L*yle stood with the potato sack in hand, staring at the man kneeling before him. Harley blinked in utter shock. She'd expected to see Ackley; instead, she saw a man she didn't recognize. The man's body shape and build had an uncanny resemblance to Ackley.

"I demand you release me at once," the prisoner insisted. "You, a false king, have no right to stand there accusing me of being a traitor." The man even spoke with the same accent and intonation as Ackley.

"I believe you know my wife, Lady Harley," Lyle said, waving her over.

She approached cautiously.

The man looked at her and sneered. "I should have known you weren't loyal to Owen."

Lyle slid his arm around her waist. "Love, verify this is Prince Ackley of Marsden—the man who brought foreign soldiers onto my land to kill me."

Harley froze, understanding that this man had been captured in Ackley's place. She wanted to speak to him privately to find out if that had been intentional or not. However, she couldn't let Lyle see her expressing any interest in Ackley—even if this man wasn't him—because it would only make matters worse.

"That is the man who traveled with my cousin, Owen," she said loud enough for everyone to hear. Not only did she want to keep the real Ackley safe, but she needed to make sure these soldiers knew Owen was still alive making him the rightful heir to the throne.

Lyle's fingers tightened on her waist, almost hurting her. "And?" he prompted. "I need his identity verified so I can dictate his punishment."

Harley felt as if she stood atop a great precipice. She couldn't decide if she should acknowledge this man wasn't Ackley or continue to pretend he was. Each option had pros and cons. If she admitted the truth, this man's life would be spared. However, it meant Lyle would continue hunting Ackley. She didn't like destroying one man's life so that another would be saved. It made her no better than Lyle. Her words would have the same consequence as if she killed the man with a sword herself.

She glanced at the imposter who continued to stare directly at her. His lips remained pressed together, not even trying to deny his innocence. Which meant he'd chosen this. If she claimed he wasn't the Marsden prince, he'd probably contradict her. Somehow his consent made the decision easier. This man had purposely taken Ackley's place to save him. A true soldier loyal to his kingdom, prince, and commander. She bit her lip to keep it from shaking. Then she sucked in a deep breath and said, "This is Prince Ackley."

Lyle patted her side, then released her.

Harley couldn't help but wonder if her warning had reached Ackley in time, thus accounting for the decoy. Maybe she wasn't as bad at being a spy as she thought.

Focusing on the task at hand, she needed to make sure she did her part to pull this off. Lyle couldn't suspect anything. "I think you should let him go," she pleaded. "He is a prince from Marsden. We don't want Marsden sending their army here to seek retribution and take control of the kingdom."

Lyle sneered. "Isn't that what they're attempting to do right now?"

She tried not to roll her eyes as she grabbed onto his arm. "Please don't hurt Prince Ackley. Owen considers him a friend, and he'd be so upset if you executed him."

Lyle's eyes darkened. "Who, exactly, are you loyal to? Owen? Or me?"

"You." Tears slid down her cheeks.

"Then don't mention Owen's name in my presence ever again." He turned to his soldiers. "I hereby sentence Prince Ackley of Marsden to death for infiltrating my kingdom and attempting to assassinate me."

The tears kept sliding down her cheeks. This was the second person her lies killed.

Harley looked at the man who'd chosen to die in Ackley's place. "This man is a traitor to our kingdom," she said, her voice soft and appearing weak. All by choice. However, she couldn't bring herself to say he deserved to die.

"Hang him," Lyle said, pointing to the same place the royal family had been beheaded.

Bile rose in the back of her throat, and she had to shove it down. She had a part to play so that Ackley remained safe.

The soldiers closed in on the fake Marsden prince. Lyle took

Harley's hand, leading her away from them and into the castle. She didn't look back. He dragged her through the corridor and up the staircase. At the third level, he turned and started up to the fourth floor. Her stomach twisted with pain. Lyle was taking her to the execution site. She was going to have to watch the fake Ackley be hanged. Her breathing sped up, and a chill spread across her skin.

They exited a door and stepped outside onto the open gorge tower. Blood still stained the stones from her family's brutal beheadings. Lyle released her and moved to the half wall.

A side door banged open, and the fake Ackley was dragged out, a noose already around his neck. Lyle stepped forward, jumping onto the half wall. One of the sentries waved a flag, gaining the attention of the soldiers camped below.

Lyle addressed his soldiers; however, Harley didn't hear a word he said.

She couldn't look away from the blood stains. Her brother's blood. She still could hear Oriana's piercing screams, see the horror on her aunt's face. So much death. All because of her husband.

Lyle deftly jumped off the wall, leaned down, and whispered in Harley's ear, "It was Russek, not me. Now get it together and stop acting like a pathetic wench."

"You invited them here." The words slipped out before she thought better of it.

"My father did. And the killing that ensued was all Russek. An unfortunate consequence."

She nodded, as if what he said made it okay. As if what he said even made sense—especially as he prepared to kill again.

The soldiers below started chanting, "Traitor! Traitor!"

A queasy feeling gripped her, and she couldn't even look at the fake Ackley.

The soldiers dragged the innocent man forward, his hands once again tied behind his back. The man holding the end of the rope looped it around one of the poles sticking out of the wall. He tugged it to ensure it held. Satisfied, he gave the okay to proceed.

Two soldiers lifted the fake Ackley onto the half wall. Teetering there, he glanced at Harley and winked.

Lyle shoved the man forward. His body fell over the side of the castle. A sickening sound cracked through the crisp afternoon, followed by a raucous cheering.

Everything turned blurry as tears filled Harley's eyes. Her legs became weak and she reached out, leaning against the wall for support so she wouldn't topple over. Would the death and destruction ever stop?

Needing to get away from the cheering, the dead man hanging over the side of the castle, and these sadistic soldiers, Harley turned and stumbled inside, not even paying attention to where she went. In a daze, she descended four levels and entered the great hall where it had all started. She still remembered Kerdan walking in with his men looking like wolves about to slaughter bunnies. Funny how the real threat ended up coming from within the castle. One of their own had betrayed them, allowing Russek to take over and slaughter them.

Heading behind the dais, she found the hidden door she'd escaped through. She opened it and stepped inside the secret passageways. After lighting a torch, she wandered through the corridors, retracing the steps she'd taken that dreadful night. When she came to the turret with the ladder, she glanced up, remembering her frantic climb to light the signal fire. Then she went to the spot where she'd been knocked out, and the key to the dungeon had been stolen from her.

If only that night had gone differently. If she'd never been struck over the back of her head, she would still possess the key.

Imagining that scenario, she took the passageways to the narrow stairwell, going down, seeking the entrance to the dungeon. Since this level had always been off limits, she'd never been here before. Dripping noises echoed through the corridor, and the stones became slick. An odd musty smell permeated the air. The passageways had never scared her. However, on the subterranean level, a cold terror set in.

She came to a dead end, a black iron door before her. Not seeing a keyhole or handle, she wondered how the door opened. At the bottom, she noticed a raised stone block. She stepped on it, pushing it down, and the door groaned open toward her. Darkness greeted her. Harley's heart pounded, and her hands shook. She had no idea if any prisoners were in the dungeon or if any guards were on duty.

Only the royal family knew about this secret entrance. The one everyone else used could be found on the first level of the castle, near the north end. That door was always guarded by two soldiers.

Shoving the torch forward into the darkness, Harley examined the long, empty hallway that extended before her. She didn't see any cells or anything indicative of a dungeon. Her entire life, she'd been told never to go near this place. It was where the royal family housed criminals and enemies of the kingdom. It had been the only place in the castle she didn't have access to.

She stepped into the hallway, her footsteps echoing. The temperature plummeted, the walls glistened with water, and the smell of dank mold filled the stale air. Harley came to another door, this one with a visible lock. Glancing around, she spotted a key hanging on the wall. She plucked it off a metal nail and inserted it into the lock. A soft click resounded, and the door swung open.

Harley stepped inside a square room, three walls made of stones and one of metal bars. This had to be one of the dungeon cells. She clutched the key in her right hand, the torch in her left. Standing in the middle of the cell, she listened for sounds, trying to determine if anyone was in the dungeon.

No voices or sounds came from within. A thought suddenly occurred to her—Hollis had spent his last hours down here before his beheading. An overwhelming need to see if he'd left anything behind seized her. She slid the torch into a holder on the wall, then opened the cell door. It squeaked, making her freeze for fear someone had heard. When no one screamed or came running, she stepped out of the cell and into a long hallway. Torches hung on the walls every fifteen feet. To her left was a dead end, so she headed to the right, moving slowly. As she passed the cells, she glanced inside, trying to see if anyone was in them. Most were too dark to see inside, and she only caught glimpses of straw, chamber pots, and the occasional blanket.

At the end of the hallway, she came to an intersection where an additional hallway extended to both the left and the right, containing more cells. Straight ahead, there was a rectangular room with a single round table, a stack of cards scattered on it. The four chairs had all been pushed back as if the people sitting there had left in a hurry. Beyond that, a staircase led up, probably to the first level of the castle and what was considered the entrance to the dungeon.

She mulled over her options. There could be nobles down here from the takeover. If so, she had to find out. "Hello?" she called out, softer than intended. Clearing her throat, she tried again. "Hello?" she said, this time louder, her voice echoing in the hallways. "Is anyone in here?"

The cells should all be locked so if there were criminals, she didn't have to worry about them. But if she found a noble person, a loyal Melenia soldier, or even a servant from the takeover that had been put down here, she had to save them. She glanced at the key in her hand, wondering if it unlocked any of the cell doors.

There was only one way to find out. She went to one of the hallways, peering down it. "Is anyone there?" No one responded. She turned and went to the other hallway. "Hello?"

Someone coughed, the sound low and barely audible.

Frozen in place, she listened, hearing a soft rustling sound. She forced herself to head down the hallway toward the noise. Outside one of the cells, an empty bowl and cup sat. Harley inched closer. The smell of body odor and fecal matter pervaded the air, making her gag. "Who's there?" she asked.

"My ears must be deceiving me," a familiar voice replied.

Harley stumbled, sure she'd misheard.

"Harley?" the familiar voice said.

"Papa?" she asked, staring at the dark cell in question.

A lump on the ground moved. Someone stood and stepped forward, into the light, and the dear face of her father appeared. His hair was rumpled from having slept on the floor, his clothes were wrinkled, and dirt was caked on the side of his face. However, other than that, he appeared unharmed.

"What are you doing here?" she asked, astonished and unable to fathom why he'd be in the dungeon.

"I didn't think he'd let me see you," Lord Silas said, his eyes warm and welcoming.

"I thought you were at home. Mother said you were sick in bed." Not only did he appear to be in good health, but she had no idea how he'd gotten to the royal castle, let alone survived the trip if he'd been as frail as her mother indicated.

"Sick?" he asked. "My health has been declining, but that's nothing new. Of course, being stuck in here doesn't help these old bones." He reached through the bars, patting her cheek. "He told me what those Russek bastards did. How they killed everyone, including Hollis."

"Is that what Lyle told you?"

He nodded.

"Did he also tell you that he's the one who struck a bargain with Russek, bringing them here?" She was furious everyone continued to blame this solely on Russek, not acknowledging Lyle's part in it.

"He failed to mention that," he replied. "However, it doesn't take a genius to understand the deal was mutually beneficial to both parties involved."

"I don't understand why you're here." She couldn't fathom a reason Lyle would put her father in the dungeon.

"I'm here as a witness," he revealed. "Lyle said when the time is right, he'll come and get me. Then I'll tell everyone the truth."

If Lyle needed Lord Silas, he should be treated better and be staying in a guest room, not the dungeon. Then she remembered that this man before her wasn't actually her father, and Lyle probably wanted him to verify it.

"Is it true?" she asked, unable to voice the words. Unable to ask if the late king had really been her father.

"Oh, my dear girl," he said, withdrawing his hand from her cheek. "I don't know what he's told you, but I am your father in every sense of the word, save one. I raised you, and I love you."

And he'd married her off to Lyle without even considering

what she wanted. That had always bothered her. "You're not actually my father?" she whispered, trying to understand it all.

"No, honey, I'm not."

Hearing him say it grounded her in the reality of it. Tears filled her eyes. "Why?" He should have told her before now. She didn't understand why it had been kept from her.

Her father took a step back, pinching the bridge of his nose. "This is a conversation your mother always wanted to have with you."

"She's had ample opportunities." Including when Harley had last been in Penlar. Her mother could have told her instead of insinuating things through cryptic words and phrases.

"She couldn't, honey. We were being threatened."

"By Commander Beck and Lyle?"

He nodded. "Now tell me what you're doing down here in the dungeon."

"I'm here to…" She was about to tell him she was there to kill Lyle, but something stopped her. She didn't know what it was, but intuition told her not to say anything.

"What are you here to do?" Lord Silas prodded.

"I'm here because I got lost and found myself in the dungeon. Curiosity got the better of me since I'd never been allowed down here as a child." She forced a smile on her lips so this man before her wouldn't think twice about what she said.

"You should get up to the main portion of the castle," he replied, "where it's warmer."

She absently nodded, about to leave when something occurred to her. "When you say you have to tell people about my true parentage, who are you going to tell?" All the nobles had been killed.

"The other rulers on the mainland."

A chill went through her body as she wondered what Lyle

had planned. Suddenly, she realized she had no idea what he intended to do with his newfound title other than rule Melenia. She hadn't considered him wanting more until now. Since Commander Beck had gone to Marsden with the intention of taking over, she had to look at all options.

"How long have you been here for?" she asked, a sick feeling taking root.

"Since just before the takeover."

She took a step back, feeling off kilter, as if a key component were missing. Maybe she'd just spent too much time with Ackley. Regardless, she decided to trust her instincts. And right now, while she knew this man before her might claim to love her dearly, she also knew there was more going on than he was telling her.

"Why isn't Mother in here with you?" After all, Lady Mayle was the one who'd been intimate with the former king and had given birth to Harley. Something nagged at the back of her mind. She was missing something; she was certain of it. "I better get going," she said, taking another step back. "Lyle's probably looking for me."

He nodded. "Don't worry about me. I'll be fine. I love you."

He'd been the one to teach Harley everything she knew. "I love you, too." She hurried from the dungeon.

Once Harley knew Lyle's daily schedule, she started actively doing things that could help Owen. First on her list, she went out to see the soldiers camped on the castle grounds. She pretended to be there handing out bread. However, she really wanted to discover if these were the men who'd traveled with Owen. He'd ordered his men to go to Lyle and swear fealty to the fake king so they could rescue their loved ones. Harley needed to discover if that had happened, or if Lyle had yet to release the people he'd been holding captive.

None of the faces looked familiar as she gave out loaf after loaf. Not that she'd paid much attention to those she'd been traveling with. She'd been so relieved Owen had returned, that she hadn't bothered getting to know those around her.

She started asking subtle questions in order to discover if these were those soldiers or not. "How long have you been camped here?" she asked the short man with stubble covering his face.

"Too long to count," he replied before taking the bread and lumbering away.

"At least this is better than being on a ship for a couple weeks," she said.

"I've never been on a ship before," another soldier replied.

On and on the questions went. Not once did anyone answer in a way indicative of being with Owen.

After an hour of questions, it became abundantly clear these were not those men. So now she needed to discover where those soldiers had gone and what Lyle had done with their loved ones.

Frustrated, Harley went back inside. She wanted to head up to her room and light the candle telling Rikter she had a message for him. He needed to know about the information she'd discovered in Lyle's room the other day. In all the chaos of having to warn Ackley of the men coming after him and the man who'd died in his place, she'd forgotten to relay the information.

She strolled along the corridor, about to pass the library, when she remembered the books on poisons. Tonight would be the perfect night to spend reading. She entered the library and went over to the section where she'd located the books. Fourth section, fifth row. She stood there staring at an empty shelf. The books were gone. Glancing around the room, she looked to see if they were on one of the tables. She didn't see them anywhere. Not able to fathom why Lyle would need books about poisons, she perused the library, thinking of possibilities.

Stopping before the romance section, she remembered she'd hidden one of the books there so Lyle wouldn't see what she'd been holding. She rushed to that shelf and quickly located the book *Plants, Leaves, and Trees: Various Uses.* Excitement coursed through her as she pulled the book off the shelf. This might be her only chance to discover what those roots and leaves were that Ledger had in his bag. She just had to make it up to her room without running into Lyle.

CHAPTER TEN

ACKLEY

*R*ema's eyes bore into Ackley. "Hostiles are approaching. I suggest you leave. Audek, Brodek, you will remain with me."

Ackley withdrew his sword. A collective *whoosh* resounded in the room as every person sucked in their breath and leaned closer, about to subdue him. "Let me remain at your side," he said to the empress, ignoring everyone else. "I'm not one to run away, and I don't want to just leave you here."

A smile slid over her face. "I'm hardly alone; and my men are more than capable of handling this situation." She pulled her shawl tightly around her body before exiting the room, Savenek right behind her.

Ackley ran after them. "While I'm sure your men are capable, I'm still not leaving."

"You're not needed," Savenek asserted.

Ackley kept pace with the empress and Savenek, their soldiers following behind them. "Where I come from, we protect and help our friends." Ackley tilted his head to the side, stretching his neck. As they headed down the staircase, he pulled his mental armor on, preparing for battle.

On the first level, they entered the great room and headed to the front of the castle toward the open windows located there. Rema's men moved around her, taking up position next to each of the windows and peering outside. The empress and her son remained safely behind the stone wall where doors would have been had this been a normal castle and not one surrounded by water.

"What's the situation?" the empress demanded.

"I see about a dozen men hidden on shore," someone answered. "No one is attempting to cross the lake yet."

Gytha remained off to the side with Audek and Brodek.

"We're deep in Emperion," Ackley said, thinking out loud. "I can understand a raid near the border, or some sort of attack in the northern kingdoms you'd recently aligned with." Something about this felt off. "But here? Being hidden so well, I'm having trouble figuring out who would attack you. Unless your kingdom is unstable, which I don't think it is."

Rema chuckled. "This isn't a raiding party or an attack."

"Then what is it?"

"A game," Savenek answered.

Ackley glanced at Gytha who shrugged, apparently just as confused as he was.

"We're running a training exercise of sorts," Rema explained. "The men out there are trying to capture me. The men in here are trying to keep me safe. At sundown, whoever has me wins."

"See, there's your problem," Gytha muttered. "All men. If you had women, it would be better."

Rema raised a single eyebrow, somehow managing to look

both beautiful and intimidating at the same time. With her striking presence, Ackley understood why she managed to command such a large kingdom despite being a female.

"Possibly," Rema replied. "However, right now, these are some of my most skilled men. We're practicing because I had a unit of elite soldiers mutilated and butchered by those Russek barbarians. My daughter was kidnapped by them as well. Neither of those events is acceptable. We are going to rectify these issues and ensure it doesn't happen again."

"So, you see, we don't need some prince with a sword trying to help us," Savenek said. "Be on your way and let us get to work."

Ackley chuckled. "Are you speaking about me or you?" The two men stood there staring at one another. Something flashed in Savenek's eyes, something dark. "Are you a prince or soldier?" Ackley asked. Maybe he'd misinterpreted and Savenek wasn't Rema's son.

"Both," he snarled.

"Savenek," Rema snapped. "Remember your role."

"Even in a situation like this?" he asked.

"Especially in a situation like this. It ensures the enemy never sees it coming."

Savenek nodded and relaxed his hand which had been gripping the hilt of his sword.

"That doesn't mean you can't command our men," Rema said, gesturing for him to take the lead.

He gave a curt nod. "Our mission is to not let anyone touch the empress," Savenek said. "We have to assume our enemy knows how to get into this castle. I want half of you monitoring the water entrance below. The rest, keep watching the shore."

Rema addressed Ackley and Gytha. "You're welcome to stay, but it's not necessary."

"Now that I know you're not in any real danger, we will go." He turned to leave and remembered something. "You never confirmed our deal." They'd been interrupted.

"Your soldiers may remain on my land so long as they do not harm any of my citizens. The second Owen requests you return, you do so immediately. Then I want to meet with Owen and his bride."

"Done."

"One last thing," Rema said. "When the situation with Melenia and Russek is rectified, I'd like to speak with you further about your kingdom. I think we should open some form of communication and peace between Emperion and Marsden."

"I agree." He took her hand, kissing the back of it. "It was a pleasure meeting you." He released her hand and exited the room, Gytha following close behind.

"With this exercise going on, how do you propose we get out of here without getting caught up in this?" Gytha still held her sword in her right hand.

"We're going to provide a distraction and help the empress out." Instead of going to the lower level where the water entrance was located, he went to the end of the hallway where a tall window had once been.

"Why would we do that?" she asked, sheathing her sword.

"To show her we're on her side and can be a valuable ally." Peering out of the opening, he estimated the water was about fifteen feet below.

"Won't we be caught doing this?"

Ackley gawked. "Caught? Never. Besides, we're going to

show her we have our own set of skills and aren't simpletons from some little unknown kingdom."

"By doing that, aren't you also declaring you're not to be trifled with?"

A wicked smile spread across his face. "Perhaps. Now let's get out of here." After making sure his weapons were secure, Ackley climbed onto the window ledge. Not seeing anyone on the shore on this side of the castle, he dove into the water. He resurfaced and watched Gytha jump in feet first. Once her head popped above the water, he pointed to the shore. Gytha nodded.

Ackley swam that way. If everyone was on the other side, no one would see them. Then, once he reached land, he could circle around and come up behind the men, surprising them.

Nearing the shore, he thought he saw movement amongst the trees. When his feet could touch, he stood, observing the shore and the nearby forest. He felt the presence of people hidden nearby. Not wanting to harm any of Rema's men, he planned to fight using only his hands and not his weapons.

He started to exit the water. When he was knee deep, a man stepped out from behind a tree. Ackley came face to face with one of his spies, Morton, the one he'd sent to the castle to assist Harley. "What are you doing here?" he asked his man, panic seizing him. Morton would only be here if there was a complication.

"We have a problem," he answered.

They were going to have a lot more than that when Rema found—he quickly counted—four of his soldiers here. He cursed.

The air shifted, and an unnatural silence blanketed the lake and nearby forest. Rema's men had to be closing in on them.

Standing in the lake, the water lapping around his knees, Ackley quickly considered his options. He didn't care to have an arrow shot through his back, so he lifted his arms in surrender. "Everyone, follow suit."

His four spies and Gytha promptly imitated him.

"No one move," Ackley said. Then, louder, "These men are with me!"

One of his soldiers cursed, his attention going above Ackley's head to the castle behind him.

"What is it?" he demanded.

"There's a handful of archers with arrows pointed at us. There's also a boat filled with soldiers heading this way."

"And now there are men behind you," Ackley mumbled. "We're surrounded."

"You don't want us to fight?" Morton clarified.

"No," Ackley replied. "Stand down." He knew it went against everything his men had been taught.

They remained standing there with their hands raised in the air.

The boat neared and Savenek jumped out before even reaching the shore. His boots splashed in the water, and he stormed closer to Ackley. "What's the meaning of this?" His face turned red like a fire and just as furious.

"These are my men," Ackley explained, speaking calmly, hoping to placate him. "They came here looking for me."

"Did they follow you here?" Savenek withdrew his sword, the sound of steel slicing through the air. "Because neither Audek nor Brodek know anything about them."

"I don't know how they got here," Ackley replied. "I was just about to ask them."

Morton cleared his throat. "We, uh, tracked Prince Ackley

to a manor. There, a woman gave us directions to a town near here. We were supposed to wait there for you. But we caught your trail and decided to follow you since time is of the essence."

"Is Harley all right?" Ackley demanded. If something had happened to her, he'd tear Lyle apart.

"I'm not sure."

"Start at the beginning," Ackley said, panic rising. He had to stifle it so he could focus and think clearly.

"A group of Melenia soldiers came looking for you," the man to Morton's right explained. "Your decoy, Ruthar, decided to let himself get captured. They took him away, leaving the rest of your soldiers alone."

That was a problem. Not only did they have one of his men, but they knew where his soldiers were camped. "Did they kill him outright?" Ackley asked.

"No. I'm assuming they took him to Lyle."

"Then there's still time to rescue him." Ackley ran his hands over his head, thinking of various plans. "How does this tie to Harley?"

"No one has seen her in days."

It felt as if the ground beneath him tilted. Then he remembered he was still standing in water. He lowered his arms. Just because no one had seen her in days didn't necessarily mean something bad had happened to her. "When was she last spotted?" he demanded.

"I'm not sure," Morton said. "She was rarely seen outside the castle. However, the kitchen staff started talking about her not eating dinner with the false king. Then soldiers started saying even inside the castle, she hadn't been seen."

Maybe she'd run away. He pinched the bridge of his nose,

thinking. "Has Harley been successful at getting any information to Owen?"

"No."

That wasn't good. Either he'd thrown her in there completely unprepared or he'd overestimated her. She'd been there long enough that she should have been able to get some information to Owen. Otherwise, it made her look exceedingly guilty. Which, she wasn't. She didn't love or support Lyle—even though he was her husband.

A sick feeling took root. Something was wrong, and Ackley wanted to save Harley. But his men also needed him since his decoy had most likely been executed and Lyle knew their location.

"We told you to arrive alone," Savenek said. "And yet, you brought Gytha. Now these men are here."

While Ackley knew Savenek was speaking, his words didn't fully register because he was busy thinking of the quickest way to get to the royal castle and extract Harley before something happened to her.

"Your orders?" Morton asked.

"I'm going to get her."

Savenek chuckled. "Are you saying you fell in love with Owen's cousin? And this cousin is married to Lyle—the man claiming to be the king?" He started laughing. "Oh, this is good."

Something in Ackley snapped. He turned and jumped, launching himself at Savenek. The two men fell over, into the water. Ackley wanted to strangle him. He was sure Savenek had no idea what it was like to be in love with someone he wasn't supposed to have or want.

Savenek wound his arm around Ackley, shoving him below

the water and holding him under. Ackley wrapped his legs around Savenek, squeezing. He tried to flip so he'd be on top, only Savenek's hold was too tight. This was no ordinary prince. Ackley brought his arms in and under Savenek's. When he flung his arms out, Savenek released Ackley's shoulders. Ackley twisted, hurling Savenek under the water. Someone grabbed him from behind, yanking him back and pinning his arms down.

Another person had Savenek similarly situated.

Brodek stood on the shore, shaking his head. "Do I need to remind you, *Your Highness*, that the drill is still going on? We don't want to jeopardize the empress's plans."

Ackley glanced at Brodek, realizing he was addressing Savenek.

"I don't need one of your lectures today," Savenek muttered. The soldier holding Savenek let go and he stood, tossing his head back to get his wet hair out of his face.

The man released Ackley, and he got to his feet, heaving in air. It had been far too long since he'd had a good fight.

Ackley chuckled. "You're not simply a prince, are you?" Savenek's build and the way he held his body reeked of a fighter, not a person of royalty. Somehow, he was the two molded into one. Like Ackley.

"Neither are you." Savenek wiped his arm over his forehead.

"Your orders, Your Highness?" Brodek asked.

Savenek glanced behind him. "Everyone but Brodek back to the castle. Defend the empress. I'll be along shortly."

Ackley got the feeling Savenek wanted to have this conversation alone. "My men, remain on shore. That includes you, Gytha."

When it was just Savenek and Ackley, the two men stood

only a foot apart, both staring into the other's eyes, as if trying to decipher a hidden code.

"You're going after the woman, aren't you?" Savenek asked.

"I am." He didn't care if it was the wrong decision.

"I would, too."

Ackley raised his eyebrows. "As a prince, you'd leave your men to fend for themselves, to go after a woman you loved?"

"Without question."

Somehow, Ackley didn't feel quite as crazy now.

"I have something that might prove useful." He handed Ackley a vial. "If anyone asks, you didn't get this from me."

A wicked smile slid across Ackley's face. "Understood." He pocketed the vial. "When all of this is over, we should meet again. Maybe go a round or two."

"If you manage to survive, I might like getting the chance to pummel you."

When they reached their horses, Ackley, Gytha, and the four Marsden soldiers parted ways from Brodek and Audek. They traveled hard and fast, making their way straight toward where the Marsden soldiers were camped just inside Emperion's border.

When it got too dark to travel, they stopped and made camp for the night. Ackley knew he had to tell Gytha what he intended to do. If his brother were there, he'd smack him on the back of the head for letting a woman dictate his actions. Even though he knew going after Harley wasn't the smartest move, he was going to do it regardless.

With Morton taking the first watch, Ackley settled beside Gytha.

Gytha crawled under her blanket. "I know you're going after her," the warrior woman said.

"I have to."

She rolled over and looked at him under the dim moonlight. "What's your plan? Go in, rescue the damsel in distress, and kill the evil guy?"

"Not quite." He'd been going over various plans. He knew if he just went in there and grabbed Harley, Lyle would go crazy. He'd hunt Ackley down with everything he had. Not only that, but it could jeopardize whatever Owen had planned. He needed to be discreet.

"Then what is it?"

Instead of revealing his plan, which included not only one but two backup plans, he told her what he needed her to do. Somehow that made it easier to deal with. As he explained it to her, she didn't interrupt or stop him once to ask questions. When he finally finished, her silence made him uncomfortable. He expected her to argue or at least tell him he was crazy.

"I hope she's worth it," Gytha finally said before rolling over and facing away from him.

"I hope so, too." He didn't even understand his own reaction to Harley or why he wanted her so badly. It made no sense. "So, you'll do it?"

"You're my prince, and you're in charge of this mission. I take orders from you."

That was not what he wanted to hear. If her heart wasn't in it, she'd never survive. "Gytha…"

"Don't. You gave me an order, and I will follow it."

"I want to explain." Not really. He just wanted her to understand or agree with him.

"I can't be here and listen to you speak of another woman.

You've made your stance clear. We're in the army together. You are my prince. I follow your orders."

It was like a knife to his heart. While he didn't love Gytha in a romantic way, he certainly cared for her like a sister. He wanted her to be happy, and he didn't want something to stand in the way of their friendship. He valued and respected her too much. She was the fiercest warrior he knew.

But he didn't love her. Not the way she wanted him to.

CHAPTER ELEVEN

HARLEY

*H*arley sat in bed reading the book on plants and leaves. She sighed, wishing she was reading a romance novel instead of this dry drivel. Half-way through, she had yet to find any reference to making something resembling any sort of poison. Maybe this book was only about plants, leaves, and trees and their uses. How droll.

Turning the page, she forced herself to keep reading. She had to stay up until midnight to meet Rikter anyway. He needed to know what she'd seen in Lyle's room so he could pass the information on. Her eyelids became heavy, and she started to nod off when she read the word *numb*. She sat upright. Finally, a section that interested her. Fully awake, she read the paragraph again. It talked about a leaf that when soaked in water, could be ground up with a pestle making a gooey substance. When the root of a cattail was mixed with it, the substance became dangerous, causing numbness for a couple of hours if it came into contact with a person's skin.

That had to be what Ledger put on the horse's reins. She still remembered touching it and the extreme pain followed by losing all feeling in her hands and arms. She shivered. Below the paragraph, a picture of the leaf in question had been drawn. Scrambling off the bed, she knelt on the floor, peeled the rug back, and pushed on the end of the wooden floorboard. It opened, revealing Ledger's hidden items. Pulling out the sack, she untied it and examined the leaves. They appeared to be the same as the one drawn in the book.

Her heart pounded. She had the ingredients necessary to make the poison. This could work to her advantage. Putting the items away, she jumped back on the bed and read the book some more, trying to see how long the poison remained effective in that form. Ten hours. Once she made it, she'd only have ten hours to use it. Otherwise, it would be nothing more than a gooey gel. Tomorrow, she would acquire the bowl and utensil necessary to make it. She'd store the items under the floorboard; that way, when she needed them, she'd have them.

She scanned through the rest of the book, not finding anything useful. When it was finally midnight, she blew out her candle and neared the door, listening for sounds. A low male voice could be heard. Tying her robe around her waist, she opened her door and entered the antechamber. Outside in the hallway, she heard Lyle speaking to someone. She only caught a few words, and it sounded as if two men were talking about horses. She rolled her eyes. They could be at it for quite some time.

Harley went back into her bedchamber, considering her options. She could wait for Lyle to finish his conversation and retire for the night. However, it might be another thirty minutes before he fell asleep. Not wanting to wait and risk rousing him, she decided to go to bed. She'd have to meet with Rikter tomorrow.

The next morning, Harley dressed and combed her hair. Once presentable, she exited her room and went to Oriana's bedchamber. While she didn't expect to find Rikter there, she hoped she'd find some clue. Standing in the middle of Oriana's room, she searched for anything out of place. One of the pillows appeared off-center.

She went over to the bed and lifted the pillow. The corner of a piece of paper stuck out from under the blanket. Pulling it out, she read the note. It was from Rikter. Since meeting at night was becoming too dangerous, he told her to leave all communication for Owen in the third guest bedchamber in the north wing. He would check the room daily.

Once she located the guest suite in question, she sat and penned a letter to Owen. When she finished, she left it there for Rikter to find. Standing in the empty corridor, she glanced both ways, ensuring no one was around before pulling out the key she'd taken from the dungeon. She slid it in the lock. It easily turned, locking the door. Her heart pounded. Turning the key the other way, it unlocked it. Excitement coursed through her. She went to the next room and tried using the key. Again, it locked and unlocked the door with ease.

She slid the key into the neckline of her dress and hurried down to the first level of the castle, eager to see if the key worked on other, more important doors. She made her way to the wing where the offices were located, wanting access to them. Unfortunately, this wing bustled with activity. She'd have to try those doors later.

Pretending to meander through the hallways, she slowly made her way to the corridor containing the library. She inserted the key into a random door. It worked. Thrilled, she went to the kitchen and the great room. No matter what lock she slid the key into, it both locked and unlocked the door. Somehow knowing she had poison and a universal key made her feel infinitely more cunning.

The following days, Harley noticed that Lyle's routine shifted. He began going outside earlier and training with his soldiers for much of the day. From her bedchamber window, she watched him run drills with his men. It reminded her of what he did most days back in Penlar.

Once Harley was certain of Lyle's schedule, she began searching the offices closest to his, assuming the highest-ranking officers would be in those rooms. Most were locked; however, her key opened every single one of them. At first, she didn't touch anything and just looked at the notes and papers scattered on desks and tables. However, when that didn't wield anything useful, she began going through the drawers. With painstaking detail, she'd open one, look through its contents, and then close it, making sure everything was just as she'd found it.

After a week, she'd learned that Penlar was the only major city to avoid destruction, and it didn't appear to be an accident. Several letters stated that no one was to enter Penlar. A few villages, like the one she'd recently visited, were intact. However, the vast majority had been destroyed, and the inhabitants killed. From the letters she'd read, it appeared that Russek took all men and boys south. Kerdan had said that

Russek needed soldiers to invade Emperion. Kerdan had also said that when his father died, he called all Russek soldiers home. He assumed the Melenia people had returned home as well. Only they had no home to go back to. Harley had no idea where all the people who'd survived had gone.

Each morning, she made her way to the guest suite to check for correspondence from Rikter. On the seventh day, she found a note stating that Owen wanted her to look at Lyle's ledgers. Owen thought that if she could follow the money, she could find out where the soldiers who'd traveled with him had gone and what had happened to their loved ones. Chewing on her bottom lip, Harley knew Lyle's ledgers would be in his office. She'd been avoiding going in there because it would be the trickiest one to navigate through. Surely, he'd have traps set throughout—similar to what he had in his bedchamber—to determine if someone stepped foot in there.

As she headed to the first level of the castle, she realized putting it off would only delay discovering information. She rolled her shoulders back. Owen wanted her to look in the ledgers, and she would do it for him. Otherwise, she had no business being in the castle. Ackley had sent her there to spy and kill Lyle. So far, she hadn't accomplished either of those tasks. It was time to see this through.

Since Lyle was still outside training with his soldiers, the wing where the offices were located was empty. If she accidentally stumbled across a soldier or servant, she would have to claim she got lost since there was no reason for her to be there. At Lyle's office, she knelt on the floor and peered under the closed door, trying to see if any leaves or feathers would be disturbed if she opened the door. Not seeing anything, she stood and pulled out the key. With a shaky hand, she slid it into the lock. It clicked open. Pushing the door, she moved slowly, not wanting to miss anything. A lone leaf drifted to the floor. It must have been placed in the door jam and fallen when she'd opened it. She picked the leaf up and set it aside. She couldn't forget to place it back when she exited the room.

A bead of sweat slid down her forehead. She stepped inside, closing the door behind her, and surveyed the room. It had changed a lot since the king's death. Lyle had removed the portraits, statues, and tapestries. The room now had a sparse, utilitarian feeling to it. Harley shivered, feeling Lyle's presence around her since everything was neat, organized, and logical—just like Lyle. Going to the massive wooden desk, she looked it over before touching anything. Several stacks of papers had been neatly arranged on top. One appeared to be maps, another letters and correspondence, and the third ledgers. That was what she needed.

Her heart pounded, and another bead of sweat trickled down the side of her face.

Focusing on the ledgers, she read the top sheet. It mostly listed quantities of food. She carefully lifted it, looking at the next page. It contained a list of weapons. She turned the page and found a list of soldiers' names and the names of their family members. Her hands started trembling. Harley turned page after page, finding hundreds and hundreds of names. On the last page, a single word had been written: Losger.

Everything suddenly made sense. Losger was the name of an abandoned castle that hadn't been occupied in hundreds of years. Occasionally, the king had used it to house prisoners since it was remote and well-fortified. Harley should have thought of this location before now. It had to be where the soldiers' loved ones were being kept. Maybe even the soldiers themselves.

She put the papers back in order, making sure they were lined up and perfectly straight. Satisfied everything was as she'd found it, she went over to the door and opened it an inch. Not seeing anyone in sight, she took the leaf and held it in the door jam, then closed the door, locking it.

With Lyle and his men still outside, Harley made her way back to her bedchamber where she quickly composed a letter to Owen, detailing what she'd discovered. Then she went to the second floor and put the letter in the guest suite for Rikter to find. Stepping out of the room, she stood in the hallway, thinking. A few doors down had been where she hid the sword and letters Ackley had given her.

Before she knew what she was doing, she headed that way and entered the guest suite. Standing before the armoire, she considered her options. Since she'd discovered where the soldiers' loved ones were being kept, it was time to kill Lyle.

Could she kill him?

While she wanted to, she didn't know if she could bring herself to do it. But if she didn't, that left the responsibility to Owen or Ackley. For them to get to Lyle, a war would ensue, and hundreds of people would die. By killing Lyle herself, she would save countless lives. She had a duty to her kingdom. A plan formed, and she knew what she had to do.

She opened the armoire and pulled out the drawer. Reaching in the back, she found the letters, quickly tucking them in her dress. Then she reached in again, her fingers coming across the pommel of the sword she'd hidden. Her fingers curled around it, and she withdrew the weapon, no bigger than her forearm. It was even more beautiful than she remembered. On the hilt, the grip had been wrapped with red leather. The guard had an intricate swirly design.

She lifted her dress and slid the sword into her boot. It was awkward and uncomfortable, but she only had to get it to her bedchamber.

Somehow, some way, she would end Lyle.

As Harley dressed for supper, she made sure to choose a dress Lyle would appreciate. Since he favored yellow—a color she despised—she picked the most modest yellow dress she could find. She arranged her hair half up and half down, just the way he preferred. Satisfied with her appearance, she went downstairs.

Making her way along the corridor, Harley moved slowly, as if in a dream. She still couldn't believe she was about to go through with this violent plan of hers. Outside the dining hall, she took a deep breath, then slowly let it out. She remembered playing that game of War with Ackley. When she'd first started, she moved pieces around with no clear plan. Then, once she understood the end goal, she came up with a strategy and enacted it. The same was true here at the castle. For weeks she'd been trying to figure out what to do and how to do it. Tonight, that changed.

While she knew what needed to be done, she prayed she was strong enough to see it through. She steeled her resolve and stepped inside. It was time to win this game.

Lyle sat, waiting for her. His left arm rested on the table; his middle finger tapping methodically against the wood surface. He glanced at her, his eyes narrowing. "I was wondering when you'd show."

Harley rushed over to her chair. "Sorry I'm late." As she sat, an ominous feeling settled over her. She didn't know if it was from Lyle and the dark mood he appeared to be in, or if it was from what would transpire tonight. In either case, she embraced the darkness and used it as fuel. "I wanted to look nice."

He sat there, his finger still tapping, astutely studying her across the table.

"My monthly bleeding finished. Since I am not with Ledger's child, we may resume relations." She had to force herself to breathe evenly, steadily. It took every ounce of effort just to keep her face serene. Her stomach rolled with nausea. She feared she'd be physically ill.

"Why didn't you tell me when your bleeding started?" His eyes narrowed, assessing her.

A servant entered, placing a plate of food in front of Lyle and then Harley.

"I wanted to surprise you," Harley answered, forcing a smile on her face. "That's why I'm dressed up." He didn't need to know she hadn't bled, and she'd only used it as an excuse to buy her some time. She prayed he didn't see through the lie.

He picked up his fork and started eating. "You don't need to bother with your clothes. It doesn't improve the way you look."

Such cruel words usually cut and chipped away at her. However, after being with Ackley, she saw Lyle for what he was —a shallow man who used words to manipulate people and situations. He wanted to always maintain control. Given what she intended to do tonight, she would let him think he had the upper hand.

She peered down at her plate, fluttering her eyelids as if on the verge of crying. Without looking at Lyle, she began picking at her food, acting sad and depressed. As if his opinion and what he thought of her mattered. Rounding her shoulders back, she pretended to put on a brave front while chewing on her bottom lip.

"What have you been doing all day?" Lyle asked, his voice softer than before.

At that, Harley glanced at him. He never asked her about her day. Either he suspected her of snooping around, or someone had seen her in a part of the castle she shouldn't have been. "Not much," she answered, taking a bite of food to stall. "I intended to go to the library. However, I ended up lost in the west end of the castle. After wandering around, I finally just went back to my room."

"Did you find anything interesting in the west end?"

She set her fork down and folded her hands together. "I stumbled into my cousin's office. I ended up standing there thinking about him." A version of the truth since his door had been the only one left open.

"He would have made a terrible king," Lyle responded. "He was too disorganized and had his father's propensities."

She tried not taking offense to that.

"Did you do anything else?"

She considered every section of the castle she'd been in today. "Yes." She took another bite of food to stall. "I went to the guest wing. To the room we stayed in when we came for Oriana's birthday party." Tears threatened just saying Oriana's name out loud.

"Why did you go there?" he demanded.

"To gather my possessions that were in there. I had a few dresses and trinkets." The room was close enough to the one she'd hidden the sword and letters in that Lyle shouldn't question her story.

"Oh." His brows furrowed and he took a drink from his goblet, as if trying to think of what to say next.

141

Harley rarely threw him off, and he hadn't expected that answer. Taking another bite, she forced the food down. She would need her strength to do what needed to be done tonight. Ackley had briefly shown her where to strike a man in the neck to kill him. There would be a lot of blood. Lyle would awaken and realize what she'd done. Her stomach rolled with nausea. She was going to kill a man. And there was no room for error. No hesitation. Or she would be the one to die.

But if she succeeded, she would single-handedly save her kingdom and countless lives.

Ackley had faith in her—otherwise he wouldn't have given her his sword.

A seed of doubt crept in. Ackley had said the best assassin was the one sleeping next to the target. Even though he'd sent her there to kill Lyle, surely he didn't intend for her to be a whore. Or had he? To get close to Lyle, she had to sleep with him. Ackley knew that; yet, it didn't seem like he hesitated to send her on this assignment. Maybe he didn't care for her the way she cared for him. Because if she knew he had to share another woman's bed, it would drive her mad.

Since the last person she'd been with was Ackley, she didn't know how she could be with Lyle again. If this had happened back in Penlar, before she'd met Ackley, it wouldn't have been a big deal since she shared a bed with Lyle nightly and didn't know any different. However, here in this castle, they had separate rooms. Plus, she'd made up that lie about sleeping with Ledger in order to buy herself time so she wouldn't have to sleep with Lyle right away.

"Is something wrong?" Lyle asked, his deep voice cutting through the room.

She almost dropped her fork. "No," she lied, forcing a smile on her face.

His eyes narrowed, sensing the lie.

"I'm sorry," she said, wanting to punch him. "I was thinking about my brother." Although she couldn't physically hurt Lyle right now, she could use her words to inflict pain—just like he did to her.

It was his turn to glance away. Even though Lyle hadn't been the one to physically kill Hollis, he might as well have because his actions led to her brother's death.

"We have a kingdom to run," he said, staring at the wall. "Most of the towns are decimated. I've only found a handful untouched." He turned the full force of his gaze on her. "We are working on getting food to those places. We must do more. We need to make sure our people have what they need to survive. I can't be bogged down with the past. We must look forward."

He'd chosen to say *our people* for a reason. He wanted her to buy into this idea of helping those less fortunate. That was why he took her to that town. He needed her compliant, sympathetic, and believing that they would be better rulers than the previous ones.

Her family.

He'd killed her family.

He'd allowed thousands to be slaughtered like farm animals to achieve his quest for power.

"Listen, Harley," Lyle said, setting his fork down. "You must understand that—"

"That what?" That this had all been his father's idea? Even if it had been Commander Beck's plan, Lyle had still gone along with it. He was equally responsible.

"Nothing." He shook his head, then took another drink from his goblet. "I find my appetite seeking something besides food. Let's retire for the night."

Her heart pounded, and she froze. This was it. It was time to execute her plan. But doing so meant she had to sleep with Lyle. A man she loathed. She'd gone over it in her head a hundred times, trying to find a way to tolerate his touch. All she'd managed to come up with was that at the end of it all, when he fell asleep, she'd withdraw her sword and plunge it into his neck.

Tonight, Lyle would die.

After dressing in her nightgown, Harley looked in the mirror. Tonight would be the last time she had to endure Lyle's touch. Once she killed him, her kingdom would be saved, and she would be truly free.

She'd hidden the sword on the right side of the bed, between the two mattresses. Once Lyle fell asleep, she'd reach down, pull the sword free, and kill him. She'd practiced pressing a knife into a raw potato. She had to push hard and fast, and there could be no second-guessing with her kingdom and freedom at stake.

Turning away from the mirror, she went over to the door leading to the adjacent room. She hesitated a moment and then reached forward, clasping the door handle. From this point forward, she had to be strong. Pushing the door open, she entered the room lit only by a handful of candles—just enough to find her way around the room. The less she saw of Lyle, the better.

Going over to the bed, she pulled back the covers and closed her eyes, remembering the night she'd spent with Ackley. He'd been so gentle and loving with her. Everything she'd imagined it could be with the right person.

And now she had to spend the night with the wrong person. A tear slid down her cheek. She wiped it away. This was her choice, and she couldn't be sad about it. This man was her husband, and she'd been with him countless times. Plus, she needed to be careful since Lyle knew her. If she acted strangely, he'd suspect something was wrong. The second he walked in, he'd expect to be the one in charge. And she had to let him have his way.

The door opened.

Harley turned and faced Lyle.

"Something's come up," he said, not stepping into the room. "My attention is needed elsewhere. Go to bed in here. If it's not too late when I return, I'll spend the rest of the night with you." He started to leave, then paused. "If I'm not back by morning, I want you to go to that village I took you to. Wait there for me."

She nodded, wondering what needed his attention so late at night and where he could be going. If he intended to return by morning, then it couldn't be too far away.

After the door closed, she let out a sigh of relief. She'd thought she was ready to go through with the assassination until she saw Lyle standing in the doorway. Now, she realized she needed to fine-tune her plan for it to succeed.

She climbed into bed and reached between the mattresses, her fingers fumbling over cold steel. Withdrawing the weapon, she pretended to strike Lyle with it. She went through the motion countless times until it not only felt natural, but she could do it with ease in a matter of seconds. Once her confidence had been restored, she stretched out on her stomach, trying to fall asleep. If Lyle didn't return tonight, she'd try killing him tomorrow.

A light feather of a touch brushed Harley's shoulder. Her eyes fluttered open. The candles had burned lower casting a soft glow over the room. It had to be almost morning. Harley rolled onto her back, rubbing her eyes.

Lyle knelt on the bed beside her. He leaned down, his mouth devouring hers. His lips felt hard, demanding, and wrong. She wanted Ackley. But to have Ackley, she needed to get rid of this man above her.

He lowered his body onto hers. His hands reached down, shoving her nightgown up and pulling it off over her head. He leaned back and focused on her.

She forced herself to stare into his cold eyes. As he usually did when they had marital relations, he broke eye contact. He shoved himself inside of her, taking his pleasures. As always, he was fast, rough, and efficient. She'd long ago learned to relax and let him have his way. If she engaged at all, it only prolonged the event. It was best to get it over with as quickly as possible.

When he finished, he rolled off her, lying beside her.

Tears welled in her eyes. Even though this man was her husband, she felt as if she'd cheated on Ackley. Which was insane since they didn't even have an understanding. The night they shared could have been a one-time thing. She had no idea if there was a future with Ackley.

The tears slid from her eyes, falling down the sides of her face, pooling in her ears. She couldn't move and wipe them away because then Lyle would know. And she couldn't let him see that he'd gotten to her.

She remained there, waiting.

Eventually, Lyle's breathing evened out, becoming heavy and smooth.

It was time for her to make her move. Her tears had dried. Her heart had hardened. Peering over, she verified Lyle's eyes were closed, his chest slowly rising and falling as he slept.

As slowly as possible, she reached down, pulling the sword free from the mattresses. Her hand trembled as she held the weapon, the weight of it suddenly heavy. Once she brought the sword up, she couldn't hesitate. She had to do it quickly. She was an assassin sent to kill a ruthless man who'd murdered her family. Fury built inside of her. This man had slaughtered her brother, destroyed her kingdom. He had to die—and she was the only one who could end him.

She'd practiced this hundreds of times. Taking a deep breath, she counted to three and moved. She pulled the sword up and twisted her body, straddling Lyle. Raising the sword, she gripped the hilt with both hands and placed the tip at his neck. All she had to do was push it into him.

His eyes flew open, and a smile slid across his face. "It took you long enough."

CHAPTER TWELVE

*A*ckley woke up early. After packing his supplies, he stood and stretched, surveying the land. He needed to head north, Gytha northeast, and his four soldiers west. A light fog clung to the land like a blanket. Navigating through it would be difficult. However, it would allow him to easily avoid his enemies.

Gytha came and stood next to him. While she wore nondescript clothing, her hair hung in its signature braid down her back.

"My spies always travel incognito," Ackley said, handing her a cap he'd stolen from the last town they'd rode through.

Without asking any questions, she wound her braid around her head, then put the cap on. With her muscular build, someone would have to look twice before realizing she was a woman. He chose not to mention that. There was no use in having her hit him before they parted ways.

"I think what you're doing is stupid, risky, and unnecessary," she said.

He nodded. He knew it, too.

She sighed. "Unfortunately, I understand why you're going." She rolled her eyes. "You can count on me to do my part."

"Thank you." He wanted to say more but couldn't find the words.

"Be careful," she said. She opened her mouth to say something else but thought better of it. Instead, she patted his shoulder. "Safe travels."

"You, too." Not wanting to waste any more time, Ackley bid his soldiers goodbye. He mounted and nudged his horse, urging it on faster. If he rode hard, he should reach the royal castle in a few days. With any luck, he'd be reunited with Harley by the end of the week.

As he rode, he went over his plans again and again. There were so many variables that could go wrong, and he'd have to improvise. He feared Harley had tried killing Lyle, only he'd killed her instead. If that happened, Owen would never forgive Ackley for sending her there in the first place. It didn't matter because Ackley would never forgive himself either. Regardless, Ackley still believed she would make a capable spy and assassin. She was the type of person the Knights scouted to be a part of the organization. He needed to have faith she could handle herself.

Only, she wasn't a full-fledged Knight.

But she could be one of the greatest with more training, of that he had no doubt.

The issue was he had no idea what she planned to do with her life. She had a place at court where she could serve as a princess and a personal confidant to Idina. However, that didn't seem enough for someone like her. Spending her time at court would be a waste of her talent. She could be a spy and work for Owen. Somehow, that didn't feel right either. Ackley wanted her to work with him. But he was from Marsden and she from Melenia.

And then there was the matter of his romantic interest in her. Though Ackley loved her, he still didn't want to marry. Somehow the thought of marriage made him think of being in chains, and he needed his freedom. Knights took an oath not to marry. If he devoted himself to Harley through marriage, he'd have to face giving up a part of himself by quitting the Knights.

He also had no idea if Harley wanted to remarry after being with someone like Lyle. The two of them needed to talk. While they'd both expressed an interest in continuing their relationship, neither had mentioned what it may look like.

Just before nightfall, he passed the spears with heads, entering Melenia. The land appeared colder and darker than before. Thick clouds rolled in, and thunder boomed in the distance. Once he found a suitable place to sleep for the night, he stopped.

Images of Harley being harmed filled his dreams. One had her being hanged, another Lyle hitting her. Ackley woke up, drenched in sweat. An urgency to get to her and save her inundated him. He didn't know where the panic came from, but he felt it in his bones. She needed him.

Ackley mounted and set out, his horse flying over the land, kicking up grass and mud as it ran. He only stopped at night when it became too dark to travel. Then he woke and rode all day. Time blurred and held little meaning. All he knew was that Harley was in danger, and he wouldn't let her down.

The royal castle came into view. It was just as his spies had described. Soldiers camped on the west end of the castle, and the roof was heavily guarded with patrols. Since he couldn't risk someone finding his horse, he led the animal about a mile away, and then released it. If he needed to make a quick escape, he'd steal a horse from the stables. With the soldiers looking down from the top of the castle, Ackley decided to wait until nighttime to make his move.

Once darkness settled over the land, he headed to the cornfield, approaching the castle from that end. He moved between the cornstalks, being careful not to rustle the leaves and alert the guardsmen to his presence. Nearing the edge, he crawled on his stomach, ever so slowly, until the camp came into view. Several fires had been lit throughout, casting the camp in an orange glow.

He needed to find his man, Galvin.

Soldiers moved through the camp, some retiring for the night, others sitting around a fire talking. After observing the area for over an hour, he scooted backward until he was certain he couldn't be seen. Then he stood and headed to the north end of the corn field. He dropped and crawled to the edge. Needing to get a hold of Galvin, Ackley found a stick and drew a mark in the mud at the base of a cornstalk. When Galvin saw the mark, he'd know it was a message from Ackley. Satisfied, he slowly inched backward.

He moved deeper into the middle of the cornfield, twenty rows from the north and twenty rows from the east. After setting up a handful of traps so he'd be alerted to someone approaching, he laid down and fell asleep.

A twig snapped, waking Ackley. He bolted upright, a dagger in hand. A rabbit hopped by. Taking a deep breath, he observed his surroundings, not seeing anything of concern. The dark clouds hid the rising sun. He guessed it was early morning, but he couldn't be certain.

He sat, waiting for Galvin. Around noon, he could feel someone approaching. Standing, he prepared to attack if necessary.

A whistle rang out.

Ackley breathed a sigh of relief and answered the whistle with his own.

Galvin approached a moment later. He stood alongside a cornstalk, trying to blend it.

Ackley did the same. "You got my message," he said by way of greeting.

"I did," Galvin responded. "I didn't expect to see you here."

"Morton found me," he spoke softly. "He told me Harley is missing."

Galvin snorted. "She's not missing."

Ackley went very still. "What do you mean?"

"She's in the castle. Where she has been this entire time. I've been wondering what happened to Morton."

Confusion washed through Ackley. "I'm not following what you're saying."

"Then let's back up a step," Galvin said. "Why does Morton think she's missing?"

"He told me no one has seen her in weeks." He ran his hands through his hair, trying to remember the exact words Morton had used.

"Rikter runs the inside intel, Morton delivers messages between the outside and inside, and I am responsible for the outside intelligence."

"What are you saying?" Ackley asked.

"If there was a problem, Rikter would have left a message for Morton who would have given it to me to deliver."

And that hadn't happened. Morton had delivered the message, not Galvin. Ackley should have realized this sooner. "The only way Morton would have brought me the message is if someone told him to." It felt as if thousands of ants crawled over his skin.

"Exactly. Which means we've been compromised." Galvin's words hung heavy in the air between them.

The leaves of the cornstalks blew, sounding like a light rain. Ackley had been so focused on saving Harley, that he hadn't stopped to analyze the situation properly. "I've known Rikter for years," he said, thinking out loud. "There's no way he would have made a deal with Lyle."

"And neither would Morton."

Ackley narrowed his eyes. "What are you saying?"

"Harley is working with the enemy." He tossed a soldier's uniform to him. "Find out for yourself."

Ackley caught the clothes. "I was told Ruthar has been captured?"

He nodded. "He was brought here and killed. The soldiers cheered, thinking it was you who'd been hanged."

Sitting in the middle of the cornfield, Ackley spent hours trying to work through it. No matter which angle he looked at the situation, he couldn't fathom Harley being on Lyle's side. Not after Ackley had been to Lyle's house and spent so much time with Harley. He knew her. And she'd sworn allegiance to Ackley and Owen, not Lyle.

Still, he couldn't figure out how Morton had gotten bad information and relayed it to Ackley. He knew Morton's family, had known Morton for years, and felt confident he couldn't be bought. Morton was a Knight through and through. Same as Rikter. However, somehow inaccurate information had gotten out of the castle, all the way to Ackley.

The next logical conclusion was that this could be a trap. The only problem with that theory, Ruthar, his decoy, had been captured and killed. Ackley had to assume that Lyle thought Ackley dead. That being the case, there was no reason to try and lure Ackley to the castle. Regardless, he'd have to be extra careful.

Galvin had said Harley was alive and well. She'd been seen walking amongst the soldiers, handing out bread. Several of the servants had also recently spotted her in the castle. No one claimed she was in any sort of distress. Ackley had to see her for himself. He needed to make sure she was okay. A seed of doubt crept in. There was a chance, granted a tiny one, that she'd been working with Lyle this entire time. As wrong as that felt, as much as Ackley didn't want to believe it to be true, he had to at least acknowledge the possibility.

It was time for him to get to work. Thick clouds covered the sky making the air crisp and cool. He needed to gain access to the castle, which meant he had to know who came and went, and what guards were on duty when. Hiding in the nearby cornfield would do him no good. He decided to put on the soldier's uniform and go into camp. Being among the Melenia soldiers would be the quickest way to learn the most information.

After changing, he headed toward camp. Enough soldiers came and went on patrols that he shouldn't have any trouble walking around the tents as long as he pretended to know what he was doing.

Galvin had told him which tent he used in case Ackley needed to hide. While he didn't anticipate that happening, he headed toward that general direction. The thick smell of mud mixed with burning wood from the fires wafted in the air. Ackley neared a group of men sitting around a fire eating their supper. He pretended to be fixing the stake of the tent while listening in on their conversation for pertinent information.

"I heard they brought in the same man who crowned King Coden," one of the soldiers said.

"When do you think they'll crown her?" another asked.

"Who knows."

Ackley had been so caught up in the men's conversation that he failed to hear the soldier approaching behind him. He should have known better. The tip of a sword nipped into his back.

"Stand," the man holding a sword demanded.

Ackley silently cursed.

CHAPTER THIRTEEN

HARLEY

*H*arley's heart pounded, and her entire body shook as she stared into the cold eyes of her husband.

Lyle snatched both her wrists. "It took you long enough," he sneered. "What? You can't possibly be surprised." He pinched her right wrist, forcing her to drop the sword.

She should have moved faster. By not shoving the sword into his neck, she'd failed at everything she'd been sent there to do. A cry escaped her lips.

He shoved her away and slid out of bed. Grabbing his pants, he pulled them on. "Get dressed. I can't have you taken to the dungeon if you're naked."

Her head pounded, and a ringing sounded in her ears. She'd failed. And now she was going to be thrown in the dungeon. People would die because of her incompetence.

Lyle chucked her nightgown at her. "I said get dressed."

She took it, putting it on, while trying to think of a way out of this mess. Eyeing the sword, she wondered if she could grab it, piercing Lyle's back as he headed to the door. After putting the nightgown on, she stood.

"Don't even try it," he said. "If you so much as touch that weapon again, I'll drag you to the tower and hang you myself."

At this point, she wasn't sure she cared to live. Ackley and Owen would be so disappointed in her.

"Okay," Lyle called out.

Both doors flew open, and a half dozen soldiers poured into the room. Two clutched onto Harley's arms, dragging her away. Everything moved so quickly she couldn't fully process what was happening.

They took her through her bedchamber. She squinted at the bright morning light. Instead of locking her in her room as she'd hoped, they took her out of the suite and down the stairs to the first level of the castle. Stopping before an oversized door with three locks, the sentry standing there withdrew a key and unlocked the door, granting them entrance. The two men holding Harley dragged her down into the dungeon. The other soldiers followed close behind. As if she were a threat. She couldn't even kill Lyle.

Disappointment, cold fear, and numbness warred within. She'd failed.

One soldier opened a cell door, and the two men tossed her inside. She stumbled and crashed to the stone floor, hitting her chin. The door slammed shut, and the sound of a lock sliding into place echoed in the dreary corridor.

"How?" she managed to squeak out.

One of the soldiers glanced back at her. "Did you say something?"

She was going to ask how Lyle knew she was going to kill him. However, that would only implicate her to treason. She had to be smart about this. "What am I being held in the dungeon for?"

"Treason," the soldier stated.

"Explain," she demanded, getting to her knees.

"You tried to kill the king."

"I didn't kill him." A fact, and he had no proof. It was Lyle's word against hers. "And Lyle is not the true king so long as Owen lives."

Something flashed in the man's eyes. Harley couldn't tell if it was hesitancy or not. Regardless, she forged on. "And he can't be the king. He has no claim to the throne."

"You're the late king's daughter."

She got to her feet, moving to the metal bars. Sliding her fingers around the bars, she said, "I haven't been crowned yet." And if she wasn't queen, Lyle couldn't be king. "Maybe you should remind my husband of that fact."

"Edgar!" one of the other soldiers said. "Let's go!"

The soldier turned and hurried away. Harley hoped she'd gotten through to him.

An eerie silence filled the dungeon.

The last time she'd been in there, she'd run into Lord Silas. Curious if he was still here, she called out, "Father!" The word echoed.

"Harley?" his voice answered. "What are you doing here, child?" He was a handful of cells down from her on the other side. Too far away to see him in the dim lighting.

"I've been arrested for treason," she replied.

"Treason?"

She started pacing in her cell, trying to think of what to do. The key that unlocked every door in the castle was hidden in the queen's bedchamber under the floorboard. Not having a way to reach it, she'd need to come up with another plan.

Hopefully, the fact that she hadn't been crowned would work in her favor. Maybe Lyle wouldn't kill her until that happened. At the very least, it would buy her time to think of something. Not that she wanted to run away and hide. She wanted to fix the mistakes she'd made.

"Harley?" a man groaned. "Harley, is that you?" It sounded like he was in the next cell over to her left.

"Yes," she replied. "Who are you?" The last time she'd been down there, she hadn't come across any other prisoners.

"It's me, Rikter."

The floor felt as if it spun beneath her. "Rikter? What are you doing here?" Panic swelled within. Not only did Lyle know she was going to try and kill him, but Rikter was here as well.

"Haven't you wondered where I've been these past few days?" he asked.

"What do you mean?" She didn't understand his question. "We've been leaving each other correspondence for the past week in the guest suite."

He didn't respond.

"Rikter?"

"What do you mean by correspondence?" he asked, his voice hard.

"Letters."

"I haven't written, nor have I left any letters in a guest suite for you. Why do you say I have?"

She thought back over everything. She'd found a letter in Oriana's bedchamber telling her to leave correspondence for him in the guest suite. What if it hadn't been from Rikter at all?

"Harley?"

"If it wasn't you, then who was it?" He didn't need to answer her question because she knew. Lyle. He must have figured it out somehow. "How long have you been down here?"

"I've lost track of time, but I estimate about a week."

If Lyle had been reading her letters and leaving replies, then that meant he wanted her to find his ledgers. He wanted her to discover the soldiers were in Losger. She had no idea why, especially if her information wasn't even getting to Owen.

"Who do you pass the information on to?" she asked.

"One of Ackley's men."

"Do you speak to him directly?"

"No," he replied tartly. "I leave him a coded message."

She thought through it. If the messages were in code, then Lyle shouldn't be able to figure them out. And if Ackley's man received one not in code, then he should be able to deduce Rikter had been compromised.

"Who else is in here?" Rikter asked. "The entire time I've been down here, I hadn't realized someone else was here."

"My father." Well, he wasn't really her father. "I mean, my stepfather." Regardless, he was the man who raised her. And he was here to announce to the kingdom that she wasn't his child.

Harley settled in, leaning against the wall. This entire time, she'd thought she had the upper hand and Lyle had no clue Ackley had sent her there as a spy and potential assassin. Instead, Lyle had figured it all out and managed to outsmart her. She'd played right into his hands, and now here she sat in the dungeon.

Pulling her legs to her chest, she rested her head on her knees. She had to figure a way out of this mess.

"I can't do it down here," a male voice said, rousing Harley from her sleep.

She rubbed her eyes and sat up, yawning. In the dim torchlight, she had no idea whether it was day or night.

"Why the hell not?" Lyle asked.

"In order for this to be legitimate, there have to be witnesses. Usually, the entire noble class is in attendance so they can swear fealty. Without these basic traditions, the line will be questioned."

"Fine. Then get out of here. I'll let you know when you're needed."

Harley held in a smirk. Her comment to the soldier about Lyle not really being the king must have gotten to him.

Lyle came and stood on the other side of the cell bars, folding his arms, and watching her.

"Is there a problem?" she said, not bothering to stand.

"Everything is proceeding as planned," he replied.

"Then why are you here?" She pushed her hair behind her ears, carefully watching him.

His right eye twitched. "I'm having you moved to different accommodations."

"Why?" He had to enjoy seeing her locked in the dungeon.

"You need to be crowned so I can legally carry the line. Once that happens, then I can have you officially arrested for treason."

She refused to go along with his plan. He was an idiot for telling her what he intended to do. Especially when her father and Rikter could hear every word he said.

"Let's go." He unlocked the door and held it open for her.

"No." She preferred the dungeon to being locked in a closet.

"Why do you have to work against me?" Lyle stepped into the cell.

The area suddenly became smaller, and the air harder to breathe. With him in there, she had nowhere to go.

He squatted, now eye level with her. "We both want the same things."

"I don't think we do." He had no idea what she wanted. He'd never bothered to learn anything about her.

"We both want what's best for Melenia. We both care about our people."

If he cared about the kingdom, he wouldn't have invited a neighboring army in to destroy it. He wouldn't have allowed Russek to kill so many of the people he claimed to care about.

"Why are you crying?" He cocked his head, studying her as if she were a puzzle he needed to figure out.

She wiped the tears from her face, shrugging. Honestly, she didn't know why the tears were falling. Maybe it was the fact that so many had died, including her family. Or that her husband didn't even know her. It could even be because the man she'd called Father her entire life wasn't even her father.

"Let's get you out of here and ready to be crowned."

She shook her head, refusing to comply. "It won't make a difference. Owen still lives."

A devious smile slid across his face. "Not for long."

Cold fear shot through her. "What have you done?" she whispered, half afraid to know.

"I haven't done anything. You, my dear, took care of that for me when you sent him a letter." He tsked.

She wanted to reach forward and strangle him. "You're a monster." She'd told Owen the soldiers' loved ones were in Losger. Lyle must have set some sort of trap to kill Owen.

He chuckled. "Maybe you need to look in the mirror." He stood. "Let's go."

She didn't want to comply. She'd spent too much of her life bowing to others.

Exiting the cell, Lyle waved at someone down the corridor. There was a shuffling sound and then Lord Silas appeared, a bruise on his cheek. "Follow instructions, or Lord Silas will suffer for your insolence."

Harley considered trying to reason with Lyle. However, at the end of the day, nothing she said or did would matter. What she needed to do was find a way out of the castle, and she'd have a much better chance if she wasn't locked in the dungeon. She slowly rose to her feet, pretending to be scared and defeated. Maybe if he thought he'd worn her into submission, he'd let his guard down.

She exited the cell. Before she could hug her father, Lyle sent him back to his own cell. She followed Lyle to the staircase. He led her out of the dungeon and to the second level.

He pushed open a door and gestured for her to enter. "Someone will be by shortly to help you prepare for the ceremony. It won't be long now until it's all over."

Harley stepped into the dark room, waiting for her eyes to adjust.

Lyle shut and locked the door.

Alone in the dark room, Harley slid to the floor, wanting to cry. She didn't think this was a closet, it felt bigger than one; however, there weren't any windows or furniture.

"If you hear any noise at all," Lyle said from out in the hallway, "I want you to investigate. I made sure word was sent a couple weeks ago that Harley is in trouble. I expect someone to try and rescue her any day now. This person is vital to me. I want him captured alive. Understood?"

"Yes, Your Majesty," two men replied.

A ringing sounded in Harley's head. Not only had Lyle set a trap for Owen in Losger, but she suspected he'd set one right here in the castle for Ackley. And she was the bait. He must have discovered the man he'd killed wasn't the real prince. Hopefully Ackley wouldn't fall for Lyle's tricks. But if he did, she didn't know what scared her more—Ackley coming for her and facing Lyle, or Ackley choosing not to rescue her at all.

Anger coursed through her. She didn't need to be saved. She could take care of herself. Granted, her current predicament didn't look so great. But she'd figure something out.

Suddenly, she saw a series of events laid out before her as if they were moves on a game board. She knew the last move she had to make to win. From there, she worked backward until it became clear. Once she had it figured out, she went over the plan, looking for holes. The biggest problem—it most likely would lead to her demise; however, it had the potential to save her kingdom.

A sly smile formed on her lips. She knew how to win.

CHAPTER FOURTEEN

ACKLEY

ckley slowly stood. "I'm just fixing it." He took a step away from the tent, letting the soldier see the bent stake.

The man lowered his sword, observing the corner of the tent. "What happened?" he demanded.

"I was in a hurry and kicked it with the tip of my boot. I'd hoped to fix it before anyone noticed." He made sure to maintain eye contact so the soldier would believe he told the truth.

He nodded. "I've done that once or twice myself. This is my tent. I'll fix it."

Ackley gave a curt nod and hurried away, reeling over what he'd heard the men say. Harley was about to be crowned as the queen of Melenia. Once that happened, she'd be guilty of treason right along with Lyle. Perhaps she didn't have a choice in the matter, and Lyle was forcing her to go through with the ceremony. Because there was no way she'd willingly be crowned. That was one mess not even Owen would be able to undo. A small part of him couldn't help but wonder if Galvin was right and Harley had fooled them all. Shaking his head, he banished that thought, unable to believe it.

He headed toward the center of the camp, wanting to have a good view of the castle so he could learn the guards' shifts and where people entered and exited.

"Looks like you could use something to eat," a soldier said, capturing Ackley's attention. He held out half a loaf of bread. "You can have this."

Ackley thanked the man and took the food.

"Come closer to the fire and warm up. We've all been stuck on perimeter duty." The man waved Ackley closer to the fire. Five men sat around it, no one talking.

Ackley took a seat between two soldiers, slowly eating the bread so he could smell and taste it for poisons. The sky turned from dark gray to black as night set in.

The man who'd given him the food sat next to him, a little closer than necessary. Ackley was about to scoot away when the man leaned in and whispered, "It looks like you just discovered the lie. Are you doing all right?" He pulled out a flask, handing it to Ackley.

Ackley shook his head. He never drank. "How could you tell?" he asked, trying to be vague.

"You have that look we all had when we learned the truth. Honestly, in hindsight, I should have known. Russek killed everyone. To believe that Lyle had our family members to ensure our cooperation...I don't know why I thought my wife and kids had been spared."

Ackley nodded, agreeing with the man. He'd gotten the information second-hand and hadn't questioned it either. To think Owen had immediately ordered his soldiers to abandon him and to swear fealty to Lyle to get their family members back. Truly, it was a genius move and exemplified the fact that Ackley had been underestimating Lyle this entire time.

"If you change your mind, let me know." The man took a swig from the flask, corked it, and tucked it in his tunic. He stood and patted Ackley on the shoulder before lumbering away.

Ackley sat there, pretending to stare at the fire, while watching the castle and tracking various shift changes. Once he knew where servants entered and exited and how often soldiers went on and off duty, he excused himself and headed over to Galvin's tent. He climbed inside and stretched out on the bedroll, falling fast asleep for the night.

When he woke up, the sun had not yet risen. He exited the tent and froze. Most soldiers were up. Instead of meandering about as they'd been doing while off duty, they walked fast and with purpose. He watched them, trying to see what they were up to. After a few minutes, it became clear. To the north, weapons were being gathered. To the south, food was being collected. Ackley knew enough about armies to understand that these men were preparing to go somewhere. If they were going to attack Owen, Ackley needed to stop them. On the flip side, with the army gone, it would be the perfect time for Owen to take back the castle.

Ackley spent the day confirming what he'd learned the previous evening. Satisfied he knew when the shifts changed, he waited for darkness to blanket the land before making his way around to the east side of the castle, being sure to remain in the shadows so the sentries on duty wouldn't see him. The guards only looked to the east every three minutes which was more than enough time for Ackley to move from one hiding place to the next. When he finally reached the castle, he snuck up to one of the windows and peered inside. Not seeing anyone in the dark room, he withdrew his dagger, shoving it between the lock and glass. The lock released, and he gently pushed the window open.

He climbed inside, closed the window, and surveyed the room. An empty table with several chairs situated around it took up most of the space. This had to be a room for meetings. Not seeing papers or anything worth investigating, he made his way over to the door, listening. No sounds could be heard, so he opened it a crack, peering into the empty hallway.

He needed to head toward the center of the castle, which should be to the left. After exiting the room, he slowly moved in that direction, peering into the rooms as he passed. When he came across an office that looked promising, he entered, snooping around for anything useful. So far, he hadn't found much.

At an intersection, he saw a light coming from one of the rooms to the left, so he headed that way. Getting closer, he heard mumbled voices, one of them female. If it was Harley, he'd have to find a way to sneak her out of the castle. Unless he discovered she was working with Lyle. Ackley slid against the wall next to the doorway, listening. Shock rolled through him—one of the voices seemed familiar, but it wasn't Harley's. It dawned on him that it belonged to Lady Mayle—Harley's mother. He had absolutely no idea why she'd be at the castle. Unless Harley wanted her here. Shaking his head, he strained to listen to the conversation.

"I told you I had it under control," a male voice whispered. "You didn't need to get involved."

"Not get involved?" Lady Mayle responded, harsh and unbelieving. "It's a little late for that, don't you think? Have you ever stopped to consider that if you had shared this information with me sooner, we could have averted this mess?"

"It was unavoidable."

There was the soft swish of fabric rustling. "Regardless, here we are. What are we going to do?" she asked.

"I'm not sure there's anything we can do." The man sighed. "Despite what you want, you do not, nor have you ever had, the upper hand."

"Everything I've done has been for my daughter," Lady Mayle snapped. "Don't ever doubt that."

Another shuffling noise sounded, closer to the door this time. "I'm not doubting that," the man said. "I am simply pointing out that you are playing the losing hand in a game you think you have a chance of winning. It's time you realize that."

Afraid the man would find him standing there, Ackley hurried to the adjacent room and slid inside, hiding behind the door. Out in the hallway, footsteps passed by. Ackley considered confronting Lady Mayle about why she was at the royal castle and what she knew about Lyle's plans. However, he decided to keep his presence a secret for now.

Instead, Ackley exited the room and followed the man, curious to learn who he was and where he was going. The man had dark gray hair and walked slightly hunched forward. He made his way along hallway after hallway, moving at a snail's pace. Based upon the way he walked, Ackley guessed he was in his late sixties. Since he remained a safe distance away, Ackley couldn't see the man's face and didn't know if there were any distinguishing characteristics about it. He wore dark pants and a tunic, finer than a commoner but not so fine as to be a member of the royal family.

The man stopped before an oversized door, pulled out a key and unlocked it.

When he opened the door, someone said, "Back already?"

"I told you I wouldn't be long."

"Most people aren't as eager as you are to be in the dungeon."

The door started to close. "I'm not most people." A *thunk* resounded as the door slammed shut, and the lock slid into place.

Ackley moved away from the dungeon door, glad he knew where it was located, but not thrilled he couldn't identify the man—especially since he seemed to know Harley and her mother.

Moving the curtain aside, Ackley found a door without a handle. He'd seen doors like this before and knew he had to find a release button. In the dim lighting, it was hard to see any wear marks. However, after a moment, he noticed a stone that seemed a little off. He pushed it, and the door opened.

Ackley stepped into a hidden passageway that appeared to be between the walls of the castle. When the door closed, darkness engulfed him. He'd caught a glimpse of a torch hanging on the wall, so he reached that way, his fingers fumbling over the stones until they found it. Grabbing the torch, he felt around until he located the lighter. Once it was lit, he glanced in both directions. There was a narrow set of stairs to the right, so he headed that way, counting his steps as he went.

On the second level of the castle, Ackley passed a handful of doors. Wanting to exit near the west end of the castle, he snuffed out the torch and used the last door. He found himself standing in a long hallway with over a dozen doors on both sides.

Peeking into the rooms, he discovered most were empty guest suites. He chose one that would likely have a good view of the soldiers outside and entered, sliding under the bed where no one would be able to see him. Lying there, he closed his eyes, trying to fall asleep.

When morning came, he crawled out from under the bed and peered out the window, observing the soldiers below. As he'd noticed the day before, weapons had been gathered in one area, food in another. He expected to see the tents being taken down and was surprised to find them all intact. Scanning the land, he took note of the terrain and planned various escape routes. When he finished, he exited the room.

The best place to hear gossip was usually in the kitchen. Not knowing the inner workings of the castle would make what he was about to do more difficult. However, he always appreciated a challenge. Ackley made his way back to the secret passageways. Not bothering with the torch, he counted his steps, easily retracing his way to the first level. After adjusting the uniform he wore, he stepped out of the passageways and walked with purpose, pretending he was supposed to be there.

Ackley located the kitchen and entered, finding over two dozen people rushing around. Some chopped vegetables, others kneaded bread, and a few tended to the ovens. After grabbing a loaf of bread and a handful of carrots, he headed for the door.

"It starts at noon," someone to his right said.

"Where's the ceremony taking place?" another asked.

"I think on the open tower," the elderly cook answered. "That way everyone can see."

"Are we serving food in the great hall afterward?"

"Yes."

Unable to stand there any longer for fear of being noticed, Ackley exited the kitchen and turned right. As he walked along the corridor, he tried to decide what ceremony was most likely taking place at noon. Probably Harley's coronation, which would explain why Harley's mother was at the royal castle. He took a bite of the bread he'd taken. Not only did he need to decide his next move, but he needed to see Harley for himself. He couldn't believe she'd willingly be crowned queen—not with Owen alive.

Outside the castle, Ackley headed toward the tents, wanting to blend in and overhear what the soldiers were saying.

Galvin suddenly appeared at his side. "A letter just arrived," he mumbled so low no one would overhear. "It's in my tent."

Ackley gave a curt nod and headed that way. Once he located the right tent, he went inside. He found a piece of paper beneath the bedroll. Unfolding it, he saw that it was from Owen. He quickly read the contents. When he finished, he cursed.

Owen had received a message from Harley stating that his soldiers and their loved ones were in Losger. However, the Kreng army refused to ride with Owen because they feared leaving Kreng unprotected. Three ships, each filled with soldiers, had docked off the coastline. Owen then proceeded to ask if Ackley would bring his men and join with him near Penlar. Then, together, they would march to Losger and rescue everyone.

There were two major problems. One, Ackley wasn't with his men; he was at the castle checking up on Harley. And two, the Melenia soldiers' family members weren't in Losger. Ackley knew it had to be a trap.

CHAPTER FIFTEEN

HARLEY

Sitting in the dark room, Harley thought of all the ways she'd love to murder Lyle. Fury consumed her that she'd allowed him to lock her in this empty room. At least the dungeon had some light. Guilt and self-loathing inundated her. If only she hadn't hesitated when he'd opened his eyes. If she'd plunged the sword into his neck, he'd be dead. Even if he fought with her, she probably would have done enough damage to kill him. Since she'd gotten herself into this mess, it was up to her to get herself out of it.

The door creaked open, and bright light shot into the room. Squinting, she watched a plump woman enter, followed by two soldiers.

"It's time to get you dressed," the woman said. "Let's go."

Harley scrambled to her feet, assuming she had to dress for the coronation. Instead of asking any questions, she quietly followed the woman out of the room, the guards close behind them.

They entered the adjacent room. A single bed and armoire indicated it was a simple guest suite, one used for less important guests. An ornate gown fit for a queen had been laid on the bed, looking out of place in the plain room.

The soldiers remained in the hallway, closing the door to give Harley and the servant privacy.

Alone with the woman, Harley assumed she was supposed to get ready, and this delightful person was there to help her. Not caring to make small talk, she removed her nightdress and stepped into the light blue silk gown. As she pulled the gown up and over her shoulders, she became light-headed and swooned. The woman grabbed Harley's arm, steadying her.

"I'm all right," Harley insisted. "It's just been a while since I've had anything to eat." She figured it had to be at least a full day since she'd had food.

The woman didn't respond. Once Harley had the gown on, the woman cinched it together, lacing the ties in the back. Then she proceeded to arrange Harley's hair atop her head. Satisfied with Harley's appearance, the woman opened the door.

The two guards escorted Harley to the staircase where Lyle stood waiting for her.

When she neared him, he held out his hand for her. She hesitated.

He dismissed the woman, but the guards remained. "Let me show you something." He waved for Harley to follow him down the hallway. Opening the fourth door on the right, he motioned for Harley to look inside.

Harley leaned in and saw Lady Mayle sitting on a chair next to the window. "Mother?" She stepped forward, about to rush into the room so she could hug her.

Lyle grabbed her arm, stopping her.

Lady Mayle stood, facing Harley, tears in her eyes, as she remained on the other side of the room.

"Lady Mayle is here as my guest," Lyle said, speaking into Harley's ear, his hot breath assaulting her. "She will remain a guest so long as you cooperate with me. Is that understood?"

Harley nodded.

"If you say or do anything I don't like, your mother will meet the same fate as Hollis."

She wanted to tear Lyle's eyes out. "I understand."

"Excellent." He released her and held out his hand for her to take.

She shivered, then slid her hand into his.

"Much better." Pulling Harley away from the room, he led her back to the staircase where they went up to the fourth level of the castle.

As they approached the open gorge tower, a deep foreboding set in. Once Harley took the oath and was officially crowned, she would be guilty of treason since she knew Owen was the true heir to the throne. If she refused, Lyle might kill her, but he would never have the throne legitimately. However, her goal was to crown Owen and destroy Lyle. The crazy plan she'd concocted last night might just be insane enough to work. Smiling, she followed Lyle onto the open tower, ready to face her fate.

The sun shone bright overhead, not a cloud in the sky. As Harley approached the half wall—the wall where her family had been murdered—she swayed on her feet. Images of her brother being beheaded, his body shoved over the side, and blood everywhere inundated her. Maybe if she hadn't been so weak from a lack of food and water, she wouldn't feel as if the floor swayed beneath her.

"Smile," Lyle purred in her ear. "Or your mother pays the price."

Standing next to Lyle under the bright, glaring sun, she forced a smile on her lips as she held her head high.

An elderly man dressed in a long tunic stood next to them. He started talking about duty and honor. Harley tuned him out as she gazed at the sight before her. Hundreds of soldiers were crowded together below, watching. She didn't know if these men liked or supported Lyle, or if they were only following him to protect someone they loved. That was the funny thing about love—it made people do things they may not ordinarily do.

The man set a heavy crown upon Harley's head. It weighed more than she thought possible.

"Repeat after me," he said. "I, Lady Harley of Penlar."

Harley said the words.

"Do hereby solemnly swear to protect the kingdom of Melenia and its citizens."

Again, Harley repeated what the man said, vowing to make good on the words. She swore to protect her land and her people, and she would stop at nothing to make sure she accomplished those goals.

The man slid a thick gold ring on her finger. It was the ring of a queen, and it had previously belonged to her aunt. The seal of Melenia had been etched on top of it.

"I hereby give you Queen Harley of Melenia!" the man announced.

The soldiers below cheered.

"I officially present King Lyle and Queen Harley!"

The cheering intensified. Lyle took her fingers, raising their joined hands in the air as they faced their subjects below.

Harley had never envisioned being a princess or a queen. The entire ceremony felt surreal to her. She tilted her head and the crown shifted, almost slipping. She had to right her head, being careful the crown didn't topple off. If it did, Lyle would accuse her of trying to sabotage him.

Lyle's arm wrapped around her waist. "The ceremony is done. Let's go inside."

That was the best thing she'd heard all day.

He led her back into the castle and downstairs to the first level. Instead of entering the dining hall as she'd anticipated, they passed it and went to the library. Tears filled Harley's eyes. Hunger gripped her. She needed food; otherwise, she feared she'd pass out.

"Don't worry," Lyle murmured in her ear. "I'll have something brought to you."

"I thought you had a meal planned to celebrate the coronation," she said as she slid onto the sofa, resting her face against her hands. Her body shook, and her head spun.

"I do." He moved over to the window and glanced outside. "But I can't have you looking ill at your first royal function. I thought we'd rest in here for a bit. Then, when you're feeling better, we'll head to the dining hall for a meal with my captains."

Once she got some food in her, she'd feel better. Rubbing her forehead, she knew his thoughtfulness had nothing to do with her well-being. He needed her to play a part and in her current state, she could barely do anything.

The sofa dipped as he sat next to her. He reached out, rubbing her back. She tried not to flinch at his touch. Lyle moved his free hand to her arm.

Feeling trapped, she went to scoot away but someone rushed in. She held still and looked up in time to see a servant set a plate of food and a cup of tea on the low table before scurrying from the room.

"Let's get some food into you." Lyle reached forward, grabbing an apple slice.

When he went to feed it to her, she leaned back. "What are you doing?"

"I'm trying to feed my lovely wife," he said, a smile plastered on his face.

Not once had he ever cared for her well-being or called her lovely. While she knew his words and actions weren't authentic, she had no idea why. There was no one around to see him. Her attention drifted to the door. Maybe he expected someone of importance to arrive at any minute, so he was on his best behavior, pretending to be someone he wasn't.

"Here," he said, regaining her attention.

She plucked the apple from his fingers, feeding it to herself. Then she quickly drank her tea and devoured the biscuit. Her head started to clear, and her strength began to return; she felt immensely better and could think clearly.

With one hand still on her back, Lyle lifted his free hand and cupped her cheek. Harley held still, not knowing what he intended to do. He could just as easily snap her neck as he could kiss her. He ran his thumb over her lips.

It took every ounce of Harley's strength to refrain from biting his thumb off. She glanced at the doorway again, not seeing anyone. She had no idea why he insisted putting on this sham of a show—especially with no one watching.

"Focus on me," he snapped, his voice low and demanding.

She did as he said, uncomfortable with how close he sat next to her. His breath assaulted her face, making her want to gag. He leaned in, his lips brushing hers. The gentleness of it surprised her. But she knew better and wouldn't be fooled by a false gesture. Lyle was anything but gentle. Harley tensed, waiting for him to say or do something to chip away at her.

Lyle carefully bit her bottom lip, holding her in place with just his teeth, while his cold eyes locked onto hers making her scared to move or even breathe. A cruel smile slid across his face, and he released her lip. "I'm going to kiss your neck. Then you will slowly remove my shirt. Pretend like you're enjoying yourself." Mischief gleamed in his eyes as he leaned forward and kissed just below her right ear.

Not once had he ever kissed her like this before. She knew he didn't do it for her benefit but rather for some other purpose, as if someone was watching. Although she didn't fully grasp the game Lyle played, she refused to be a pawn he could control.

"Your turn," he whispered, his hands moving to her waist, half pinching her.

"This isn't our bedchamber," she chided him. "We're in the library, and anyone can walk right in." She would not remove his clothing and do as he said, especially when she didn't know why he wanted her to behave so scandalously.

"We're alone," he ground out, his voice laced with irritation.

"We may be alone, but I am now the queen of Melenia." She spoke with conviction. "I will not behave so untoward in a public setting. If you wish to have relations with me, it will be in our bedchamber as custom dictates."

He pinched her side, hard. "If that's the way you want to behave, so be it. For not cooperating, your mother will lose a finger."

Tears filled her eyes, but she had to hold them in so Lyle wouldn't know he'd gotten to her. Someone cleared his throat from the doorway. Harley glanced over to see a soldier hovering there.

"Your Majesties." The soldier bowed, then looked at Lyle. "He didn't come down this corridor as you'd hoped."

Lyle released her and abruptly stood. "Then this was a total waste of time. Escort my wife back to her room." He strode from the library without a backward glance.

It felt as if a gust of wind had blown through the library, erasing all the tension that had been there.

"Let's go, Your Majesty," the soldier said to her.

Even though she outranked him, she decided to listen to him. Not only did she want to create sympathy so others might come to her aid, but she didn't want Lyle to harm her mother on her account. She had a plan and needed to stick to it. Standing, she plucked the apple off the tray, devouring it as she followed the soldier back to the empty room she was being temporarily kept in.

"Harley," a deep voice crooned. "Wake up."

Lying on the hard floor, Harley rolled onto her side and opened her eyes, unable to see anyone in the pitch-black room.

"There are a few things I must know."

She immediately tensed, recognizing Lyle's voice. In the darkness, she couldn't see him, but she could feel him mere inches in front of her. If he had a knife pointed her way, she wouldn't know until she felt the tip pressed into her. She blinked, wishing she could see him. Her heart pounded, and a dull ringing sounded in her ears as fear flooded into every inch of her body.

"Love has never been a part of our marriage," he said, his voice a soft whisper laced with the lethalness of a slithering snake.

Harley shivered. "No, it hasn't." She wondered where he was going with this and what he intended to do with her. In all her careful planning, she hadn't accounted for him sneaking in and striking her dead. She figured she had at least a week until he killed her.

"You have always been a means to an end."

There had never been any love or kindness between them. "I knew you married me for political reasons," Harley stated. "I just didn't understand how ambitious you were."

A low chuckle rumbled through the room. "Tell me, have you always been this strong-willed?"

Honestly, she didn't know if it had always been there and Ackley brought it out, or if she'd changed after living through the bloody takeover. "You wouldn't know since you never tried to get to know me." Not once had he taken any interest or even asked her anything about her life.

"There was no point." The truth and brutality of his words stung like a venomous bite. "I'm merely pondering whether you have always been this way, or whether you became this way after you met a certain someone."

Sweat beaded on Harley's forehead, and her heart pounded so loudly she could swear it echoed in the room. Afraid Lyle referred to Ackley, she decided to keep her mouth shut and not speak. The last thing she wanted to do was incriminate Ackley. As far as Lyle knew, Ackley was dead, and she intended to keep it that way.

"You have nothing to say?" Lyle asked, his voice even deeper than before.

"I have no idea what you're talking about." She prayed he didn't sense the lie.

Lyle chuckled. "Where was this feistiness before?"

It had always been there hidden below the surface,

simmering. She bit her bottom lip to refrain from speaking the nasty comments forming on the tip of her tongue.

"No matter." It sounded as if he stood. "I will make sure it is drained from you before the end." His footsteps echoed in the room, then the door opened and closed.

Harley found herself alone once again. This time, she welcomed the silence.

A sliver of light shot into the room. Sitting up, Harley rubbed her eyes. Without a window, she had no idea what time of day it was. Her back stung from having slept on the hard floor. "Who's there?" she asked.

"His Majesty requests your presence in the great hall," a plump woman said. It was the same one who'd helped Harley dress for the coronation.

"Do you know what the occasion is?" She stood and stretched, her muscles protesting and her stomach growling from hunger.

"I think his soldiers are swearing fealty to you." She held the door open for Harley.

Harley exited and made her way to the adjacent room where a gown had been laid out for her. As before, the guards waited outside while the woman helped Harley dress.

It was time to enact her plan.

"What's your name?" Harley asked, wanting to distract the woman.

"Emma," she replied.

Stepping into the gown, Harley made sure her foot landed on a chunk of the fabric. "Can you help me pull it up?"

Emma stepped closer and grabbed the back while Harley

clutched the front. Together they pulled it up. Harley made sure to yank it with all her might. The fabric ripped right down the center of the skirt.

She had to hide her smile. "Oops," she said, looking down in feigned shock. "Lyle will be so upset when I show up in a ruined gown." She bit her tongue, and tears formed in her eyes.

"I'll run to the queen's room and get you another one."

"Then we're going to be late." Harley started crying.

"Hush, it'll all be fine." Emma patted her back.

"I'll accompany you," Harley suggested. "That way we won't waste any time." She slid her arm around Emma's, leading her to the door. "We must hurry. Lyle hates when people are late. I'd feel awful if he killed you over something so silly." She glanced sidelong at the woman.

Emma's face paled. "That's a good idea. Let's be quick about it."

They rushed to the third floor and entered the queen's room, the guards waiting outside.

"I'll remove this ruined gown while you pick another one," Harley said, standing in just the right spot. As soon as Emma entered the dressing room, Harley knelt, pulling back the area rug and lifting the wooden board. She grabbed the letters, sacks of leaves and roots, and what she wanted most—the key. Setting the items aside, she put the board and rug back. Then she removed her dress, placing it atop the items so they couldn't be seen.

Emma hurried over, carrying a dark red gown. She opened the laces and held it for Harley. Harley stepped into the gown, and Emma cinched it up.

"I'll need a necklace," Harley said. "And a pin for my hair. Both are in the queen's dressing room on the right. Can you please get those items while I put my shoes on?" She slid her one shoe off and pushed it out from under her gown.

"Yes, of course." Emma rushed back to the dressing room.

Harley grabbed the key, shoving it into her bosom. Then she tucked the sacks up her gown and under her waist band. Lastly, with the bulky letters, she had to split them in half to hide them in her undergarments. She stood just as Emma ran back in with a necklace and hair pin.

"Thank you," Harley said, gathering her hair and holding it up so Emma could attach the necklace. "I don't know what I'd do without you."

A loud grumble sounded.

"Is that your stomach making those noises?" Emma asked.

Harley released her hair. "It is. I haven't eaten today."

Emma shook her head. "I'll make sure something is brought to your room for you."

"Thank you." Harley clutched the woman's arm and squeezed it in appreciation. "Now we must go before Lyle becomes angry."

Together, they exited the room. With the items stashed in Harley's gown, she felt extremely uncomfortable walking and feared something would slip out. However, she forced a smile on her face as she made her way down the stairs and to the first floor of the castle. They stopped outside the great hall and the doors swung open, revealing a room packed with soldiers.

CHAPTER SIXTEEN

ACKLEY

*I*n the great hall, Ackley made his way over to the side to be near one of the exits. Just in case. Thankfully there were well over a hundred soldiers in attendance, and he could easily blend in amongst them. At the front of the room, two throne chairs sat on the raised dais. He wondered if Harley would be attending today's event— whatever today's event was—and if she'd sit in one of the throne chairs.

Yesterday, he witnessed Harley crowned. She'd been even more beautiful than he remembered. As she'd taken her oath, she looked confident and poised, as if she wanted to be crowned. A week ago, he wouldn't have thought it possible. But given all he'd learned since being there, he realized he didn't know Harley as well as he thought he did.

Ackley listened in on the conversations of those around him, trying to learn as much information as he could. The snippets he caught had to do mostly with troop movement. It sounded as if they intended to leave the castle in two days, marching north.

A hush descended over those gathered, and the soldiers stood a little taller. Movement came from the front of the room. One of the side doors opened, and Lyle entered the great hall. He strode to the dais, climbed the steps, and then turned and faced those present.

Ackley's fingers itched to withdraw his dagger and impale it into Lyle's eyeball.

The back doors swung open, and Harley stepped forward. She glided toward the dais looking like a queen. Holding her head high, the dark red dress swayed around her body. Her golden hair cascaded down her back. Lyle proffered his hand, and she took it, climbing the steps to stand alongside him.

It felt as if Ackley had eaten a handful of worms. Seeing Harley on the dais alongside her husband made him want to vomit.

"Thank you all for coming on such short notice," Lyle said. "Before you swear fealty to your new queen, there is an issue we must address."

It felt as if Ackley stood in quicksand. This room was filled with soldiers there to swear loyalty to their new queen. If Harley wasn't a willing participant, then she wouldn't be cooperating. Instead, she would be fighting for Owen.

Maybe there was something going on that Ackley wasn't aware of. Some vital piece of information he had yet to discover. His legs wanted to run from the great hall, to do something to discover what the missing piece was. Because he knew Harley wouldn't have betrayed him.

Unable to tear his gaze away from her face, he remained rooted in place, watching.

"I'd hoped to have written proof of Queen Harley's birthright," Lyle said. "Until the late king's possessions can be found, Lord Silas of Penlar has agreed to be a witness."

The side door opened, and Lord Silas entered the great hall. Ackley recognized his gait right away—he was the man from the other night. The one Ackley had followed to the dungeon. Which meant Lord Silas had been talking to his wife, Lady Mayle.

"As many of you know," Lord Silas began, "I raised Queen Harley as my daughter. However, I've known since before she was born that she is not my blood. Lady Mayle conceived Harley with the late King Coden. Harley is the late king's illegitimate child, putting her in line for the throne." Lord Silas looked over his shoulder at Harley. "I've loved her as my own, but she is not mine."

Harley's eyes glistened with tears, but she quickly blinked them away. It was the first crack Ackley had seen in her facade.

"Since there can be no objections to Queen Harley's line to the throne, let's begin with the oaths," Lyle said.

It felt as if Ackley sunk deeper into the quicksand, his legs now stuck, unable to move.

"Pardon me," an older officer said. "There are rumors Prince Owen is alive."

Lyle shook his head. "I wish that was the case," he said. "However, the entire royal family was executed during the Russek takeover. I know most of you saw the executions."

"Are you suggesting that those claiming Prince Owen is alive are simply mistaken?" the officer asked.

"I am," Lyle responded. "It's imperative that we move forward quickly. I received information that ships arrived carrying an army from a kingdom called Marsden."

Ackley's skin prickled at the mention of his own land.

"We believe Marsden is trying to exploit our weakness to overtake our kingdom. They mistakenly assume we are defenseless and without a leader. They are wrong. I'm sending all of you to join with our troops up north to deal with this threat. If the leader of the Marsden army is claiming to be Owen to make it easier to take our kingdom, I will make him pay. Owen is dead, and I am king." Lyle gave no room for questions.

Harley's eyebrows raised ever so slightly, as if doubting her husband. Of course, Ackley could be reading too much into it, seeing things he wanted to, rather than what was there.

"I'll go first," Lord Silas announced. He turned and knelt before Harley. With great flourish, he took her hand in his. He swore his oath as the leader of Penlar, speaking slowly and with conviction.

When he finished, the soldiers began lining up. Harley clutched Lyle's hand and smiled at him. The simple act felt like a dagger through Ackley's heart. That smile, the one she so rarely bestowed, she'd just given to Lyle—her husband.

Ackley's fingers curled inward, forming two fists. He wanted to rush forward, smashing Lyle's face. He wanted to grab Harley, throw her over his shoulder, and run from the room. Relaxing his hands, he forced himself to calm down and not do anything rash.

Soldier after soldier stepped up to the dais, declaring his oath. Ackley couldn't get that close to Lyle. Someone as shrewd as him would notice Ackley's darker hair and eyes. Ackley needed to sneak out of there without anyone noticing. But he had to look at Harley one last time.

Just then, Harley turned Ackley's way, and their eyes locked for a brief two seconds before she blinked and glanced away. During those two seconds, she hadn't shown any indication that she recognized him. The blank look on her face made it seem as if he appeared to be just another soldier.

It felt as if he sunk deeper into the quicksand, it now covering his mouth and nose, swallowing him up. Either Harley played her part exceptionally well, or she'd been fooling him this entire time.

Ackley exited the tiny storage room, hoping it was late enough that the activity in the castle had died down. He needed to find Harley and talk to her. He had to know if she wanted to be extracted. Cracking his knuckles, he went over various plans in his head, accounting for different contingencies.

Remaining in the shadows cast by the intermittent torches hanging on the walls, he made his way along the corridor. The place almost felt too quiet.

Soft voices came from the room up ahead on the right. Ackley slowed, being careful not to make a sound as he approached the doorway.

"Are we certain Owen got the message?" a man asked.

"Yes."

"How can you be so sure?"

A low, dark chuckle rumbled from the room. "Harley, the idiot that she is, thought she was communicating with Rikter when she wrote it. I took the message and put it where Owen's other man would find it."

"I know you caught Rikter, but what of this other man?"

Ackley knew Rikter would never give up information, which probably meant he was dead.

"I let him go to make sure the news reached Owen. I'm

keeping tabs on him though. That's why I believe another one of Owen's men is here."

"Is that why you have Harley locked up?"

Fury filled Ackley at the thought of Harley being locked up like an animal. He knew what being stuck in the closet did to her.

"One of the reasons. The wench tried to murder me. As if she could kill someone."

Pride filled Ackley along with a sense of relief. Harley had tried killing the bloke. That meant he could trust her, and it had all been an act with Lyle.

"Are our men in Losger ready for Owen?"

"More than ready. Once Owen goes near the place, he'll be killed. My soldiers have direct orders."

"Aren't you concerned he'll manage to raise an army?"

"Who's going to help him? All the soldiers who traveled with him are in Losger."

"What about the Marsdens?"

"That's why my soldiers here are preparing to head north. If the Marsden army tries to help Owen, my men will circle in behind them, effectively surrounding them. They'll all die. All seven hundred of them."

Ackley stepped away from the room, turning down the adjacent hallway. He needed to think. Everything seemed to be unraveling. Owen was walking into a trap, and Ackley's army was going to be slaughtered like pigs if they went to Losger.

Time was of the essence. Even though Lyle claimed he had someone watching Galvin, Ackley had to find him. He needed Galvin to stop Owen from going to Losger.

Not seeing anyone in the next hallway, Ackley slunk along the corridor, making his way toward one of the side exits. He passed the kitchen and library. Both were eerily empty.

If Ackley had learned one thing during this past year, it was to never underestimate those seeking or clinging to power. Lyle had managed to take the throne by force and therefore, couldn't be discounted as reckless. If there weren't guards on duty, there had to be a reason. Considering that Lyle had managed to flush Rikter out, Ackley knew he needed to be more careful.

Instead of taking the side door as planned, he entered the servants' passageways. He doubled back and headed toward the other end of the castle. Something felt off. Usually, Ackley never doubted his abilities or what he had planned. However, tonight he hesitated. Not wanting to discount his gut, he decided to find another way out and seek Galvin immediately.

He hadn't been in the south end of the castle before. He knew there was an exit nearby since he'd seen it from the outside. A single soldier stood guard granting people entrance. Since Ackley was exiting, he doubted the soldier would look too closely at him. And if he did, Ackley would have to dispose of him.

A sound came from the corridor to his right. He paused, listening. The sound stopped, but he heard someone breathing about eight feet away. Sliding his dagger from his sleeve, he crept toward the sound. If someone was tracking him, he needed to kill that person so his movements couldn't be reported.

A shadow shifted. He lifted his arm, prepared to throw his weapon.

There was a soft *thump* followed by a whispered curse.

Taking a step back, he melted into the shadows. "Who's there?" he demanded, his dagger still poised and ready to strike.

"Ackley?" Harley whispered.

Someone had to be playing a cruel joke on him.

Harley peered around the corner. "What are you doing here?" she asked, her eyes wide. She reached out, gently touching Ackley's arm as if to make sure he was real.

Her touch practically undid him. "I came to check on you," he whispered, sheathing his dagger, and pulling her toward him. Even her smell unraveled him further.

"I thought I saw you earlier." She slid her arms around his waist, hugging him. "Is Owen here with you?"

He shook his head, holding her against him. They couldn't stand in a hallway having a conversation—it was too dangerous. "Let's go somewhere we can talk."

Taking his hand, she led him to a door ten feet away. She opened it, pulling him inside a small storage closet. When she closed the door, darkness engulfed them. He wanted to see her face so he could read her expressions which usually revealed so much of what she was thinking and feeling.

"You're here for me?" she asked, her voice a whisper. Her fingers trailed up his arms, sending a shiver through him.

He reached forward, grabbing her hips, and yanking her body against his. His hands slid up her back, over her shoulders, to her face, her lips. He lowered his head, kissing her. She tasted the same as he remembered. Her hands wound in his hair, holding him against her. She moaned in his mouth.

If she'd been wearing a dress, he would have pulled it up so he could caress her soft skin. However, she had pants on so he couldn't feel her smooth curves. It was probably better this way since now was not the time, and here was definitely not the place. He pulled away. "I've missed you." His fingers lightly traced over her face. The swell of her cheeks hinted at a smile on her lips. He rested his forehead against hers. "Harley," he said her name with a caress, hoping to convey his own emotions. "Are you okay?" So much had happened since the last time they saw each other.

"Yes. I'm actually in the process of escaping. I have a plan."

"You have a plan?" he repeated, trying to think clearly with her this close to him.

"Yes."

"Tell me what it is."

"First, I'm going to the dungeon to rescue Rikter."

He blinked; surely, he'd heard her wrong. "My Knight, Rikter?"

"Yes. He's been imprisoned."

Relief coursed through him. He hadn't lost a man. "And once you've freed him?"

"I'm going to make sure Owen isn't killed."

She had to know about the trap. "I have the feeling you aren't telling me something."

"I doubt you'll approve of what I'm going to do. So, I'm not going to tell you. And I plan to go at it alone." She spoke with confidence, as if daring him to challenge her.

A moment of uncomfortable silence stretched between them. She reached up, cupping his cheek. "Say something," she whispered.

He had no choice but to let her go on the mission alone. If he insisted he go with her, then he'd be abandoning his army, his sister, and his friends. It would also indicate he didn't trust or believe in Harley. As difficult as it was, he had to let her go. "At least let me rescue Rikter."

A soft laugh escaped her lips. "Okay." She fumbled for his hand, then placed a piece of iron in it.

"What's this?" He curled his fingers over it.

"A key that unlocks every door in this castle, even the dungeon and the cells in it."

That would definitely come in handy. He slid it into his pocket.

"I don't think you should go in through the main door to the dungeon. There's a back entrance accessible through the secret passageways. I can tell you how to get there."

He stood there amazed at how far Harley had come in such a short amount of time. He always thought she had it in her to be a successful Knight; now she was proving to be more than capable.

"After I rescue Rikter, I'm going to meet up with my army."

"I figured." She wrapped her arms around him. "Please be careful. While we may think we know what Lyle has planned, he's already proven he is a step ahead of us. His plans could be fake ones. By trying to circumvent a trap, we could be walking right into one."

He held her tightly against him, smelling her hair, feeling her warmth. He didn't want to let her go. But he couldn't keep her locked up. "Why do I feel like this is goodbye," he murmured.

"Because it is—for now. We'll see each other soon enough."

A feeling of dread settled in him. He leaned down, gently kissing her.

"We need to get going," she whispered against his lips.

He knew they needed to part ways. The problem was, he didn't want to.

"I'll show you how to get to the dungeon." She took his hand, pulling him from the dark closet.

Harley crept to the left, down the corridor. At a tapestry, she shoved it aside, revealing a door. Pushing it open, she stepped into the secret passageways.

She lit a torch, then handed it to Ackley. "You're going to take this corridor fifty feet that way." She pointed to the left. "When you come to an intersection, go to the right. Just before you reach the dead end, there will be a stairwell to your left. That will take you down to the dungeon. You have the key. You should be able to figure out the rest on your own. To leave, backtrack to where you found me. The exit is at the end of the hall."

He had a million questions for her.

"Don't look at me like that," she said, studying his expression. "Otherwise, I won't be able to leave you and do what needs to be done." Tears shone in her eyes. "I've been so lonely. I've missed you."

He set the torch in the holder on the wall. "Harley." He slid his arms around her, pulling her close.

Her body shook as she started crying. "I lost Sword of Rage."

"What do you mean?" He rubbed her back, trying to soothe her.

"When I tried killing Lyle, he took it from me. I'm so sorry."

He kissed the top of her head. "Then I guess it's a good thing I still have its match." He released her, then withdrew Sword of Desire. "I can't have you traipsing off on a mission without a weapon."

"I can't take it. What if I lose this one, too?"

"If you're going to lose it, make sure it's on purpose." He held the sword out to her.

She hesitated a moment before taking the weapon. "Thank you." She clutched it against her chest. "Someone is going to notice I'm missing. I need to be long gone before that happens."

"And I have someone who needs to be rescued before they

195

find you missing." Otherwise, he'd never be able to escape the castle with Rikter.

Taking a step closer to him, Harley went up on her toes and gently kissed Ackley's lips. "The next time we meet—"

"Owen will be king, and you will be mine." He devoured her lips and sealed his promise with a kiss.

CHAPTER SEVENTEEN

*W*alking away from Ackley as he stood all alone in the secret passageways had to be one of the hardest things Harley ever did. However, she knew if she didn't leave, Owen wouldn't stand a chance of regaining control of the kingdom.

Clutching Sword of Desire, she entered the main portion of the castle. Sliding the sword under the tunic she'd stolen, she secured it along her back so no one would see it. She'd spent about twenty minutes with Ackley, which meant her schedule was slightly off. However, since she no longer had to rescue Rikter, she was probably still on track.

After shoving her hair under a cap, she exited the castle, giving a quick nod to the soldier on duty. He didn't even look at her as she hurried past him. She quickly made her way to the stables. With shaking hands, she pulled the flask out of her pocket and removed the lid as she neared the guard on duty. Tipping her head back, she pretended to take a drink from the flask, then wiped her mouth with her sleeve.

Three feet from the guard, she held the flask out to him. "Want a swig?" she asked, making her voice as deep as possible. "It's the good stuff."

"Sure." He grabbed the flask, took a drink, and then handed it back to her.

She carefully put the lid back on and went inside the stables, waiting on the other side of the door. The next minute seemed to drag on forever. Finally, she heard the man fall to the ground. Relieved it had worked, she went out and clutched onto his tunic, dragging him into the stables so no one would see his body.

After depositing him in the first stall, she ran to the back of the stables, quickly locating her horse. She entered the stall, cooing and saying soothing words, wanting to keep the animal calm. Satisfied it would cooperate, she put the saddle on the horse, her fingers fumbling with the straps as panic started to set in.

The book on poisons had worked. Not knowing how long the guard would be unconscious for, Harley needed to get out of there as soon as possible. She tightened the girth strap, then led the horse from the stall and out of the stables. She tried to stay close to the building so she wouldn't be spotted by the sentries patrolling the roof of the castle. At the back of the stables, where the shadows were thicker, she picked up the pace, leading the horse away from the castle. Her heartbeat quickened.

Once the castle was no longer in sight, she hoisted herself onto the horse and steered it toward the road, knowing she wouldn't have the luxury of sleep that night. While riding in the dark would be dangerous for the horse, she had no choice. Harley had to put as much distance between herself and Lyle as possible. As soon as he learned of her disappearance, he would be furious and hunt her down. She urged her horse to run faster. Normally, she'd want to stay off the roads in case they were being watched. Tonight, she would have to risk it. Since she was dressed as a man, if anyone saw her from afar, they wouldn't question her. Up close, she couldn't be certain. Regardless, she kept the cap on as she rode the horse through the dark night.

Hours later, when the sky had lightened, she came to a fork in the road. Pulling her horse to a stop, she withdrew the page she'd ripped from one of the books back at the castle and examined the map. Tracing the road she took from the castle to the fork in the road, she saw that she needed to head to the left. Not too much farther, there would be a turnoff to Losger. She'd have to be careful not to miss it.

Shoving the map in her pocket, she urged her horse to the left, toward the forest. As they traveled along, she started worrying that the soldiers staying in Losger would have some sort of watch. While she didn't think they'd kill her on sight, it was probably best to arrive at the abandoned castle with her hair down so the soldiers could see her better. Hopefully, they wouldn't think her an immediate threat and strike her down. She only needed five minutes of their time to enact the rest of her plan.

She shook her head, unable to believe she was going through with this.

Harley also couldn't believe she'd run into Ackley in the castle of all places. It still felt like a dream. She'd just been sneaking along, about to enter the secret passageways, when he slunk into the same corridor as her. He looked every bit as handsome as she remembered. It had been beyond tempting to consider abandoning her plan and running away with him. However, Lyle was her husband, and Melenia was her kingdom.

These were her problems to solve, and she couldn't allow the responsibility to fall to someone else. She was perfectly capable of dealing with this mess. It was the only reason she'd allowed the damn crown to be put atop her head. By taking the oath, she committed treason. She knew perfectly well that Owen was alive and the true heir. Not her. However, by being sworn in, she had a shot—albeit a small one—at saving everything. She just hoped she was strong enough and brave enough to go through with it.

Which was why she hadn't shared her plan with Ackley. He never would have allowed her to carry it out. Or, at the very least, he would have insisted on accompanying her. As tempting as that would have been, she couldn't rely on him to fix this. And, if she was being honest with herself, there was a part of her that didn't want him to. She needed to prove to herself that she could do this. That Lyle hadn't destroyed her spirit, that she was more than just a wife or daughter, that she could be a lady Knight.

As she rode closer to Losger, she felt the weight of her plan. When she'd tried killing Lyle the first time, she failed miserably. If she didn't succeed this time, she'd be the one dead. At the end of this, it would be either Harley or Lyle, but not both. Only one would survive.

Based upon the map and her calculations, the turnoff for Losger should be coming up. She had to assume the second she found it, guards would be watching her every move.

On both sides of the road, the trees thickened and the vegetation became denser. Green moss covered the trunks. The air turned colder. Even though the sun had started to rise, the deeper she traveled into the forest, the darker it got. The branches extended above her head, forming an arch over the road, blocking out the light.

Between two of the trees on the right, a four-foot space opened up. It had to be the turnoff to Losger. She steered her horse that way. The leaves rustled from a wind she couldn't feel. It almost sounded as if the trees were whispering secrets from the past. The hair on her arms rose. She sensed a presence here. Whether it was ghosts or soldiers hidden amongst the vegetation watching her, she couldn't be sure. She wasn't sure she wanted to know.

After a few miles, a dull light shone up ahead. Harley headed toward it. Suddenly, the trees abruptly ended, and she pulled her horse to a halt as she observed the view before her. She was at the edge of over a mile long forest wall. To the east and west, open land. Two miles directly ahead, an abandoned castle was situated on grassy land. Parts of the castle had collapsed in on itself. Green moss and ivy grew over the stones and up the turrets. Up ahead, on the other side of the castle, steep rocks shot up into the air, forming a massive cliff and shielding the castle.

"You came in the back door," a man said from behind her.

Harley slowly turned her head, watching as two men slunk out of the forest, cautiously approaching her. "I didn't realize there was more than one way to come here." She wanted them to hear her voice, so they knew she was a woman, not a man. "The book from my library showed no other path."

"Your library?" the man on the right asked. "Where's that?"

She smiled. "The royal castle." Holding her head high, she said, "I'm Queen Harley of Melenia. Who's in charge here?"

The two men looked at one another. The one on the left shrugged. "We'll take you to our leader. I'm not sure what good that'll do."

She held out her hand, the one with the queen's ring on her

finger, ensuring they saw it. "Would you please help me dismount?"

Both men rushed forward, helping her off the horse.

After riding for so many hours without a break, Harley wanted to walk to stretch her legs. Neither man spoke as she led her horse toward the castle. Since she was the queen and outranked them, trivial chitchat was uncalled for.

Harley felt uneasy. Not a single person, other than the two soldiers accompanying her, was in sight. Since the royal castle had hundreds of men and tents on its grounds, she assumed the same would be true here. However, the place appeared lifeless.

Drawing closer, the two men led her over a rickety wooden bridge toward the front entrance. They were about to step across the threshold when Harley paused.

"I want you to swear fealty to me," she said to the two soldiers.

Both turned and faced her. One had his eyebrows pulled together, and the other tilted his head as if considering what she said.

She needed to be strong to pull this off. She held out her hand displaying the queen's ring, making her expectations clear. Both men immediately dropped to one knee, bowing their heads.

She kept her hand outstretched. "Your oath."

The one on the right took her hand, said the words pledging his life to her, and then he kissed her ring. When he finished, the other soldier did the same.

"You may stand."

Both did as she said.

"Now take me to whomever is commanding this portion of the army." She felt more confident this time knowing these two men had an obligation to protect her. For some reason, nervous anticipation along with fear rose within her. Being here, doing this, had monumental consequences.

The two men led her past the threshold and into the center of the castle. Here, the ceiling had long ago collapsed leaving just the shell of the building standing. At first, Harley thought the place completely abandoned. However, she knew the hundreds of Melenia soldiers she'd traveled with across the kingdom had to be here. Once she realized that, she felt the presence of hundreds of people, all hidden in the castle walls.

That was when she realized the soldiers' families weren't here—just the soldiers. This was all a trap to lure Owen to Losger, thinking he was rescuing his people when instead, Lyle planned to kill him. If Owen came here with Ackley's army, then Ackley's men would be slaughtered as well.

Harley intended to stop it all.

"I'll take your horse and feed it," one of the men said.

She absently nodded, and he led the animal away.

"And I'll go and get the commander," the other soldier said.

"No need," Harley replied. She had no intention of standing there all alone, reacting to what happened. She needed to be proactive. To be the queen, she had to act like the queen.

Several boulders were scattered throughout, so Harley went over and climbed on one of them. Standing tall, she raised her voice and addressed those hidden behind the walls. "I am here so that you can swear fealty to me."

The lone soldier who remained at her side knelt on the ground. "Hail, Queen Harley!" he yelled, ensuring everyone heard him.

She held out her hand.

He took it, kissing her ring.

She didn't release him from his kneeling position. Instead,

she stood there wanting every single person hiding in this castle to come out and swear allegiance to her. She knew they'd already done so with Lyle.

Waiting felt like torture. At any moment, someone could shoot an arrow at her chest, killing her. This was the riskiest part. She kept her head high, as a queen would do, with the expectation of being obeyed clear on her face. Minutes passed.

Just when she was about to say something to the man still kneeling before her, she heard a low rumbling sound coming from behind her. She slowly turned. At the back of the castle, out of the dark archway, soldiers started pouring out, filling the area around her. Hundreds of them. No one spoke. When they got as close as they could to her, the men knelt.

Standing on the boulder, Harley observed the hundreds of men surrounding her, all of them on their knees before her. Then, one by one, each man came up to her, recited the oath and kissed her ring, officially swearing fealty to her. She didn't know how long she stood there for, but it felt like hours passed.

Once every single soldier had pledged his loyalty to Harley, she knew she had to address them. She was about to tell them to stand while she said a few words when one last person walked out from under the archway. As the man got closer to her, she recognized him. "What are you doing here?" she demanded.

A slow smile formed on his face. "Who do you think is leading all these men?" Lord Silas stood before Harley. His awkward lumber and stiff body movements had vanished.

"As of now, I am," she said boldly, firmly. "As the queen of Melenia, I hereby appoint myself as the commander of the Melenia army."

She heard a slight intake of breath as the men around her

reacted to her decree. She couldn't let Lord Silas's presence change anything. Her hands started trembling, so she clasped them together.

Lord Silas's eyes narrowed, but he didn't respond. Since he'd already sworn an oath to her, he didn't need to do so again. While she had a thousand questions for this man who'd raised her, with so many soldiers around, now was not the time.

She lifted her chin, addressing her subjects. "I want to meet with my captains. Everyone else, as you were."

She stepped off the boulder, unable to believe she'd just taken control of the army. With her fate officially sealed, she moved herself into the second to last position in this dangerous game with high stakes. There was only one play left to make.

"You've been in charge of these soldiers?" she asked Lord Silas, as if he was just another soldier in the army and not someone she'd known her entire life. It seemed as if pieces of her heart were being chipped away. As they headed toward the back archway, she got the feeling she knew nothing about this man beside her.

"I have," he answered.

The frail person she'd come to know had vanished and in his place, a cunning man as healthy as any other. She couldn't let it rattle her, not when she was so close to ending this. "Lord Silas, take me and my captains somewhere we can talk."

"Of course, Your Majesty." Silas bowed with a flourish, then led her through the archway and to the right.

Harley and twenty men followed him up a narrow flight of stairs and to a room at the end of the hallway. One of the walls was gone, leaving the room exposed to the north. She had so many questions for this man whom she had called Father.

While she wanted to speak to him privately, she feared being alone with him because she no longer trusted him.

Right now, her priority was to make sure Owen was safe and protected. Whatever traps had been set, had to be revised. Since she was now the queen, she couldn't order her soldiers to kill Lyle because ordering the death of a monarch was punishable by immediate death. Instead, she'd have to be cunning about it.

She turned to Lord Silas. "Since I am now the commander, you are hereby relieved of your duty. You," she pointed at the man closest to her, "escort him to the adjacent room. I'll be along shortly to give additional orders."

"Yes, Your Majesty." The man bowed and did as she instructed.

With Lord Silas out of the room, she could think clearly. "I am now your commander. I want to know what your plans are. Tell me everything."

"Forgive me, Queen Harley, but you're a woman," one of the soldiers said.

"And?" She knew there was no law prohibiting her from doing this. "Just because a woman has never commanded the army, doesn't mean it can't be done now." She looked at each man in the room. "All of you swore to protect me, obey me, and you are all loyal to Melenia." Again, she made eye contact with each soldier. "It's time for us to save our kingdom and ensure what happened with Russek never happens again. As I said before, I am Queen Harley, and I am your commander."

CHAPTER EIGHTEEN

ACKLEY

With the key Harley bestowed to Ackley, getting Rikter out of the dungeon had been easy. The two men now stood near the exit closest to the stables. Other than a few bruises and a slight limp, Rikter seemed to be in decent shape.

Earlier tonight, watching Harley walk away had been one of the hardest things Ackley had ever done. It had taken every ounce of strength not to go after her. The only reason he'd let her go was because she had a plan and seemed confident in it. Ackley had never been prouder. He'd always known she was strong and capable. Now she knew it, too.

Focusing on the task at hand, he said, "Galvin received word Owen and Idina reached Penlar where they intend to meet up with my army." Too bad Ackley's army was nowhere near there.

"Traveling on horseback won't take me long to get to

Penlar," Rikter said. "I will find Owen and stop him from going to Losger. You can count on me."

He pulled out a piece of paper, handing it to Rikter. "Here are three scenarios. Once you have Owen and Idina, give this to Idina and let her decide how to proceed from there."

Rikter took the paper, sliding it in his pocket. Then he opened the door a crack and peered outside. "Are you sure you don't want me to find Galvin before I leave?"

"No, I'll do it," Ackley insisted. Rikter needed to get out of there before anyone discovered he was missing. Ackley would have an easier time escaping since no one knew him.

Rikter placed his right fist over his chest, then left the castle.

Ackley turned and headed the other way, wanting to exit closer to the tents so no one would think twice about why he was there. When he reached the correct door, he slouched and pushed it open. Heading straight for the camp, he tucked his hands under his arms, pretending to shiver from the cold night. At this late hour, no one paid him any heed as he wound his way between the tents, a few fires still burning low. Most sentries on duty kept their focus on the front of the castle, not this side where the soldiers were.

When he reached Galvin's tent, he opened the flap and went inside, clicking his tongue four times.

"I almost killed you," Galvin said. "Good thing you gave the signal when you did."

"I have a mission for you." Ackley knelt next to him.

Galvin sat up. "What is it?" He started pulling weapons out from under his bedroll.

"I need you to head south to Landania. I have a group of fifty soldiers camped there."

"Only fifty? Where are the rest?"

Hopefully hidden from Lyle. "I moved them and sent Gytha on a secret mission."

Galvin attached his weapons belt, tightening it. "Consider it done." He started pulling on his boots. "And you?"

Ackley had a mission of his own. "The next time I see you, Owen will be king."

As far as plans went, this was definitely one of his dumber ones. Ackley knew he should just leave the castle and do what needed to be done to put Owen on the throne. But he couldn't walk away. He wanted his sword back because it had sentimental value to him, and he couldn't stand the thought of it being in Lyle's possession. Granted, he could wait until Lyle was killed and then retrieve it, but he didn't want to. Just the thought of Lyle having it grated on Ackley's nerves.

He shouldn't even call what he was about to do a *plan* since he didn't know where the sword was located. All he knew was that Harley had tried killing Lyle with it. Ackley suspected Lyle had stashed it in his office. If not there, maybe his bedchamber. Starting with the office seemed the safer of the two options.

Ackley entered the castle, heading to where the offices were located on the first floor. As he crept along, he slid a dagger from his sleeve, palming it. Thirty feet, then he turned right. Fifty feet, then he made a left. Lyle's office was supposed to be the fourth from the end. When he approached the door, he stood there, listening. No sounds came from within. Regardless, Ackley needed to proceed with caution. He went to insert his dagger into the lock when he remembered the key

Harley had given him. She said it unlocked every door in the castle. Pulling it out, he slid the key into the lock and turned.

A soft *click* chimed. Standing off to the side, Ackley twisted the knob and opened the door. Nothing happened. He peered around the corner and into the room. A leaf floated to the floor. He rolled his eyes. This had to be the right office. Back in Penlar, Lyle had used the same archaic technique to determine if anyone had been in his rooms. He shrugged, not caring. By the time Lyle realized Ackley had stepped foot in there, he'd be long gone. He entered the office, searching for his sword.

On the bookshelf in the back of the room, he spotted a sword lying on the third shelf from the top. Moving farther into the room to get a better look, he heard the door behind him softly click shut and then a bolt slide into place. He spun toward the door. Light shone from underneath out in the hallway, illuminating the shadows of a pair of boots.

He'd stepped into a trap.

He sprinted toward his sword only to discover it was an empty sheath. He cursed, pulling on his mental armor and preparing to fight. With a dagger in one hand and a short sword in the other, he surveyed his surroundings. There were three windows to his left, so he moved away from them, not wanting to be shot by an arrow. Sidling up to the bookshelves, he slid along them, moving closer to the glass, wanting to know if soldiers were approaching from outside. He didn't see anyone.

Ackley felt something across the room though he didn't see anyone. He sucked in a deep breath, trying to calm himself as he prepared to fight. Fifteen feet by twenty feet. The ceiling four feet above him. He quickly took note of each item that he could use as a weapon.

The bookshelf directly across from him opened like a door. It had to lead either to a hidden room or serve as an entrance to the secret passageways. Ackley widened his stance, preparing to face whoever was coming for him.

Footsteps sounded as a shadow emerged from the dark opening. The shadow hardened, revealing the outline of a man. He stopped before the desk, and the moonlight shone on a man with broad shoulders, blond hair, and a sword in hand.

"Looking for this?" Lyle asked, lifting the sword.

Ackley immediately recognized it as Sword of Rage. Instead of diving for the weapon like he wanted to, he remained rooted in place, observing his opponent.

"It's a beauty if you like used things. But you can't have it. It's mine." He tilted the sword, as if admiring it.

Ackley wanted to smash his fist into Lyle's face, making his nose bleed. Ackley wasn't an idiot and didn't believe for one second Lyle was referring to the sword. "I assume you're talking about Harley?"

"I am." He lowered the sword and focused on Ackley.

"Of course, I can't have her." Not because she was married to Lyle, but because she was her own person and not an item to be owned. A man like Lyle would never understand that.

The false king moved to the side of the desk, closer to Ackley.

If Ackley also moved to maintain a safe distance and keep the desk between them, it would put him directly in front of a window. Not wanting that, he remained in place, knowing he would have to fight.

"You're delusional if you think she loves you," Lyle said.

The funny thing was, Ackley didn't think Harley loved him, he knew she did. Instead of responding, he smiled.

Lyle's upper lip curled in disgust.

Ackley shrugged. "I don't know who you think I am or why you're implying I have anything to do with Harley."

"Like you, I am not a fool and would appreciate you not treating me like one." Lyle readjusted his hand on the grip.

Ackley shrugged. If he threw his dagger quick enough, he could impale it into Lyle's neck, killing him. He twisted his fingers, getting ready to throw it. "Then besides sleeping with your wife, I assume you know I killed your father." He was about to throw the dagger when Lyle shifted.

Ackley reacted before he even realized what he was doing. He lifted his short sword, blocking the strike. Their swords clanked. Lyle came around to Ackley's side of the desk, his sword moving rapidly in short, precise movements. Ackley had no time to think, only to block each blow as it came. Twisting, he rolled over the desk, getting away from the windows. Lyle grunted and came at him. When he got close enough, he spun and kicked. Ackley barely had time to step to the side, avoiding the strike. Ackley countered with one of his own, and Lyle deftly moved out of the way.

They were evenly matched.

Ackley wanted his sword, but he didn't want to stand there fighting for an hour to try and get it.

Lyle backed off. "What do you want?" He wiped his arm across his face.

"Owen on the throne where he belongs." Ackley noticed Lyle's boots—he was in an attack stance. Ackley kept his sword raised, ready to parry any blows coming his way.

"What did Owen give you for your help?" Lyle demanded. "He doesn't have any money. Did he say you could have Harley?" He shook his head in disbelief. "Some men can be so fooled by beauty."

"Owen didn't give or promise me anything."

"Since you're not from Melenia, you probably don't understand how incompetent the late king was. Squandering money, not ensuring his people had food. I plan to help my people. I will be a good ruler. So why are you fighting against me? Why try and put a man on the throne who doesn't know how to lead?"

All good questions. "Because life doesn't work that way. You can't get rid of someone—especially a monarch—just because you disagree with him."

"What if he's killing his own people?"

"You must be speaking about yourself." Ackley ducked, the sword narrowly missing his head. When he righted himself, he pressed forward, going on the offensive instead of the defensive. "What's pathetic," Ackley said, pushing Lyle back toward the bookshelf, "is that you don't even love her." He wanted to steer the conversation back to Harley.

Lyle chuckled. "She's a means to an end. Always has been, always will be." He twisted and moved to the other side of the desk, putting a buffer between them once again.

Ackley stood there, his chest heaving, as he considered his options. When he'd played that game of War with Harley, she told him that sometimes the point wasn't to beat your opponent. That it was more about strategy and avoiding an all-out war. Did he truly trust Harley to do what needed to be done for her kingdom? He did. He knew she would put Melenia, including Owen and Idina, above herself. She'd told him she had a plan, and he believed in her.

Ackley made his move. "You know Harley isn't here in the castle, don't you?"

Something flashed in Lyle's eyes, indicating that he hadn't been aware Harley left.

Raising a single eyebrow, Ackley forced a sly smile on his lips. "Didn't it occur to you that I'm a distraction so she could get away?"

Lyle's eyes narrowed. "Where would she go?"

Ackley's smile grew wider, this one genuine when he finally realized what Harley intended to do. "You haven't figured it out yet? You shouldn't underestimate Harley." She was a genius and deserved to be a full-fledged Knight. He leaned his head to the side, stretching his neck, preparing to go another round.

"It seems we're at an impasse." Lyle sheathed Ackley's sword.

"I don't see how that's the case." Ackley couldn't let his guard down, despite what Lyle wanted him to do.

"It seems I've lost my wife, and you've lost your army." His eyes gleamed with mischief.

Ackley hadn't lost his army. He knew exactly where it was and what his soldiers were doing. He'd instructed Morton to break them into smaller groups of fifty, like before, so they could travel quickly. Then he sent them into Russek, telling them to stay near the border, as they made their way north. While they traveled, Gytha was going to meet with Kerdan's man and seek permission for their passage.

The air shifted, and Ackley felt someone approach from behind him. He refused to turn his back to Lyle. He widened his stance.

Lyle leaned on his desk. "I'll make you a deal. You tell me where Harley is, and I'll tell you where I diverted your army to."

Trusting that Harley wanted Lyle to go after her, Ackley pretended to mull over it before answering, "Losger."

Lyle's brows raised in surprise. Then he lifted his hand and waved.

When Ackley spun to face his oncoming attacker, something slammed into the back of his head, knocking him to the floor.

"Excellent job, Lady Mayle," Lyle said. "You've proven you can be trusted."

Ackley was about to groan when Lady Mayle knelt next to him. "Let me make sure he's knocked out." She placed her hand on his face, tilting it toward her.

He kept his eyes closed and his breathing slow and steady.

"He's out."

"Good work. Have him taken to the dungeon. I'm going after my wife. When I get back, I'll deal with Prince Ackley of Marsden."

Ackley heard Lyle rush from the room. He silently cursed since Lyle still had Sword of Rage. He swore the next time they met he would get his sword back.

As Lady Mayle spoke to someone in the hallway, Ackley felt a person grab his ankles and drag him from the room. He continued to pretend to be unconscious, not wanting to fight several guards at once. A few minutes later, someone grabbed his arms, lifting him off the floor. He felt his body being carried down a flight of steps. Metal clanged, and then Ackley was set down on a rough stone floor.

It smelled of hay and fecal matter. Ackley assumed he was in the dungeon.

Lady Mayle thanked the men for their help, then it sounded like everyone left.

Ackley wanted to confront Harley's mother and ask why she chose Lyle's side instead of her daughter's. However, he didn't have precious time to waste. Peeling one eye open, he glanced at the corridor. Not seeing anyone, he opened his other eye and sat up. After a few minutes, all remained quiet. He withdrew the key Harley had given him and unlocked the cell door. Since he'd already been down in the dungeon when he rescued Rikter, he knew the way out. Pocketing the key, he exited the cell and made his way to the secret passageways.

When he entered the main portion of the castle again, he headed to the side entrance closest to the stables. He needed a horse. Opening the door, he peeked outside and saw a flurry of activity going on. In the chaos, Ackley could easily blend in.

He stepped outside and headed toward the stables. On his way, he noticed all the tents had been taken down. Men were lining up, getting ready to march out. Lyle and a few of his captains rode on horseback, organizing everyone. They had to be going after Harley.

Ackley hesitated a moment. He could blend in with this army and march with them. Then he could make sure Harley was okay. *No*, he chided himself. He trusted Harley and her plan. Ackley needed to check on his army. He had no idea if what Lyle said was true.

He wondered where Lyle would have diverted the Marsden army to and why. That was when it hit him. Lyle had looked surprised that Harley had gone to Losger—because that's where Lyle wanted everyone to end up. Lyle had purposefully fed Harley false information to get Owen to Losger where Lyle could set a trap and have him killed. Lyle must have a portion of the Melenia army already in place there. Then, if the Marsden army arrived and this Melenia army here showed up behind them, they'd be trapped, completely boxed in, ensuring a brutal battle to the end.

Which meant Lyle had somehow diverted Ackley's army to Losger.

Ackley had to get there before Lyle did so he could warn his men.

He sprinted to the stables and cursed.

Not a single horse was left.

CHAPTER NINETEEN

HARLEY

*H*arley exited the room, leaving her captains behind to work out the details of her plan. Her hands started shaking, and beads of sweat covered her forehead. She couldn't believe she just did that. Now she was not only the queen of Melenia, but the commander of the entire army as well. While her men had seemed hesitant at first, the more she spoke to them, the more comfortable they appeared.

Outside the room, two men waited for her. "Are you my guards?" she asked.

"We are," the one on the right answered. "That is, if you wish to have guards," he added quickly.

"Both of you, with me." While she didn't want an audience for what she was about to do, she couldn't be alone with Lord Silas. She entered the room where he was being kept. When the guard watching him went to leave, she insisted he stay along with her two guards. The three men spread out in the room, giving her space to speak with Silas. Like the other room, this one had a missing wall, leaving the room exposed to the elements.

"Why are you treating me so disrespectfully?" he asked. "I've done nothing but support you your entire life. I educated you, took care of you."

And he'd lied to her. She couldn't trust him. As she stood before him, she tried to get her thoughts in order.

"What do you hope to accomplish?" Lord Silas asked. He stood near a cluster of stones that had caved in from the missing exterior wall.

She gazed out of the castle, looking at the cliff in the distance. This castle used to house the royal family hundreds of years ago, long before the newer one had been built. "I want what's best for Melenia."

"We all do," he replied.

"Good." She faced him again, wondering how she'd ever thought him a frail, feeble man. All his coughing, walking hunched over, and fits that rendered him bedridden had been a lie. "Tell me how you came to be the commander here."

The corners of his lips curled up, and his eyes shone with shrewd intelligence. "King Lyle needed a commander after his father was brutally murdered. The position naturally fell to me."

Mulling over his words, she tried figuring out what he left unsaid. "You're not a military man, you're the leader of Penlar, and you're elderly. Being appointed as the commander makes no sense."

"To you."

Folding her arms, she started tapping her foot, trying to work through this. It had never made sense that her parents married her off to Lyle. Even if Commander Beck came to Silas demanding a union between their children, her father didn't have to agree. If Beck threatened to expose her true parentage, Silas could have gone straight to the king and gotten his help. Realization dawned on her. "You're involved with Beck and Lyle." It was the only reason that made sense, and it explained why Penlar had been the only major city unharmed.

Silas chuckled. "*Involved* is an interesting word to use." He rubbed his chin. "Tell me, how do you think Commander Beck came by the information about you not being my child?"

It felt as if she'd fallen into a cold lake, and she had no idea which way was up. "You told him?" She remembered reading through the letters Beck had sent Lyle. Beck said he discovered the king's secret, but he never mentioned how.

Lord Silas took a step closer to her. "I did."

"I don't understand." Silas was already in charge of Penlar and one of the most powerful men in the kingdom. There wasn't much more he could gain by putting Harley on the throne, especially since she wasn't even his child.

"I've been planning this for years," he revealed. "I put everything in motion the day I sent your mother to seduce King Coden. Then I raised you, groomed you, and put you right where you needed to be so I could get what I want."

Harley rubbed her temples, sorting through all he said. Particularly the part about sending her mother to seduce the king—which would have been her mother's brother-in-law. Harley's stomach cramped, and she felt ill.

"Then my next move was years later with Marsden."

She didn't understand how Ackley's kingdom fit into all of this.

"Oh, darling, don't look so confused." He took another step closer. "Marsden is a rich kingdom, despite how poor most of the people are. We started exporting their stones here, selling them off for money. Marsden can finance anything we want. Since Melenia is so impoverished, we needed their wealth."

Growing up, her father always seemed so loving. He'd insisted on her getting an education, he treated her well, taught her to think and be her own person. She didn't understand how this man before her could be so cold, calculating, and cunning. Not at all like the man who raised her. "You did all this just to put me on the throne?" It seemed extreme, but then she'd never really understood why people sought power in the first place.

"It's not so much that I want *you* on the throne," he said, taking another step toward her so their toes now touched. He leaned down and whispered in her ear, "It's my son, Lyle, who I want on the throne. You are simply a means to an end."

Everything went eerily silent as Harley tried to process the words Silas had just said. Since he'd whispered them, no one else heard. No one else knew his secret.

She sucked in a breath, shocked. "What?" She must've misunderstood him. It couldn't be true.

He leaned back slightly, watching her, a devious smile on his face. "You heard me."

Harley had no idea how to respond as undiluted anger rose within her. Her life had been built on one big lie. Well, no more. When she'd first learned Silas wasn't her father, she had a hard time reconciling the truth with what she'd believed her entire life. Now, discovering Silas was Lyle's father, equally disturbed her. She'd always wondered about Lyle's mother. He never spoke about her. She didn't even know if the woman was alive or not.

Instead of love and fatherly affection, the man who raised her only saw her as a way to get what he wanted. And her mother had known and done nothing all these years.

Harley was a means to an end.

"So, you see, my dear, you are nothing." He placed his left hand on her shoulder, squeezing it slightly. "You think you're in control, but you're not. You never have been and never will be."

Her anger snapped. She was done being a pawn in this game. Now that she was the queen and commander of the army, she would be silent no more. Ackley had shown her another way, she just had to believe in herself. "I don't think, I know." She stepped away from him just as he reached out to grab her with his other hand. "Don't touch me."

Her guards rushed forward.

"I want Lord Silas detained," she said. "I believe he is working against Melenia's interests. Tie him up and keep him here. Two of you will guard him until I return."

Silas shook his head. "You fool. You have no idea what you're doing."

One of the guards grabbed Silas's hands, yanking them back and tying them together.

Harley exited the room without a backward glance. She had more important matters to attend to.

CHAPTER TWENTY

ACKLEY

Standing in the middle of the empty stables, Ackley ran his hands through his hair, trying to remain calm. He needed a horse, and Lyle was outside readying his men to march out within the hour. All of Lyle's captains were on horses. Ackley just had to figure out how to get one of them without anyone seeing or knowing.

The fact that he'd released his animal a few days ago didn't matter since it was too late to change that. Right now, he needed a horse. He leaned his head to the side, stretching his neck. He'd just tag along with the army. Then, when they stopped to sleep, he'd steal one. Granted, it was the middle of the night right now, so he wasn't sure when exactly they'd stop. And then he'd be even farther north, away from where he needed to go.

He had that strange feeling again, the one where he was

sinking in quicksand. Everything was happening so quickly around him, and he felt powerless to stop any of it.

He started pacing, trying to work through everything. He got the feeling he was missing something. Lyle had teased him about the Marsden army for a reason. Maybe Lyle wanted Ackley to take off after them. He rubbed his face. Lyle had to know that was exactly what Ackley would do. Before he decided on the best course of action, he needed to think logically about this. It seemed as if Lyle had been setting traps all along, and everyone was falling for them.

Ackley had to look at the big picture to figure this out. Since the five hundred soldiers who'd accompanied Owen to Marsden and back weren't at the royal castle, Ackley had to assume Lyle had sent them to Losger. Then Lyle had managed to get Harley to think the soldiers' families were there, thus sending Owen there as well. Then Harley had gone there herself.

Lyle also knew where the Marsden army was camped inside Landania's border since he'd managed to kidnap Ackley's decoy. That was why Ackley had ordered for his two men to relocate the army. If, as Lyle implied, he'd managed to move the army before Ackley's men did, Ackley needed to figure out where Lyle would have sent them. Probably somewhere in Melenia since Lyle couldn't attack them on foreign soil. Since Lyle had five hundred soldiers in Losger and two hundred at the royal castle about to head there, the only place that made sense was Losger. Since they'd be evenly matched with numbers, Lyle either had a plan or something in place there that would give him the advantage.

Ackley couldn't help but wonder if Harley knew what she was up against.

Voices came from outside the stables. Ackley ducked into a stall, squatting so he wouldn't be seen.

"I can't believe he expects us to march out in the middle of the night like this," a man said.

"I don't question orders," another man said, "I just follow them."

"Here's the horse food," the first one said. "Grab it and let's go."

There were some shuffling noises, and then the stables went silent again.

Ackley decided to hide in the stall until after the army left. Sitting on the floor, he grabbed a piece of hay and started twirling it while he thought through various plans.

Even if Lyle had managed to send a message to Ackley's army to move locations, with the decoy being kidnapped, he didn't think the army would comply. If anything, the army might have already moved once Ruthar disappeared. That had been weeks ago. Ackley tossed the piece of hay, then rubbed his face. His army could be anywhere in Melenia by now, especially if they were traveling in smaller groups.

So, Morton would have gone to organize and move the army, only to find them already gone.

Somehow, Ackley didn't think traipsing all over the kingdom would solve anything. It all came down to three choices. He could stay there and wait to see what happened, he could go to Losger to help Harley, or he could go to Penlar to meet up with Owen.

Rumbling noises came from outside the stables. The army had to be marching out. With only two hundred soldiers, it wouldn't take Lyle very long to reach Losger. Harley probably had a day or two at most there before he arrived.

"Blasted," a man said.

The voice sounded familiar. Ackley peered over the stall door. "Finnegan?" What was he doing there? Ackley stood and jumped over the stall door, greeting his fellow Knight. He hadn't seen him since he'd given him the letter to take to Empress Rema.

Finnegan clapped Ackley's back. "Man is it good to see you. I've been searching for you for the past two days. I came in here to steal a horse. Didn't expect to find you here."

"Where have you been?" Ackley asked. While the Brotherhood said they hadn't harmed Finnegan, Ackley didn't know what had happened to him.

"After Brodek nabbed the letter and said he'd take care of it, I started following him to make sure he took it to the Empress."

Ackley would have done the same.

"But then Tarnek and Olek doubled back and got me. They said since they weren't monitoring the border, someone needed to ensure no one came after you. I agreed to go to one of their posts and remain there."

Ackley raised his eyebrows. "You didn't go back to camp?"

"From the post, I could monitor the camp. That's how I saw the men coming for Ruthar." He ducked his head. "I wanted to save him, but it would have jeopardized everything."

It was Ackley's turn to pat Finnegan's back. "He died protecting my identity." If anyone should feel guilty, it was Ackley.

"After that, I rejoined the army and began moving them."

Ackley's heartbeat quickened. "Where is my army now?"

"All but fifty are on our war ships sitting off the coast."

With his hands on his hips, Ackley started pacing. "They're safe?"

"They are."

"And the fifty still on land?"

"They're nearby, just a couple of miles away."

He'd never felt so relieved in all his life. "Any word from Owen?"

Finnegan shook his head.

"Take me to my men. I want to send a small contingent after Owen." Then it dawned on him he didn't know why Finnegan was there. "What do you need the horse for?"

"No one has seen or heard from Gytha."

Ackley waved his right hand. "I sent her to Russek on a mission." One that was no longer needed. Regardless, he had to get a message to her to return to Melenia.

"Word just came that Kerdan seized control of Russek. He is now the king."

This was good news, and Ackley didn't feel so panicked about Gytha being in a foreign kingdom during a civil war.

"You know what, I have a better idea. Instead of taking me to my men, bring my men here. Lyle is gone. It's time to take the castle for Owen."

CHAPTER
TWENTY-ONE

HARLEY

*H*arley pulled on the thick riding gloves one of the soldiers had procured for her. She flexed her fingers, ensuring she could move sufficiently. Satisfied, she attached Sword of Desire to her back. Not wanting her hair to get stuck on the handle, she gathered it to the side and braided it.

"Your Majesty," one of the captains said. "The king and our fellow Melenia soldiers are nearing from the east."

Lyle and his men were arriving just the way her captains expected them to. "Excellent." She stepped onto a boulder, then mounted her horse.

"Are you certain you want to ride out to meet them?" the captain asked. "We don't know where the Marsden army is, and the king was adamant they would show up here to overthrow him."

"Yes, I'm certain." She would not show weakness before her men. She had a part to play so her plan would work, and she would see it through no matter the cost.

It wasn't that she hadn't been able to kill Lyle before; it was that she'd been too focused on killing him the way Ackley had shown her. Now, she was doing this her way. She might not be stronger or faster than Lyle, but she was smarter than him.

As she rode her horse out of the castle and to the pasture, she considered how quickly Lyle and his soldiers had arrived there. She thought she'd have a couple more days to prepare. Lyle's plan had been to ride in behind Owen and the Marsden soldiers, boxing them in and then slaughtering them all. Since Owen hadn't arrived, Lyle must have changed his plans. Regardless, neither Owen nor the Marsden soldiers were there, making her plan a little easier to execute.

Harley pulled her horse to a halt as she waited for Lyle to reach her. He had to be furious that she'd gotten away from the castle. Somehow, he must have discovered she was there in Losger. She braced herself for his fury. When things didn't go according to plan, Lyle became violent. Especially when Harley challenged him. Rolling her shoulders back, she prepared to play the part necessary to get the outcome she desired.

She glanced over her shoulder, marveling at the rows and rows of soldiers lined up behind her. Truly, it was a thing of beauty. And it made her feel infinitely more powerful.

About five feet away from Harley, Lyle pulled his horse to a halt, giving the command for the three long lines of soldiers marching behind him to stop. "What's the meaning of this?" Lyle demanded. "I'm the king and the one in charge." The soldiers began fanning out.

Harley surveyed the men. It appeared all the soldiers from the royal castle were there, all two hundred of them. She had to hide her smile. "When the soldiers announced you were approaching Losger, I decided to come out to greet you," Harley answered. "Welcome, husband."

Lyle pursed his lips, his eyes scanning the soldiers behind her. He moved his horse's reins to his left hand, his right hand rubbing his chin. She could tell she'd thrown him, and he was trying to decide what to do.

Her horse whinnied, prancing to the side a little. Harley patted its neck, calming the animal. It was time to move into the next phase of her plan. "Shall we go inside?" She started to turn the animal around.

"What's that on your back?" Lyle asked, his voice low and lethal.

"Sword of Desire. I see you have its twin, Sword of Rage." She pointed at the sword strapped to his waist.

His eyes narrowed, assessing her.

She pressed on. "A friend and fellow warrior gave it to me."

"Fellow warrior?" He snorted. "You're not a warrior." He spoke with disdain. "I'm a warrior. My entire life has been dedicated to training, learning how to command an army, wield a sword with precision, and kill without hesitation. You know nothing of these things."

No, she didn't. If she did, she would have killed him that night in the bedchamber. However, she did know other things. Like the fact that he was furious with her but had to be careful since the entire Melenia army was gathered there watching. If he harmed her in any way, he'd be guilty of treason and killed on the spot. The same went with her, which was why she had to execute this so carefully.

It was time to push again. "As the commander of this army, I think that makes me a warrior."

"Commander of the army? You must be joking. I've always known you were dumb, but not that dumb." He moved his horse alongside hers. "Whatever you think you're doing, don't. You can't outsmart me."

His words sent a sliver of fear down her spine. "Who said anything about outsmarting you?" She wanted him dead.

Glancing around, Lyle surveyed his surroundings before leaning closer to her. "What do you think is going to happen right now?" he murmured.

She blinked once, twice. "That depends on why you're here."

He adjusted himself on the saddle. "It just so happens that there's a foreign army in Melenia."

"Are you referring to Russek? The army *you* invited into our kingdom?"

He narrowed his eyes. "I'm talking about the Marsden army."

"Oh?" She licked her lips. "Marsden you say?"

"Yes. I came here to collect my soldiers so I can lead them into battle. We will destroy these foreigners and claim victory."

"And what of Owen?" she asked.

Lyle shrugged. "As far as I know, Owen is dead. That is why you're the queen, and I'm the king." His fingers curled around her upper arm. "Cede the army to my command. Then go inside Losger and wait until I return."

Their noses were only inches apart. She could feel his hot breath on her face.

"No." She shook her head, emphasizing her decision.

He dug the tips of his fingers into her arm, hurting her. She let out a yelp.

"Commander?" one of the captains said. "Is everything all right?"

Before she could respond, Lyle withdrew his sword, pointing it at the captain. "Everything is fine. My *wife* is going inside where it's safe. You can escort her there."

"Commander?" the captain said again.

"I'm your king," Lyle said. "You take orders from me, not some woman."

"That is true," the captain responded. "However, we do take orders from our queen and our commander. Queen Harley is both."

Lyle's knuckles turned white as he gripped the hilt of the sword even harder.

Harley almost had him where she wanted him. "The royal line is through me," she reminded him, "not you. Therefore, I will not cede command."

"Excuse me?" Lyle's horse shook its head, agitated by the rising tension. Lyle released Harley, pulling his horse's reins to get the animal under control. Lyle raised his voice and yelled, "I hereby strip Queen Harley of her title as commander of the Melenia army. I am the king and commander. Escort her inside. The battlefield is no place for a woman." He sheathed his sword, then steered his horse next to hers, grabbing its reins to ensure she didn't try to make a run for it.

Two officers approached.

"You won't be needing this." Lyle grabbed the sword strapped to her back, unsheathing it. He released her horse's reins.

Harley turned her horse and followed the two officers toward the castle. She had to force herself not to look back at her husband.

Lyle grunted.

"The king!" someone shouted.

At that, Harley and the two officers accompanying her glanced back in time to see Lyle hunch forward, dropping the sword.

"Your Majesty," one of the soldiers said, rushing to him. "Is something the matter?"

"My hand." The sword laid discarded on the ground.

"What's wrong with your hand?" the soldier asked.

Lyle looked directly at Harley. "What did you do?" he snarled. "My hand feels like it's on fire."

"I have no idea what you're talking about." She slid off her horse, rushing over to her husband. "Were you stung by something?" She reached down, picking up Sword of Desire. She made sure to twist the hilt in her gloves, wiping the rest of the poison off as she pretended to inspect it.

"Queen Harley," the captain said, "can I see the weapon in question?"

"Of course." She handed the sword to him, then pulled off her gloves, tucking them into the waistband of her pants.

"Arrest the queen," Lyle demanded.

The soldiers closest to her looked at one another, unsure what to do.

"What for?" Harley asked.

"For treason. This isn't the first time she's tried to harm me. She tried killing me with this other sword as well."

Harley's brows drew together. "Why would I kill my own husband? Are you not feeling well?" Tears welled in her eyes.

"There's nothing wrong with this sword," the captain who'd been inspecting it said. He handed it back to Harley.

She slid it in its sheath still on her back. "Maybe it's his own sword there's a problem with? Let's look at it."

Two soldiers had to help Lyle dismount since he no longer had use of his hands. Lyle's arms hung limp at his sides, his face contorted in a mixture of pain and fury.

Harley reached forward and unsheathed Sword of Rage, then inspected it. "This sword looks fine as well. I really think something must have stung him. Let's get him inside."

"I'm fine," he ground out.

"I don't think so. You and you," Harley pointed at two soldiers, "escort King Lyle inside immediately. Let's have a healer inspect him."

"You did this," he said to Harley.

"It hurts me that you would say something so mean and cruel." She gave her horse to one of the nearby soldiers so she could accompany her husband into the castle. The last thing she wanted was to leave him alone with his soldiers. She didn't know what he'd say or do. It was best for her to stay at his side so she could monitor him.

Inside, they escorted him to the room on the third level where she'd stayed last night. The two soldiers helped Lyle to the makeshift bed.

"Thank you for your assistance. One of you remain in here with me, the other get a healer."

"Your Majesty, we don't have a healer," one of the guards said.

She'd suspected as much. "Very well. Both of you can remain here with me." The soldiers stood guard near the entrance to the room.

This was one of the few rooms that had four intact walls and a ceiling. Harley went over to the rickety straw mattress to check on Lyle.

If his eyes could shoot daggers at her, they would have. Harley tried to ignore the hatred seeping from him as she sat next to him on the bed. "Let me see your hands. I'm going to inspect them for a bite or puncture wound."

"Like hell you are. You did this to me. It stings like hell."

"I love you." She leaned forward, kissing his forehead, and whispered so neither guard could hear, "I know how painful it is. I experienced the same thing the night Ledger brought me to the royal castle for you." She leaned back.

He flung his body up, trying to smash his head against hers.

Harley yelped and fell off the bed. Both guards rushed forward.

"Queen Harley, are you okay?" The one guard helped her to her feet.

Tears welled in her eyes. "I don't understand why my husband is being so cruel. He tried to hurt me."

The soldiers looked at one another.

"What is it?" she asked.

"We don't think it's safe for you to be so close to the king in his current state."

Lyle started laughing, the sound cruel. "You're right," he said. "She shouldn't be anywhere near me right now. The second I have use of my hands and arms again, I'm going to kill her."

Both soldiers looked at her, awaiting her orders. She wiped the tears from her eyes. "He's my husband," she murmured. "But I'm the queen, and I have a duty and responsibility to my people." She stood straighter. "I hereby place King Lyle under arrest for treason. The two of you are my witnesses."

"I'll secure his hands and feet together," the soldier on her right said.

"I can't even use my hands," Lyle sneered. "I've been poisoned."

The guards went over to Lyle. One held his legs down while the other secured his ankles together. Then one tied Lyle's wrists together.

Harley watched Lyle staring at her as all of this happened. She knew he'd do far worse things than kill her if he got the chance.

"I know there is a proper procedure for a situation such as this one," Harley said. Normally, Lyle would have a chance to speak before the noble families to plead his case. Too bad all the noble families were dead—except hers. And there was no way Lord Silas would side with Harley. He would protect Lyle at all costs.

Now she just needed to find a way to get Lyle to willingly ingest the poison she'd put in the water beside his bed. It was only a matter of time.

She was about to address both guards when a soldier burst into the room.

"Queen Harley!" he shouted far louder than necessary. "There's a problem. Come quick."

Those were the last words she wanted to hear right now. Dread filling her, she followed the soldier out of the room. The two of them ran to the second level and down a long corridor.

She recognized this place. "Is it Lord Silas?"

The man nodded and ushered her into a room. Six soldiers stood near the edge.

"Don't tell me he jumped," Harley said as she rushed to the edge and peered over the side. All she saw was green grass and a few boulders. "Where is he?"

"He escaped," one of the soldiers answered. "We're conducting a search of the castle and perimeter as we speak."

"All of you, come with me." Harley exited the room and headed back up to the third level as panic set in.

"What's the matter?" one of the soldiers called after her.

Lord Silas wouldn't want to leave his son here at her mercy. She ran faster. When she reached her room, she burst inside only to find her two soldiers on the floor, blood pooling around both their heads, and Lyle nowhere to be seen.

CHAPTER TWENTY-TWO

ACKLEY

*E*ven though the soldiers had left, there were still a handful of servants roaming around the castle. No one dared go near the third level, so that was where Ackley spent most of his time. He went through the queen's room, Lyle's room, and several others that must have belonged to the royal family members. He inspected the passageways and made note of things he wanted to discuss with Idina before he left her there.

As promised, it didn't take long for the Marsden soldiers to arrive. When they did, Ackley immediately had them set up a perimeter, keeping watch for any soldiers from the Melenia army in case they returned. He also sent a handful of his men to Penlar to help escort Owen and Idina to the royal castle. This was the longest he'd ever been away from his sister, and he missed her terribly.

He had his soldiers go through the offices on the first level. To keep his mind from thinking of Harley, Ackley focused on making sure the castle was safe and secure. A few servants questioned him; however, he simply explained how he was there to help Owen who would be arriving shortly.

By the sixth day, Ackley started pacing. He'd expected Harley would have been back by now based upon where he estimated Losger to be. If something had happened to her, he'd never forgive himself for not going there to aid her.

There had been no word of Lyle or the Melenia army either. He contemplated sending some of his men to investigate but decided against it. If Harley still hadn't returned by the time Owen and Idina arrived, then he'd know something was wrong, and he'd send men to see the state of things.

Ackley had taken to sleeping in one of the guest rooms on the second level. One morning, he woke up to find dark clouds in the sky with the promise of rain. Thunder boomed and lightning flashed across the sky. After dressing, Ackley stood at the window, staring outside, contemplating what all needed to be done. His six hundred and fifty men sitting on those three war ships would need enough food to make the two weeks journey home.

Just thinking about those ships made Ackley's stomach roll with nausea. He didn't think he could step foot on one again.

Something outside caught his attention. He squinted, noticing a dozen or so people on horseback near the castle. One of the riders had bright red hair. Ackley took off running.

He bolted outside and sprinted to the stables where he found Idina already off her horse. He grabbed her, swinging her around as he hugged her.

"Brother," she said. "I see you've missed me."

He set her on her feet, examining her. "You appear to be in one piece."

Owen came over, joining them. "Where's Harley?"

That was a question Ackley would like answered. "I believe

238

she's in Losger." He rubbed the back of his neck. "It's a long story. Come inside, and we'll talk."

"Why do I have a feeling I'm not going to like whatever it is you have to say, Ackley?"

"Because people rarely like whatever Ackley says," Idina teased, taking Owen's hand and pulling him from the stables. "I'm sure it's not that bad. Otherwise, we wouldn't be at your home. If there was a serious problem, Ackley would be off fixing it." She glanced over her shoulder at her brother. "Am I right?"

He nodded. He'd told himself that if Harley wasn't here by the time Owen and Idina arrived, he'd go after her.

Thunder rumbled and lightning shot across the sky. A light rain started falling.

Owen led them inside and to an opulent sitting room. Idina flopped on the sofa, seemingly exhausted. Ackley went over to the hearth, starting a fire to warm the space, all the while trying to figure out how to start this conversation.

"Are you okay?" Idina asked when Ackley sat on the chair across from her. "You seem a little tense."

The rain picked up, now coming down hard.

Most of his soldiers were on those ships. He couldn't even fathom being on the open ocean during a storm.

"You look like you're going to be sick," Owen said, sitting next to Idina. "Why don't you tell us what's going on?" He leaned forward and rested his elbows on his knees, looking pointedly at Ackley.

Ackley sighed, about to tell them all that had happened when Lord Silas walked through the doorway.

Silas's boots were wet, his hair tousled, and his chest rose and fell in quick successions. He quickly scanned the room, then his attention went to Owen.

At that moment, Ackley knew Silas couldn't be trusted and something was wrong. Not wanting Silas to get too close to Owen, Ackley jumped to his feet, putting himself in front of Owen but trying not to be too obvious about it.

"Lord Silas," Ackley said. "I'd like to introduce you to King Owen's wife, the lovely Queen Idina." He gestured to his sister still sitting on the sofa.

"Where's Harley?" Silas demanded, his voice hard and unforgiving.

"Uncle." Owen stood. "Why don't you join us for some tea? You look like you could use it."

Ackley gestured to the chair across from Owen, and the old man sat. A moment later, a servant rushed through the door carrying a tray of tea. She set it on the low table, then hurried from the room.

Ackley reached into his pocket.

"I didn't know you were here at the castle," Owen said to Silas. "You look well."

"I'm trying to find Harley," Silas said. "Is she here?"

"I don't know," Owen replied. "We just arrived ourselves."

Ackley leaned forward, poured a cup of tea, then handed it to his sister. "I plan on looking for her," Ackley said as he poured a second cup. He handed this one to Owen. "When's the last time you saw her?"

"I don't remember," Silas replied. His hands gripped the armrests harder than necessary.

Ackley poured the third cup of tea, handing this one to Silas. "What about Lyle? Have you seen him? When we all arrived here, everyone was gone."

Silas took a sip of the steaming tea. "I haven't seen him."

"You don't seem all that surprised to see me," Owen commented. "Did you know I was alive?"

"I did." Silas took another sip. "Harley told me."

"I heard you allowed, encouraged even, Harley to be crowned as the queen of Melenia." Owen finished his tea, setting his cup on the low table before them.

"I've had a long day," Silas said. "I think I need to rest."

"Isn't it only morning?" Idina asked, taking a sip of her tea.

The rain started pouring, pounding against the windows.

Silas stood; his shoulders hunched forward. "My old bones aren't what they used to be. I must rest. We'll talk more later."

"Tell me," Ackley said, leaning back in his chair and crossing his legs, "were you in Losger with Harley?"

Silas swung around to face Ackley. "Is she here?" He now stood tall, no longer hunched forward.

"You didn't answer my question, so I won't answer yours." Ackley winked.

Silas took a step toward Ackley, then he swayed.

"Are you all right?" Ackley asked.

Silas took another step, this time losing his balance and crashing onto the low table, breaking it, and sending the teacups flying.

Idina yelped in surprise and jumped to her feet.

"I…can't…" Silas wheezed.

"You can't what?" Ackley asked. "Breathe?" He stood and went over to Silas, crouching next to him. "Maybe that's because you're about to die."

"What did you do?" Idina demanded.

"I laced his tea with poison." Ackley withdrew the vial from his pocket. "At least, that's what I think this is." He'd have to thank Savenek for that.

"Was that necessary?" Idina asked.

"I agree," Owen said. "We're all armed. We weren't in any danger from my elderly uncle."

"I think there's more to your uncle than you know."

Harley barged into the room, breathing heavily. "Silas can't be trusted!" she yelled. She bent over breathing hard. "Where's Lyle?"

Owen sprang to his feet, rushing over to her. "Are you all right?"

"I'm fine. Just exhausted from riding and then running in here. I was afraid Silas was going to kill you. I had to stop it."

"Silas?" Owen asked.

She nodded. "We'll get to that later. Right now, I have to find Lyle." She glanced up at Ackley. "Did you kill him?" She pointed at Silas's body.

"I did."

She righted herself and smiled. "Thank you." Then she reached under her cape and withdrew a sword. "I believe this is yours." She extended Sword of Rage.

A smile lit up his face. "She's a thing of beauty." He winked at Harley, meaning both the sword and the woman before him. "What about its match?"

She removed her cape and twisted, revealing Sword of Desire strapped to her back, right where it should be.

"It looks like you and I have a false king to find." Ackley leaned down and kissed Harley's cheek. "Let's go."

CHAPTER TWENTY-THREE

*E*xhaustion consumed Harley. As soon as she'd discovered Silas had taken Lyle and fled Losger, she'd gotten on a horse and tracked them. Well, she'd tried tracking them. Honestly, she had no idea how to do it. Since she assumed they'd be heading back to the royal castle, she went there. It would have been easier if she didn't have a dozen soldiers chasing after her, trying to guard her.

"Is Lyle still incapacitated?" Ackley asked, pulling her from her thoughts.

"I doubt it." The poison only lasted so many hours, and it had been days. Water dripped from her hair, though her clothes remained dry thanks to the cape she'd worn.

She and Ackley headed along the corridor. "Fletcher and Dalton," Ackley called out as two of his Knights approached. "Owen and Idina are in the sitting room with the rest of my Knights. The two of you need to organize my soldiers. Lock down the castle. No one comes or goes until we find Lyle. Oh, and someone needs to locate Harley's mother, Lady Mayle. Understood?"

"Yes, Your Highness." Both men placed a fist over their chests before hurrying away.

"My mother was here in a guest suite." She couldn't remember if she'd included that detail when she'd told Ackley and Owen everything that had happened since the last time she saw them.

"I'm aware of that fact seeing as how your mother knocked me over the head."

"She did?" Harley had a hard time envisioning her mother behaving in such a way.

"She was helping Lyle," Ackley revealed. "I don't know if she can be trusted—which is why we need to find her."

Harley doubted her mother would have left the castle on her own. She wasn't even certain Lady Mayle could ride a horse. However, after discovering her father wasn't her father and the man who'd raised her wasn't what she thought, she couldn't be sure about her mother either.

They entered the kitchen. "What are we doing in here?" she asked, her teeth chattering.

"This is the warmest room in the castle." He pulled her closer to the hearth. "Stand here for a few minutes and warm yourself. Then we'll start hunting."

"I'm sorry I didn't kill Lyle myself." She'd had two opportunities and failed both times.

"There's nothing to be sorry about." He started checking the weapons hidden throughout his clothes.

"I thought I could either poison him or bring him here and put him in the dungeon. I wanted Owen to have the chance to question him."

"Why?" After tightening his weapons belt, he leaned against the table and folded his arms, watching her with curiosity.

She shrugged. "It seems Owen and I deserve an answer."

"Sometimes there isn't one."

She wanted to tell him Silas was Lyle's father but didn't feel like getting into that at the moment. She was still reeling over the shock that she'd been fooled all her life.

"You look better," Ackley commented. "Your lips aren't blue any longer."

The warmth from the fire had seeped into her body. "I know Lyle has to be near here; I just don't know where."

"Your soldiers?"

She rubbed her eyes, warding off the increasing tiredness. "A dozen came with me. The rest were leaving as soon as they could. One of the captains said he'd organize them. They're supposed to form a perimeter or something around the castle once they get here."

Ackley nodded. "They're probably a solid day behind you."

"What do you think we should do?"

He tilted his head to the side. "What do *you* think we should do?"

She was too tired to think. She rubbed her face, trying to work through everything. She'd explained to her men that Owen was alive and well. Most of them seemed wary about the news, especially since that meant Harley was a traitor. She'd told them she only took the throne to ensure Owen's safety and that when they returned to the castle, they would have proof. Thankfully, Owen was here and most of the captains knew him. She'd deal with the part about her being a traitor later.

"The only way Lyle wins, is if Owen's dead." Harley started pacing, imagining what needed to be done as if each event were a move on a game board. If she strategized through this correctly, she could figure out a way to win.

"I agree."

"Silas and Lyle came here because this castle is safe. It is where the royal family lives." And it was where Owen would come. "He's going after Owen."

Ackley nodded.

"Your Knights?"

"Will protect Owen. But we need to kill Lyle before he takes off and regroups."

"So, we need to set a trap of our own?" Harley asked.

"Exactly."

An idea suddenly came to her. "I know what to do."

Harley and Ackley rode their horses through the pouring rain, heading for the small village Lyle had taken her to what felt like a lifetime ago. She couldn't explain how she knew Lyle was there, but she'd bet her life on it. In fact, with this crazy plan of hers, she was.

Ackley had asked a few questions, and she got the impression he wasn't sold on this plan. However, he said he trusted her, and he let her take the lead.

It felt strange for the two of them to be traveling alone. It had been a long time since they'd been together like this, reminding her of when they'd gone to Russek. So much had changed since then.

She hoped the men she'd sent north to intercept her Melenia soldiers arrived in time. She hoped Ackley's Knights kept Owen and Idina safe. And she hoped she would survive what she was about to do.

The village came into view. The area around the huts had

turned into a muddy mess from the downpour. Harley slowed her horse and squinted, trying to see the area better through the rain.

Ackley came up next to her, also slowing his horse. "Before we go through with this, I want to make sure you fully comprehend the consequences of your actions."

"I know them." She'd gone over it a hundred times in her head. And, truthfully, it was something she'd been considering for quite some time now.

He reached over, grabbing her arm. She pulled her horse to a halt and looked at him.

"Harley."

The way he said her name sent a jolt through her.

"You're already guilty of treason for taking the throne knowing Owen is alive."

"I know." She'd done it anyway to save her kingdom. It was the only way she could gain control of the army to ensure Lyle didn't attack Owen or the Marsden soldiers. She'd prevented a battle.

"If you kill Lyle, it will seal your fate."

She nodded, knowing all of this already. "Maybe Owen can pardon me."

Ackley's eyes remained focused on hers, not flinching. "Maybe."

She knew he didn't believe Owen could fix this. No matter. She'd made her choice long ago. It was time to end this. She nudged her horse and continued on, nearing the village.

No one was about, making the place appear abandoned. They'd probably been spotted already. In this downpour, she doubted an archer would be able to strike them down. Not only was it hard to see, but the wind and rain would alter the trajectory of the arrow. At least that was what she assumed. It made approaching the first couple of huts easier if she told herself that.

Harley and Ackley both dismounted, leaving their horses near one of the huts as they walked to the center of the village.

Ackley withdrew Sword of Rage, and Harley withdrew Sword of Desire. Together, they stood in the middle, surrounded by the huts. Ackley nodded for her to begin.

She sucked in a deep breath, calming herself so she'd have the mental strength to do what needed to be done. Through the rain, she could just make out the Melenia soldiers getting into position far enough away not to interfere, but close enough to see what transpired.

"Lyle!" Harley shouted. "I know you're here. Come out and face me, you coward!"

"Well," Ackley mumbled, his voice barely audible above the rain, "that's one way to antagonize him."

No movement came from within the village. It almost seemed as if no one lived there. However, Harley knew better.

"I thought you were a great warrior!" she yelled, trying again. "Is the almighty king of Melenia terrified to face his queen?" Maybe Lyle was afraid of Ackley being there. She'd considered going without Ackley but knew he'd never agree to it. And honestly, with Lyle's skills, it would be dumb for her to face him alone.

One of the doors opened. Through the rain, she couldn't see into the dark hut. Someone stepped forward. Immediately, she knew it was Lyle. With a long sword in hand, he closed the door behind him and slowly approached.

"He has a dagger in his left hand," Ackley mumbled. "Be careful he doesn't throw it at your neck."

She nodded, unable to see the dagger and wondering when he'd withdrawn it since she just saw him close the door with that hand. She swallowed, scared and excited at the same time. No matter what happened, all of this would end today.

Lyle neared, stopping ten feet away. "Afraid to face me on your own?"

Harley didn't know which one of them he was speaking to. She didn't care.

"Look at you holding a sword," he said, not coming any closer. "You're not even holding it correctly." He glanced at Ackley, then focused back on Harley. "I would love to know what you're thinking."

"Why? You never cared before."

"Is that what this is about? Your feelings are hurt I didn't worship the ground you walked on?" He shook his head. "You're pathetic."

"This was never about me," she said. "It has always been about Melenia."

He chuckled. "I don't think so. If you cared about Melenia at all, you would help me, not fight me. The late king stole from his people. They were starving to death." He moved in closer. "You know it's true. You saw how people lived in Penlar. The poverty. The desperation. I don't know how you are okay with any of that."

"Instead of killing the royal family, you could have worked with the king to try and change things." If she'd understood all of this before, if she hadn't been so sheltered, she would have tried to make changes. Harley was confident Owen would be the change needed. He would right the wrongs of his father.

"You don't think my father tried that?"

It was Harley's turn to take a step closer to Lyle. She could feel Ackley tense behind her. "Which father are you referring to? The man who raised you or your birth father?" She knew Ackley was probably trying to piece it all together as he silently watched this unfold before him.

"Did Silas finally tell you the truth?" The corners of Lyle's lips rose slightly.

She realized he didn't know Ackley had killed Silas. "He did." She took another step closer, so they now were only a couple of feet apart. "It's funny how Ackley managed to kill *both* of your fathers."

Fury raged in Lyle's eyes, the only emotion he revealed. His focus never wavered from her. She had no doubt that the second he killed her, he would go after Ackley. Ackley was the one he'd want to take his time with. Not her. She was simply a pebble in his shoe that needed to be dealt with. It was time for her to make her final jab.

"I assume Naia is here." Then she raised her voice and said to Ackley over her shoulder, "You can deal with her while I take care of Lyle." She remembered reading Naia's name in one of the letters Beck had sent Lyle. Naia had been the woman Lyle loved. He'd even been engaged to her before he was forced to end that relationship so he could marry Harley.

That was the last push she needed to force Lyle's hand. He growled and closed the short space between them, reaching forward and embedding his dagger into her stomach. The force of the hit was more than she'd intended, and her eyes widened in shock. Not wanting him to withdraw the weapon, she staggered back from him, collapsing to her knees. As she did so, she dropped Sword of Desire next to her.

Ackley stepped forward, kicking the sword up with his boot. He caught it in the air and flipped it over, attaching the pommel of her sword to his, forming a double-edged weapon.

Kneeling on the ground in the rain, Harley couldn't hear what the two men said as they battled one another. The pain was intense, her ribs screaming from the impact. She fell forward, the palms of her hands on the ground. Not wanting to pass out, she forced herself to focus on Ackley. She turned her head in time to see him parry a blow from Lyle. Lyle spun and kicked Ackley, Ackley stumbling backward a step. Lyle tossed his long sword and withdrew two wicked looking knives, coming in close to Ackley.

Ackley ended up using the double edged sword as a bow staff, blocking the lightning-fast strikes Lyle threw at him. The two men took a step away from each other, both panting heavily as they circled one another. Blood dripped from Ackley's forearm while Lyle had a gash in his thigh.

"I thought you would've been more upset when I dealt Harley that killing blow," Lyle said.

Harley's head swam, and she felt about ready to pass out.

"I guess she must not mean as much to you as I thought," Lyle said.

"As you've claimed time and time again, Harley is simply a means to an end," Ackley said.

Harley felt her heart constrict with pain at Ackley's words. She heard the *clank* of steel as their weapons struck again.

The rain let up. Harley dug her fingers into the mud, trying to hold on long enough to see the end.

Lyle grunted, then fell to his knees.

Ackley had his sword pointed directly at Lyle's chest as he said, "Harley *means* the world to me, and she is the one who will finally *end* you." He plunged the sword into Lyle, killing him.

Harley fell face forward into the mud, the dagger still in her.

Ackley rushed to her side.

"Is it done?" she squeaked out.

"It is."

Satisfied, she swallowed and allowed the darkness to take her.

CHAPTER TWENTY-FOUR

*U*nlike his predecessors, Owen stood near the front of the castle, ground level with his men. He'd told Ackley he couldn't do this from the place where his family had been murdered. This was the start of something new, so it was only fitting for this ceremony to be held amongst his people.

Ackley stood off to the side, watching. Once the crown had been placed atop Owen's head, the man turned to Idina. Ackley had never seen his sister look more beautiful or radiant than she did at that moment. Even though the ground remained muddy from yesterday's rain, the sun shone overhead, shining on Idina's red hair. She took the oath, swearing to protect Melenia. After the crown was placed on her head, Owen and Idina held hands.

The man performing the ceremony then went ahead and joined Owen and Idina in matrimony. Even though they'd already been wed, they wanted to perform the act again before their soldiers, showing they were united as one.

Ackley had a hard time concentrating on Owen and Idina

since Harley's body was next to Lyle's not far from where the ceremony was taking place. Owen wanted to make sure everyone could see the traitors were dead. There would be no questioning the succession of the royal line. While Ackley understood all of this, it was still hard to watch.

Lady Mayle had been found dead in one of the guest suites. Her body, along with Lord Silas's, had been burned yesterday after Owen declared them both traitors to the crown.

Owen and Idina kissed, and the soldiers surrounding them cheered.

Owen raised his hand, silencing everyone. "I would like to thank everyone for your support and dedication to Melenia. These last few months have been trying ones. In the coming months, we will restore what we've lost."

Ackley tuned him out. He already knew that Owen planned on sending everyone home to rebuild their houses and lives. Then, once the people had taken care of themselves, Owen would call up his army. A handful had volunteered to stay on and serve as the king and queen's personal protection. It would be enough for now.

When Owen finished, the celebration began. A few musicians played music; some people danced. The traitors' bodies were removed from the area, taken around back to be burned. That was Ackley's cue to go.

He quickly found Idina.

"I wish you could stay longer," she said. "But I understand you have duties."

"There's been one slight change," he told her. "I'm not returning to Marsden."

"Gordon is going to be furious with you, but I can't say I'm surprised." She wrapped him in a hug. "I knew you'd never step foot on a ship again." She released him.

"Maybe one day." He shrugged. "After my men are off, I'll touch base with you."

"Please keep me informed of how things are going," she said, looking pointedly at him.

"I will." He kissed the top of her head.

Owen joined them. "Thank you for all you've done. Melenia is eternally grateful."

"Just take good care of my sister." They shook hands.

"I will. I promise."

Ackley turned and walked away. He had a slew of things that had to be taken care of. Since his sister was married and crowned, he no longer had to worry about her. Granted, he'd always keep an eye on her, but Owen had it covered. Owen was a good man and would make Idina happy.

At the stables, Ackley greeted his Knights. "Is it done?" he asked.

"The bodies are taken care of." Rikter nodded to the building fire not far away.

"And your horse is saddled and ready to go," Galvin said, handing the reins to Ackley.

He took them, then mounted.

"Are you sure this is what you want to do?" Finnegan asked.

"I'm certain." He readjusted himself on the saddle since the bags attached to it took up so much room. "Rikter, you're in charge of my Knights and soldiers until you reach Marsden."

"And in Marsden?" he asked.

Ackley smiled. "I left someone in charge. Give her a full report of what happened here."

"Her?" Fletcher asked.

Ackley nodded. He'd left one of Reid's sisters in charge. He hoped things were going well. Since he was staying on the mainland for some time, he'd have to leave her in charge a little longer. "Make sure you get every man on that ship. Leave no one behind. Safe travels."

Each of his Knights placed a fist over his chest. Ackley lifted his right fist, placing it over his chest as well. "It has been a pleasure serving with each of you." With that, he nudged his horse and took off. He had no doubt Rikter would ensure every Marsden made it home safely.

Even though Ackley knew every man would make it on that ship, there was one woman who would not. He needed to discover what had happened to Gytha. She'd be furious he'd sent his army home without her. However, she could easily make the journey later. Owen and Idina planned on opening trade with Marsden. Gytha could hop on one of those ships if she wanted to. Ackley wasn't convinced she'd want to return home yet.

He traveled for two days. When he came to the dilapidated barn he'd spent the night in with Harley, he decided to stop and stay there for a few days. Not that the place was particularly appealing, but it had sentimental value. He unloaded the supplies off his horse, taking particular care of one of the items.

He unwrapped the blankets and found Harley still knocked out from that root concoction she'd made. He easily slung her over his shoulder as he carried her up the rickety ladder to the loft, then carefully laid her down, setting her head on a pillow of hay.

He sat at her side, waiting for her to wake up. She'd told him it could take a few days. He had plenty of food and water nearby for when she returned to him. While she'd been asleep, he'd done a lot of thinking. Mainly, he didn't want to go on without her in his life.

Another lonely day passed. Ackley sat and watched Harley. The leather armor she'd worn under her tunic had prevented the knife from embedding into her. However, it hadn't stopped the nasty bruise from the hit. It looked as if a rib was broken, so he'd wrapped her torso just in case.

He kept holding her hand, feeling her warmth, trying to assure himself she was alive.

Finally, on the fifth day, her eyelids fluttered and opened.

"Did it work?" she rasped out.

He nodded.

She closed her eyes and smiled.

He leaned down and kissed the tip of her nose. "I've missed your beautiful eyes."

She opened them, her smile deepening.

"Everything went just as you planned," he told her.

"I didn't want Owen to have to deal with me committing treason."

"He probably could have pardoned you."

She sat up, although the movement was obviously painful. Ackley couldn't help reaching out to touch her hair cascading around her shoulders.

"Possibly," she said. "But then he would have been seen as weak. I didn't want him to start his reign that way."

"I'm not arguing with you." Now he had her all to himself.

"I can go anywhere now, be anyone." Her smile deepened. "I can do anything."

"Anything?" he teased. He leaned forward, kissing her bare shoulder.

"Where's my shirt?" She gently touched the bandages wrapped around her torso.

"I removed it so I could keep an eye on that."

"It hurts pretty badly."

He assumed it would. "I guess that means I'll have to be extra gentle with you." He kissed her other shoulder. "At least until you heal." He kissed her right ear, then her left. "We're all alone with nothing to do."

"I can think of plenty things to do," she said, her voice breathy.

His mouth devoured hers.

When Ackley woke up, his legs were tangled with Harley's, and her hair covered his face. He'd never been happier. He started kissing her neck, trailing his lips down to her stomach.

"How long do you plan on us staying here?" she asked.

"I have no plans."

She snorted. "You? No plans? I don't think so."

He raised a single eyebrow. "Then I revise my answer. I plan on us enjoying each other whenever and however we want." And as soon as she was strong enough, they'd figure out what to do about Gytha. Together.

"Now that I'm no longer a lady," Harley said.

Ackley bit her shoulder. "Oh, I don't know about that."

"Stop, I'm trying to be serious. I have no name or identity."

He leaned on his elbow, propping himself up to look at her. "Do you want one?" Was she trying to ask about marriage?

"I don't know." She bit her bottom lip, momentarily distracting him. "What about being a Knight?" She sounded unsure.

"Do you want to be one?" Because right now, she could be anything she wanted.

She nodded.

"Then I would love to make you a Knight. But there are a few things you must know."

"Like what?"

"Knights can't marry." He watched her, wanting to see her reaction.

"Oh." Her brows drew together. "I don't think I want to marry again."

"I've never wanted to marry," Ackley admitted. He'd always felt it would chain him down and suffocate him. He traced a line up her arm and across her chest, feeling her soft, smooth skin. "But I also want you in my life." He just didn't want people to know how much she meant to him. He didn't want the enemies he'd accumulated to use Harley as a weapon against him.

"What about children?" she asked. "Do you want them?"

Truthfully, he hadn't given it much thought. He shrugged. "Why do you ask?"

"I'm just curious."

He laid back, thinking about it. "I wouldn't mind having kids, so long as it's with you."

She rolled over, climbing on top of and straddling him. "I'm glad you feel that way because there's something I must tell you. But first, I want to do this." She leaned forward and kissed him.

CHAPTER TWENTY-FIVE

GYTHA: SOMEWHERE IN RUSSEK

*G*ytha had never been so bloody cold in all her life. If she had to describe Russek in one word, it would be miserable. Why anyone chose to live there was beyond her. She continued to follow the man up the mountain, her thighs stinging in pain from the steep ascent. At least he had a fur wrap draped over his shoulders to keep him warm. She had nothing but the pants and tunic she'd been wearing for over a week now.

When they reached the top of the summit, snow started falling. Gytha couldn't feel her toes any longer. Up ahead, a small shack came into view. It didn't even have a chimney. When she saw Ackley again, she planned to pummel him with just her fist. He'd probably start laughing at her and call her *soft* for complaining or being upset. Apparently, the only one who could express such things was him.

"We're almost there," the man said, his thick accent making it hard to understand him.

"Good," Gytha replied. "But I didn't ask."

"Sorry," he said. "I thought I heard you say something."

She hadn't. Maybe a muttered curse for Ackley, but that was it.

"We're just heading to that house." He pointed at the shack.

If the wind blew hard enough, Gytha was certain it would fall over. "What will be happening in that shack?" It barely looked big enough for the two of them, and this tree of a man wasn't her type.

If she even had a type. Between Dexter and Ackley, she was done. She didn't care who she met or what she felt for any man. The next year would be all about Gytha. She intended on becoming a more proficient fighter, learning to use two swords at once, and practicing with her daggers more. While using daggers in close quarters was easy enough, she wanted to be able to throw them at longer ranges and with greater accuracy.

"Here," the man said.

Like she couldn't have figured out they'd arrived as they stood before a door.

The man kicked his boots on the porch—really, a board—and then stepped onto it, opening the door.

Gytha did the same, ridding them of what little snow they'd accumulated. When she entered the room, she blinked, trying to get her eyes to adjust to the dim lighting.

"It's about time," a familiar voice said.

Gytha squinted, just to be sure. "What in the hell are you doing here, Brodek?" she asked. He should be in Emperion where he belonged, not Russek.

"Funny you should ask." He stood from the table. "I have a proposition for you."

She eyed him. He had on some sort of furry hat and a wrap similar to what her guide wore, making him look ridiculous.

On the Russeks, the fur clothing seemed fitting. On Brodek, not so much.

"I'll wait outside," the Russek man said. "When you're done, let me know."

Brodek nodded. Once the man left, Brodek gestured to the chair across from him.

Gytha sat. She had so many questions for Brodek that she didn't even know where to start.

"My empress is impressed with you," he said. "She would like to employ your services."

Gytha folded her arms, trying to hide her shock. "Why are we in Russek?" She originally came to the kingdom as a favor for Ackley. He wanted her to meet with Kerdan's man and get permission for the Marsden army to travel through Russek. Somewhere along the way, all that changed, and she ended up following that man here, to Brodek. If a meeting was what he wanted, she would much rather have done it somewhere more convenient, not in the middle of a mountain range. It was too bloody cold there.

"The job Empress Rema would like to employ you for is here in Russek." He removed his furry hat, running his hands through his hair. "I told her you wouldn't do it. That you'd want to return home with Ackley. But she insisted I bring you here and show you."

When Gytha had met Rema, she hadn't thought much beyond her being a pampered ruler at first. After listening to her talk to Ackley, she started to realize the woman was shrewd. If she wanted something from Gytha, and Gytha didn't want to give it to her, would Rema order her execution? She shivered. "Show me what, exactly?"

"First of all," Brodek said, standing, "I'm only the

messenger. I will not be working with you at all. Kerdan will assign someone."

Gytha stood, suddenly nervous.

He went to the corner of the small shack, kneeling on the floor. He pushed on a floorboard, then popped a trap door open. He climbed down, disappearing from her sight.

Gytha went around the table and peered inside the hole in the floor. She saw a ladder and the top of Brodek's head. Silently cursing Ackley for getting her into this mess, she started to descend the ladder. It felt like she went down at least five levels. Thankfully, the air turned warmer. At the bottom, Brodek grabbed her arm, pulling her forward in the darkness. She heard what sounded like a door. He pushed it open, and light burst out.

Gytha stepped into a massive cavern lit by hundreds of torches. "What is this place?" Pathways had been carved into the sides and there were several holes which appeared to lead to rooms. At the bottom, a large, flat surface.

"If you accept the position, this will be your training ground," Brodek said.

"Training ground for what?"

"An elite unit of women fighters. So, what do you think? Emperion will pay you handsomely for your services."

This place was enormous and would be perfect for training people to fight. But she wouldn't be training people. She'd be training women. She still had so many questions. "I don't understand." Why was she here in Russek and not Emperion? She didn't want to be caught up in some political mess and train women to assassinate rulers.

"It looks like Princess Allyssa will be marrying King Kerdan. Empress Rema wants her daughter well protected. She thinks that men won't be able to serve Princess Allyssa as well as a trained unit of women. The empress isn't comfortable with her daughter living here among these Russeks without some form of protection. She's hoping you can ensure her daughter's safety. So, what do you think?"

Reaching back, Gytha pulled her braid over her shoulder, running her hands down it. "How many?" She'd never trained a unit of all women before.

He shrugged. "You'll meet with Kerdan and discuss the details with him. The empress is thinking around fifty. Then you can pick the top twelve to serve. The rest can do something else. The empress also wants a few Russek warriors to assist you so you can become familiar with their customs and fighting techniques."

Turning in a slow circle, Gytha took it all in. "And if I refuse?"

"I'm to escort you to Ackley in Melenia. Then you can hop on a ship and go back to Marsden and resume your life."

If resuming her life in Marsden meant watching Dexter and Reid, she'd rather not. And if Ackley brought Harley with him, she wouldn't care for seeing the two of them either. Returning home left little appeal. She'd just been talking about how she wanted to spend the next year training. Well, here was an opportunity. By training women to fight, she'd also be working on her own skills. Especially if she'd be working with a couple Russek warriors. She might actually come out of this a better fighter than Ackley. She smiled as she envisioned being able to outfight him.

The idea of remaining on the mainland started growing on her. It wasn't like she'd be there forever, just temporarily.

"I accept." The words were out before she could talk herself out of it.

"Really?"

"Why not?" She shrugged. How hard could it be? She'd trained men before. Women couldn't be that much more difficult.

Brodek chuckled. "All righty. I'll let the empress and Kerdan know." He turned and headed out of the cavern.

Gytha took one last look at the place before following him. Instead of returning home and throwing herself into her job, she would stay here and train an elite group of women fighters. Excitement coursed through her.

ABOUT THE AUTHOR

Jennifer Anne Davis graduated from the University of San Diego with a degree in English and a teaching credential. She is currently a full-time writer and mother of three kids. She is happily married to her high school sweetheart and lives in the San Diego area.

Jennifer is the recipient of the San Diego Book Awards Best Published Young Adult Novel (2013), winner of the Kindle Book Awards (2018), a finalist in the USA Best Book Awards (2014), and a finalist in the Next Generation Indie Book Awards (2014).

Visit Jennifer at:
www.JenniferAnneDavis.com

facebook.com/AuthorJenniferAnneDavis
twitter.com/authorjennifer
instagram.com/authorjennifer
bookbub.com/authors/jennifer-anne-davis
goodreads.com/jenniferannedavis
pinterest.com/authorjennifer

CPSIA information can be obtained
at www.ICGtesting.com
Printed in the USA
BVHW030218161121
621758BV00005B/196